HUMOR ME

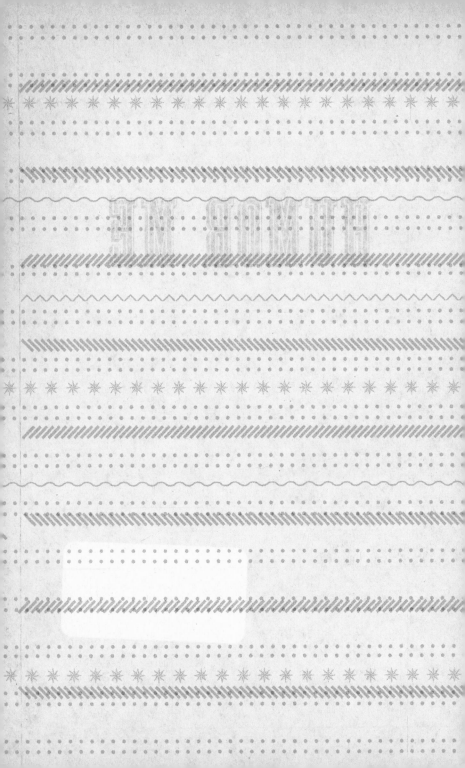

HUMOR ME

AN ANTHOLOGY OF FUNNY

CONTEMPORARY WRITING

(PLUS SOME GREAT OLD STUFF TOO)

Edited by

IAN FRAZIER

ecco

An Imprint of HarperCollinsPublishers

HarperCollins books may be purchased for educational, business, or sales promotional use. For information please write: Special Markets Department, HarperCollins Publishers, 10 East 53rd Street, New York, NY 10022.

A hardcover edition of this book was originally published in 2010 by Ecco, an imprint of HarperCollins Publishers.

FIRST ECCO PAPERBACK EDITION PUBLISHED 2011.

Designed by Mary Austin Speaker

Library of Congress Cataloging-in-Publication data has been applied for.

ISBN 978-0-06-172895-2

12 13 14 15 WCF 10 9 8 7 6 5 4 3 2

CONTENTS

✳ ✳ ✳

PART II. SOME GREAT OLD STUFF

INTRODUCTION

✳ ✳ ✳

BY IAN FRAZIER

OK, I'm under control now. I did kind of lose it there for a bit, laughing and all, coffee going up my nose, etc. What your old-time Protestant types might call "excessive mirth." But I'm cool now (h-h-h-h-h). No! I'm not going to start (h-h-h-h-h-h) again. (H-h-h-h-h-spb-spb!) Control! MAINTAIN RIGID CONTROL! No laughing any more! I have to explain about this—Ha!—stop laughing!—this—Ha! Spb! Sputter!—this anthology—Oh hahahahahahahaha heeheeheehee sorry I just can't help it the thing is so FUNNY hahahahahahahaha oh help me!

STOP! GET A GRIP! OK, now take a deep breath, start again. I can do this. I'll give myself a stern talking-to: You, Ian Frazier, do not have all year to finish this introduction, and if you keep breaking up like this you'll be here forever, and you'll be wasting your own time and the publisher's time and the editor's time and everybody's time and none of us wants that. You are an adult, and a professional writer, and more, quite frankly, is expected of you. So—are you feeling better now?

Yes. All right. I think I've got the thing back in the box. No more hilarity or hysteria.

I'll proceed.

This anthology, which you, the reader, hold in your hands, has been assembled of the very best humorous essays of this or indeed of any age. The anthology, called *Humor Me*, is a special publication whose proceeds will benefit 826 Seattle programs, which provide free after-school tutoring and writing workshops to students of all ages. This is not only true but important: 826 is great! Thanks, praise, and kudos to 826 Seattle!

Now let us turn our attention to the anthology itself, and its (h-h-h-h-h-h).

Start again: Now let us turn our attention to the anthology itself, and its contents, which include an eminent piece by the eminent writer Mark Twain on the subject of Shakespeare farting. Hahaha-hahahahahahahahahahahahah, oh God why did I start with that one? There's no way I can describe the farting piece without breaking up completely, oh God oh jeez. What now? Heeheeheeheeheeheehee! A-hee. A-ha. A-hee. Deep breath. Breathe . . .

This may be hopeless. I do apologize. I should have better command of myself than to fall apart laughing this way. It's just that, for example, when I describe the wonderful piece by Roy Blount where he's heeheeheehee in the army and living hahahahahaha in married officer housing and he's hanging up diapers on a clothesline and his haahaahaa superior officer walks by and Roy—hahahaha—and Roy has this diaper on his HAT oh hahahaha this one is even harder than the Twain to describe without howling heeheeheehhhhheeeegasp, gasp, gasp, oh please . . .

OK, sorry. Won't happen again.

SPB! SPUTTER! HAHAHAHAHAHAHAHAHAHAHAHAHA the Lynn Caraganis piece where the rat comes out hahahahee and the

HOHOHOHOHOHOHO and Bill Franzen with all the weird twister ruination, and the HAHAHAHAHAHAHEEHEEHEEHEEE Veronica Geng *Godfather* parody, the best parody of all time, hohoho oh help me hehehehaahoo and Scott Gutterman's "Gum," where Susan Sontag has a hilarious cameo if you can believe it hoohoohoohoohoo and "What I'd Say to the Martians," by Jack Handey, the funniest piece of the last ten years, ahaaahahhaaaahaaa and Jamaica Kincaid's heeheeheeheehee "Girl" with that incredible recurring line, hahahahaha, the line about "the slut you are so bent on becoming" hohoho hahahahahahahaha and the *Glengarry Glen Ross* scene with the guy named James Lingk why does that name aways crack me up hahahahahah? *Glengarry Glen Ross* is a piece of writing from our time sure to survive, and hahahahaha Steve Martin a-haa, a-haa, a-haa-ha-ha-ha-heeheehee on the subject of the Third Millennium and how it's been going so far hoohoohoohoo and, and, and Ian Maxtone-Graham's "Fair Warning," which HAHAHAHAHAHAHAHAHA-HAHAHAGHA AHAAHAAHAAHAAHEEHEE (this is an exact transcription of my laughter) AHAHEEHEEHEE, A-HOO, A-HEE AHAHAHAHAHAHAHAHAHAHA HEEHEEHEE HEEHEEHEE HEEHEEHEE, a-gasp, ghik, gasp h'h'h'h'h oh help me. . . .

Gasp. Gasp. Pant. I'm exhausted from all that laughing, and I've only made it, alphabetically, to the early M's. I can't go on. The pieces after the early M's, and the Old Stuff in Part II, are all just as hilarious as the ones in Part I, if not more so. If I go on I might injure myself. In my overview just now I skipped a lot of pieces in this anthology, and when I made the anthology I left a lot of good pieces out of it entirely. (I'm sorry, Thurber.) If I'd put in all the good ones I skipped, I'd've risked my own health, what with all this laughter's stress and strain on my diaphragm.

Also, unconnected to anything, here's a note, just FYI: The John Updike piece, "A Mild 'Complaint'," which concludes Part I, was famous at the *New Yorker* as the piece that the magazine held on to the longest before it was published. Updike wrote the piece, and the magazine bought it, in the mid-1950s, when he was a young man. For inscrutable reasons the *New Yorker* then kept the piece for twenty-some years and finally ran it in the 1970s, when Updike was in his middle years. The piece is included here as a testament to the resilience of literature, and as a wave to Mr. Updike, wherever in the afterlife he may be.

Now to conclude this introduction, let me say this: I hope you, the reader, will enjoy this anthology as much as I have. There are great pieces in here, so you SHOULD enjoy it. If you don't, the problem is with you. I hope you will get a lot out of delving into this anthology, and you will learn from it, and grow, and become a wiser person as a result. But most of all, and most deeply, I hope you will BUY this anthology. And I don't mean buy just one copy on Amazon for a penny or on Kindle or any of that noise—I mean multiple copies, each at 100 percent full non-discount price. I will not be satisfied (as Mr. Mamet's salesmen say) with anything less than TOTAL COMMITMENT! Twenty-five full-price copies, at the very least, is what I am asking of you. Do not disappoint me, please.

HUMOR ME

PART I

NOW

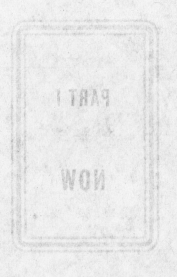

HENRY ALFORD

HENRY ALFORD

* * *

Fall Fashion Report from a Local Correctional Facility

THE RECENT ARRIVAL

For the woman who suddenly finds herself in a new place in life, this unlawful assembly of crepe and acid-washed denim puts a new spin on the old jumpsuit classic. While the strappy slingbacks with shiv heel merely hint that she may be someone who likes to mix pleasure with business, the jumpsuit's jaunty bodice takes a far more aggressive stance—think shantung and shirred georgette, all in moody tones of bruise and second-degree-burn aubergine. The net effect is pure mystery and myth. First-time offender, or career? Assault and Battery, or Man. 2? She's not telling, and Fashion is doing his job by accentuating these unanswered questions while posing a few memorable ones of his own. Meanwhile, the removeable skirt adds a bit of flirty flounce and distraction to the architectural severity of the ribbed corselette—it's a witness protection program in griege and persimmon voile. At her extremities, Elsa Perretti-ish wrist and ankle bangles hewed from dented tin drinking cups make a memorably swoopy and daft impression: the New Girl. Is she already spoken for? Watch for her in the yard.

JADE JAMMIN'

Nunchuk tie-ups and toggle bolts ensure a sprightly lockup on this all-season stunner; and you can pop up the vicuna-lined hood for a definitive Lights Out. But at the end of the day, she's all about the shimmer. Texture begets form begets dazzle begets *hello* with this jumpsuit's heavily encrusted surface: Swarovski crystals and oodles of striated Tasmanian topaz are complemented with gobs of toothpaste-left-to-harden-in-the-sink for a glittering *mosaico* tribute to haut-boheme sophistication—you're a teenage Jade Jagger, running barefoot through the alleyways of Ibiza; you're Ellen Barkin, and you have bitten someone who is now bleeding. The guards may try to confiscate the skinny lizard belt and the ribbony, fringed peplum, but just give those wage slaves a good look at all that luxurious ruching and beadwork and they'll collapse in the shade like a bunch of espadrille-wearing pêcheurs on a late-arriving dayboat. That oh-so-mod, super-chunky jewelry? It's bits of license plates, twisted into nautilus and dollar-sign shapes; Fashion is telling you that even though everyone around you has a bad case of the drearies, all it takes is a little imagination to be absolutely hoose-gawgeous.

G.I.T.

Drag your bully stick against the metal bars of this crepe-and-organza catsuit with caftan cover-up, all trimmed with bedsheet and leatherette-Bible-jacket cuffing. One thing's clear—she's a Girl in Trouble. Note the slashes of embroidery at the wrists—this cry for help is *all* elegance, as befits thread that has been harvested from vealed mergansers and then triple-dyed with strawberry Jell-O stolen from KP shifts. What's in the concealed pleather holster? Fashion isn't telling. But every garment quietly tells a story, and the story here is, Keep Your Distance—I Am Only a Phone Call Away from a Network of Highly Responsive Colleagues. Rusty water and lighter fluid have been used on the caftan to distress a patchwork of washcloths and old jeans into a nubblescape of faded cotton romance: Fashion speaks in the gangsta patois of raw terry and unborn denim. And every story, they say, has a happy ending—while the 300-pound titanium ball with matching chain gives new meaning to the charge, Accessory After the Fact, the matching Cleopatra anklet-booty assures us this teenage Queen is all Nile and no denial.

THE GOER

Fashion is definitely aiding and abetting with this camouflage print of money green and Hilfiger khaki, especially stunning when backlit by the searchlights near the western wall. The ample play of the palazzo pants is perfect for sudden movement, and the outer shell of the jacquard-lined canvas keeps its starched, architectural silhouette intact whether you're wiggling through dank, underground tunnels or zigzagging tree-to-tree through a wooded glen like a woman with a strong sense of mission. Yes, at last—a piece to take her from day *into* evening. And she'll need all the help she can get—this one's making a beeline for a place where she won't have to stand in line for dinner; a place where Arts and Crafts is an artistic movement and not a protracted Tuesday-morning battle for control of the scissors and gluepot. Fashion counsels those in his sway to jettison their struggle with the appellate system. So now this one's on the move. She's going home.

ROGER ANGELL

✳ ✳ ✳

This Old Bod

(*In this rerun of the familiar series, our host, Doc, and his pert nurse, Doris, have begun the checkup by walking around the exterior of a ramshackle, two-story frame structure, with sagging shoulders, silvered brows, and a heavy, old-fashioned front porch. Some attempts at renovation seem to be in progress, but even our indomitably cheerful experts, in their hard hats and snowy medical coats, don't look very upbeat today.*)

Doc: Watch your step, Doris. There's a lot of old siding and under-wear piled up back here. (*As he speaks, there is a warning cry from above and a load of debris comes crashing down.*)

Doris (*She is wearing a handy carpenter's apron, in the pocket of which we can glimpse a stethoscope, a rubber hammer, surgical shears, and the like.*): Yowee! Is that Bob and his Hair Club Boys up there, tak-ing a preliminary look-see?

Doc: Sure is, Dor, and they can do a bang-up job, as we know, with that new styrene shingling, absolutely indistinguishable from the real thing. (*He calls up to Bob.*) How's it look up there, big guy?

BOB (*From the roof.*): Not so hot, Doc. It's your standard horror show—advanced alopecia, spotty pate, and what looks like unsightly spreading lichen. Most places, we're right down to the original dermis.

DOC: But you guys can fix all that up good as new, can't you, Bob? Better than new!

BOB: Not this time—you know what these original owners are like. I've told this one what seventy years of hot showers, plus our New England winters, have done, but if I know him he'll shrug and just say leave it be. If he could see it from up above, the way we do, he'd sing a different tune!

DOC: Great to see you, Bob, but now we've got a date down cellar with Ace Axhelm and his Kardiac Krew, from over in Attleboro. (*He hurries around to the front door.*) Watch your footing coming in here, Doris. It's kind of slippery. Hang on to the molding there.

DORIS: Ee-yew, what is this we're walking on?

DOC: Hard to believe, but I think that's original tongue. But look, there's some picturesque dental filigree, here along the wall. Could even be gold, if you can imagine that.

(*We cut to the basement, where our hosts join several colleagues who are standing around a bulky, looming old-style oil furnace, which seems to heave and sigh as it goes on with its work.*)

DOC: Hey, look at this quaint prewar mitral valve, Ace! And down here's the good old right ventricle—right? Listen to her knock!

ACE AXHELM (*Icily.*): That's the lower vena cava, guy. The tatty old asbestos-foil wrapping fooled you.

DORIS: But Dr. Axhelm, your people can rip all this out in a minute, can't they, and put in brand-new tubing? Why don't you do it for us right now?

ACE AXHELM: All in good time, Doris. All in good time. (*He puts one hand on the side of the furnace and smiles quietly.*)

DOC: Well, Doris, it's on to the sub-basement for us! Got your flashlight? Here we go!

DORIS (*To herself.*): I always hate this part.

(*We are in a damp, poorly lit space crammed with interlocked pipes and twisted wiring.*)

DOC: Golly, Dor, it's always a wonder to me why the original architects arranged things this way—so many different, well, functions, in so little room. You'd think they'd have learned something from Mies.

DORIS: Ow! I hit my head.

DOC: This is pretty claustrophobic, I gotta say. Cripes, what's that yucko bulging overhead object? I can't even recognize it. You know, this is all just semi-functional wreckage down here, Doris. Let's get back up to the sunshine.

(*As we say goodbye, our hosts are out on the front walk, looking back at the gallant, gawky structure.*)

DORIS: Next week, Doc, we're going to visit some great new deltoids, over at the Twenty-first Century Gym. I look forward to that!

DOC: Me, too, Doris. But let's hand it to some of these stylish, pre-Depression bods, like this one, before we go. They still sort of get you, don't they?

DORIS (*She's off camera, heading for her car.*): Right, Doc. Anything you say.

1994

ROY BLOUNT, JR.

❋   ❋ ❋

Salute to John Wayne

A few years ago, before nakedness became old hat, I was standing near Times Square looking at an opaque storefront behind which, according to a boldly lettered sign, you could talk to a nude woman. It wasn't the kind of thing I would do, but I stood there wondering what it would be like, what I would say to her, whether she would feel obliged to respond.

As I began to move on, I found myself surrounded by green arms: an army colonel and a staff sergeant materialized, passed each other and me at the same time, and exchanged crisp salutes.

Although these two may have been the only servicemen in the entire midtown area, their eyes did not meet. You can tell by looking at a person's eyes whether they are meeting someone else's. Both men were in fact angling their attention toward the TALK TO A NUDE WOMAN sign, but at any rate each of them addressed himself, quite properly, to the uniform, not the man.

I sensed an epiphany, or at least a *déjà vu*. Except that there seemed to be an element missing. I turned back to the storefront. What if the woman were actually quite good company: hearty, secure, at peace, her skin tautly billowy like a flag?

Still, you might be at some pains to give her the impression that so far as you were concerned, she was not the only fish in the sea. And she might want to convey that although you might be with a large accounting firm, and her own occupation was being talked to nude, she was not your bit of fluff.

It hit me. What was missing.

Then she came out, slightly but not unfetchingly cross-eyed, and wearing—something loose. I can never, except where they are revealing, describe women's clothes. But hers reminded me of the time in seventh grade when I showed up at my girlfriend Amy's house unexpectedly the afternoon before a Methodist hayride I was taking her to and she seemed more domestic than she did at school. She smelled of hand lotion, something I did not understand the appeal of. Her hair was wet, and she was wearing the kind of flapabout clothes one's mother wore while giving herself a home permanent. Then, through fabric, I descried the unsegmented line of Amy's whole flank. I didn't recall having seen that line, moving and unbroken by band or ruffle, before.

Amy, flustered, offered me a Coke. While she was getting it, I sat down. Her orange-and-white cat jumped into my lap and started kneading my crotch in an embarrassing way. I half stood, but the cat clung. I pulled at the cat, the cat sank its claws into me, and I was hopping, hunched, trying to wrangle the cat loose, when Amy came in with my Coke.

"Mister Fluff!" she cried, and her eyes filled with tears.

Well, that was the element. When this nude woman in mufti came out of the storefront, she was carrying a plush but alert-looking gray cat. You know how hard it is to pin down a cat's focus, but this one gave me a look, I thought, as his mistress went pitter-pat on high heels right by me, sprang into a taxi, and was gone.

Did she hold the cat, stroking it, in her lap or at her bosom, as she was being talked to? Did she let visitors touch it? Certain visitors? When I am trying to concentrate on something, cats drive me crazy, and yet I am drawn to them. To pet the cat of a not unfetching woman who is tangibly unavailable, as she watches, I imagine would be exciting but not salutary.

Associations were gathering quickly now. The salutes by which I had just been bracketed were the first I had seen in some time. They took me back to the mid-sixties, when nudity and antimilitarism were growing rampant among the young, and I was a callow, married army lieutenant. Other twenty-three-year-old Americans were daubing "Peace" and "Love" on their foreheads and filling the picture magazines with Human Be-Ins. I had grown up imprinted with sentiments like "Do your bit" and "If you must talk to a nude woman, start a family."

What adults did, I had gathered, was marry, for life; Paul had told the Corinthians that it was better to marry than to burn. I had been burning since the seventh grade. So I married. And suddenly the conscience of America was single, anti-grown-up, and running around naked at Make Love Not War rallies.

These youths must have come along a few years too late to be affected, as I had been in 1949 at the age of eight, by *The Sands of Iwo Jima*, in which John Wayne plays a sergeant who turns raw recruits into fighting men. Since I was palpably raw, and I loved playing gun battle, and John Wayne was John Wayne, that movie struck me with the force of an imperative.

Looking at it today, you might think that *The Sands of Iwo Jima* would put a decent-minded boy off warfare, since it features the broiling of what John Wayne calls "little lemon-colored characters" in pillboxes. But you don't have the feeling that John Wayne enjoys that kind of thing. The movie's great theme is the difficulty of getting through to people.

Wayne keeps trying to strike a rapport with John Agar, who plays a raw recruit whose father, a legendary colonel, was killed in action. Wayne's own son (from whom he is now estranged) is named after Agar's father, under whom Wayne once served. Agar, for his part, is bitter toward his father, who regarded Agar as "too soft." At mail call Agar learns of the birth of *his* son. When Wayne tries to congratulate him, Agar tells Wayne, coldly, pointedly, "I won't insist that he read the Marine Corps manual. Instead I'll get him a set of Shakespeare."

Wayne's eyes narrow, but with feeling. "I've tried every approach to you that I know, and got nowhere," he tells Agar. Eventually the two of them become close, after Agar saves Wayne's life by dispatching an impending Asian with an entrenching tool. Agar says, "There's something I've been trying to say, but I just can't seem to find the words."

Wayne says, "You mean you been to two universities and still can't find the words to say you been out of line?"

Then we see Wayne get killed by a sniper, and the famous flag-raising scene. Inside Wayne's shirt Agar finds a letter to Wayne's son that says, "Always do what your heart tells you is right."

I don't say, even in retrospect, that this is bad advice. But it doesn't clear up the obliqueness in *The Sands of Iwa Jima*, which I never quite got out of my system. Furthermore, the notion that becoming a fighting man was profoundly connected with adulthood stuck with me, through two universities, all the way up until I entered the army. It was ROTC camp that took the pleasure out of weapons for me. To get our attention, one Korea-vet instructor went *fwooof* with a flamethrower and said, "Presto! Chinese hamburger!" By then I was already sworn in.

I embarked upon two years of bureaucratic lieutenancy. The Vietnam buildup began. I was unable to see the point of burning villages in order to save them. I *could* see a certain appeal, for a guy my age, in friendly nude anarchy. I was living in married-junior-officer quarters and exchanging salutes.

When saluted by young men who had the good taste to be not only disaffected soldiers, like me, but also uncommissioned, I felt what is known as role strain. And they knew it. Once I fell from a bicycle in front of a leaf-raking detail—three stockade prisoners whose sudden salute I tried to return while pedaling, balancing, and holding on to some papers. I and the papers fell into the leaves. The prisoners remained at attention. "Let's all desert!" I felt like saying, but I was in no position to.

What you were supposed to say when you ran into a knot of enlisted men who were engaged in the accomplishment of their mission was "Carry on." I didn't like the sound of it. Even when not climbing out of a pile of leaves, I tried to give "Carry on" a tongue-in-cheek twist, but then it seemed to imply too racy an authorization. What if some specialist 4, caught body-painting a general's daughter, were to exclaim, "But this lieutenant said I was to carry on"?

What really bothered me, though, was being saluted by a topkick or a sergeant major who looked as if he might have served with John Wayne at Iwo Jima. Clear as it was to me that the army at the upper levels did not know what it was doing, it was just as clear that this sergeant was my superior in years, training, job responsibility, and devotion to duty. He would signal himself officially beneath me with a salute snappy enough to cut ice, a salute that, however, leaned over backward not to contain any hint of "You mooncalf, sir." I tried to develop a *wry* return-of-salute, but that is difficult.

I was myself required, of course, to salute superior officers—not as an oppressed person, which would have fit my mood, but as an accomplice. Here I showed some sixties spirit. Once, I saluted a major who was using one hand to take a last drag on a cigarette and the other to hold his hat on against the wind. A colonel would just have nodded, but this major, a young one, lost his hat and bit through his cigarette. Even a full bird colonel could be made to feel overacknowledged, I found, if saluted from fifty yards away, or while he was playing golf, or while the saluter was having a tooth filled.

A general, on the other hand, could not be made to feel that he was being shown undue respect. A general could seldom be made to feel that he was being shown anything. On Governors Island, New York, where I was stationed for a year, it was my good fortune never to serve as officer of the day, in charge of emergencies. A friend of mine named Swardlow drew that duty on the day of the big blackout of 1965, when electrical power went out all over New York City and its environs. Governors Island lies just below the downtown tip of Manhattan. Swardlow looked out his window, saw the Wall Street skyline go dark, and immediately heard the phone ring. "Brief me," said the voice of a general.

Swardlow was at a loss. "We still have phone communications, sir," was all he could think to say. The general was outraged.

In saluting a general the trick was to wait, perhaps humming tunelessly as he bore down, until the last split second before he could legitimately bring you up on charges of ignoring him. Since a general didn't want to admit the possibility that it would enter into anyone's mind to ignore him, you had a certain amount of slack to work with. It was bracing to feel that you had frustrated a general for even a moment.

You could also say to a general, "Good morning, sir," quite confidently, at, say, 1900 hours. I found that a general so addressed would never exclaim, "Good God, Lieutenant, it's getting dark!" If some general had, I could have looked at him blankly and said, "Yes, sir," and I doubt he could have made a case stand up against me in any proper court-martial.

That's the way I handled generals at Governors Island, where in those days (the coast guard has it now) First Army Headquarters was based. Because so many generals came and went there, and because I never had to brief any of them, their effect was like that of Norse gods on someone raised a Methodist: entertaining. For the second half of my tour, however, I was transferred to Fort Totten, New York, in Queens, where there was only one general. He was often alluded to as The General. He gave the impression from a distance of being that uncommon sort of officer who could have made it as a sergeant if he'd wanted to. I developed a fear that he would enter into my life.

It was at Fort Totten that Emmy, a white cat, came through our kitchen window one day fully grown: a sizable, fleecy, impure but robust Persian, fluffy even to the bottoms of her feet. No one could say where she had come from. She took up with us, and soon became widely known on the post for all the things she was seen chasing. "If it moves, run it up the flagpole" was her attitude.

There was a pheasant whose periodic appearances from out of the woods bordering Fort Totten made him something of a post institution; Emmy chased him through a softball game. The paper girl, collecting at our door one evening, looked over at Emmy admiringly and said, "She chases all the *doougs*." A captain's wife reported having seen Emmy scooping something up out of Little Neck Bay "and struggling with it."

Emmy would also chase, or at least run out at, officers emerging from the Regional Air Defense Command building at close of day. She would lie in wait under the Command building until they came down the front steps. Like a big, somehow sinewy powder puff she would pounce and light right in front of them and then scurry back to her hiding place, having shaken their composure. But The General did not rattle easily. He took a shine to her.

I didn't work in the Command building, but we were quartered right across from it. Through our kitchen window I would see The General poking playfully at Emmy with his swagger stick and hear him calling her "WP," which stands for white phosphorus, a particularly loathsome kind of explosive. She would loll when he came at her, and then she would slap at his stick. Once, she and I were out walking. Emmy was the only cat I ever had who would go on long walks with me, and keep up; but she always acted as if she only happened to be heading in the same direction I was. We passed the garden-plot area. There was The General, digging. I veered toward a grove of trees, but Emmy ran over to him. As I looked on, frozen, she wet his mustard greens. It didn't faze him. Word did get around that he disapproved of her chasing the pheasant, whose appearance in some way pleased him, but months passed and he never took that matter, or any other, up with me.

Then one afternoon I was outside in full uniform hanging diapers. Regulations prohibited doing such a thing without changing into fatigues or civilian clothes, but I was in a hurry because the diapers had to be dry before the hour at which, pursuant to post regulations, you couldn't have any laundry in view.

So I was contending with a flapping damp diaper and a high-tension clothespin when I caught a glimpse out of the corner of my eye of a specialist 6 approaching with a gleam in his.

When a superior fails to notice that you are saluting him, you are supposed to say "By your leave, sir," and he is supposed to look up and return your salute. I had the clothespin and the diaper in my hands, and my hat was resting unevenly on my head, and I was pivoting slowly so as to keep my back always to the advancing spec 6, when I heard him say, "By your lea— YO!"

Emmy had made her only recorded spring at an enlisted man, and had timed it perfectly. I said, "Carry on, soldier," with relish, over my shoulder, and made to get on with my work.

Then I saw The General coming up the hill from the other direction. It was the closest I had seen him. He was one of those people who are overweight but stay in pretty good shape by dint of the vigor it takes to carry themselves as if in excellent shape. He appeared to be bursting out of his uniform. Wind caught the diaper and wrapped it around my head.

Well, maybe I should have peeled that diaper off forthrightly, faced up to The General, and cried:

"Sir! I shouldn't be here. I got married too young and I don't believe in the war. I want to be skinny-dipping and taking consciousness-exfoliating mushrooms with someone who looks like Grace Slick."

I just stood there. Obliquity saved me. Just as I did not want to admit to myself that I was in the army, The General may not have wanted to admit to himself that I was either. Or maybe Emmy struck a pose so beguiling to The General's eye that he was loath to spoil the moment by taking into account a diapered lieutenant. (She may have represented to him a freedom beyond even a general's: she could be soft, she could be fierce, she could simply choose.) Either way, he must have angled his eyes so as to make it credible, even to himself, that I was not in his field of vision.

"Quite some cat!" I heard The General say to the spec 6. "Got a bit of the devil in her."

"Yes, sir!" I heard the spec 6 say.

When I unwrapped my head, they were all three gone.

The next time I saw Emmy, I told her, with, I am afraid, some reediness of tone, "Quite some cat is right." She was intent on something under an armored personnel carrier and didn't return my salute.

What if I had buttonholed The General, and a dialectic had been wrought: I accepting that America was not cut out for a state of nature, he that napalming Asian peasants was not going to liberate them. The spec 6 might have joined in and reminded us that at heart this was a nation of shifting and mingling middle, not rapidly diverging upper and lower, classes. Together we might have charted a wholesome course toward the seventies, and the eighties might have had some soul.

But how often do people really face up to each other, flush? And how well does it turn out when they do? We are all slanty-eyed.

Even John Wayne in *The Sands of Iwo Jima*. On liberty, and planning to get polluted and fight some MPs because he is divorced and his son never writes him, he meets a quite attractive and decent-seeming woman named Mary in a bar. She gets him to lighten up a bit, and takes him to her apartment.

The two of them see something in each other—in the sixties it would have been no cheap encounter. But at her place, from a back room, a cry is heard. It's a baby. Nice-looking kid, well taken care of. Mary is picking up soldiers, inferably talking to them nude, and getting money from them so she can feed the baby—whose father, she tells Wayne when he asks, is "gone." She adds, "There are a lot tougher ways of making a living than going to war."

Oof. Wayne gets that grim-wry look in the corners of his eyes, softens and toughens all at once, tosses all his cash to the baby in the crib, and moves his essentially compassionate gruffness to the doorway, which he fills.

"You're a very good man," Mary tells him.

Looking off, Wayne vouchsafes a quick, grave near-grin. "You can get odds on that in the Marine Corps," he rumbles, and then he moves on toward Iwo Jima.

Women have told me that I am too oblique. "Tell it to John Wayne," I should have replied. All these years, and it has only just lately begun to occur to me: if he is so good, how come he can't keep any loved ones? Here he is, putting distance between himself and the very things—women and children—whose absence is driving him to drink.

What if Mary's cat had done a quick figure-eight around John Wayne's ankles, causing him to stand there in the doorway for a while and then to come back and sit on the couch; and the cat had jumped up next to him and stared at the side of his head intently, the way cats will do, and caused him to reflect.

We may think of cats as oblique, because by our standards there is an odd cast in their eyes. But insofar as a cat is interested at all, a cat is at least as un-hung-up and up-front as the sixties. If a cat spoke, a cat would say things like, "Hey. I don't see the *problem* here."

What if this cat had moved John Wayne to reflect, "Yuh know . . . the truth of the matter is, gettin' shot by people, and burnin' 'em alive . . . It's a tougher dollar than bringin' 'em home with you for . . . intimacies and . . . considerations. And—dag burn it, it's less *savory*. Now, I'm not sayin' what you do is *right*, but . . ."

And Mary had seen his point, and then . . . I believe *The Sands of Iwo Jima* would have had a healthier formative effect on me if John Wayne had petted the cat, and exchanged looks with it, and done the same with Mary, and she had undressed. I *like* it when women undress in movies—okay, it has been run into the ground, but I'm glad it got started.

And John Wayne had said, "I've got something else to get off my chest. You know how, a lot of times, I am aware of something that other people aren't, something that can't be told, so that I have to appear less caring than I am? And a lot of times . . . like in *The Man Who Shot Liberty Valance*, I let it be believed that Jimmy Stewart shot Liberty Valance, when actually *I* did, but that's all right; but I *also* let Jimmy have the woman I love, because . . . well, because even though he can't handle a gun, he's better for her than I am."

"Oh, who says?"

"Well, the thing of it is . . . Here's the thing: I can't get over the notion that honchos and women aren't *right* for each other."

"That's not *true*."

"Oh, no? Why do you think I gravitate toward raw recruits? You can *get on* a raw recruit, that's why. The way you can't with a nude woman. You can *bark* at a raw recruit—in such a way that it's tougher'n hell but six months later the raw recruit, well, he realizes it was for his own good. To a raw recruit you can say—excuse me— you can say, 'You better shape your ass up, mister!' That doesn't work with a nude woman."

"Well . . ."

"Yeah, and nude women always want you to say such obvious things! Things that kinda go without saying: 'You have beautiful breasts and I love to touch them!' Well, I'm touching them, aren't I?"

"Mm . . ."

"Nude women think it's easy to talk to a nude woman. It's not! It's so personal! And there's a woman present!"

"Yes, but . . ."

"It's *hard*."

"I know. Shhh. I know."

And after a while Mary had added, "Isn't this better than bashing and being bashed by MPs?"

"Well . . . *yeah*. *Sure* it is."

And still later Mary had made the observation that people should not enter upon a family ("or a war," John Wayne had put in) until they have talked nude with enough members of the opposite sex ("or nationality") to dispel some of that virulent *defensiveness* that cats don't have.

I know what would have happened the next morning, though. Because it happened to me in civilian life, with a brand-new leather jacket, not long after I got divorced. John Wayne and Mary would have waked, stretched, smiled a little abashedly at each other, reached for their clothes, and found that Mary's cat had sprayed foully—and that stuff will not come out—on John Wayne's Marine Corps tunic.

Frankly, having been in the situation myself and having given some thought to what he would do in it, I don't think John Wayne could have come up with an expression in the corners of his eyes potent enough to return that salute. I think he would have tried to murder the cat, and Mary would have screamed and the baby would have waked up and screamed and John Wayne would have screamed and the cat would have screamed, lap dissolve to beachhead, projectiles shrieking.

What *is* the problem?

1985

ANDY BOROWITZ

✳ ✳ ✳

Theatre-Lobby Notices

WARNING: In Act II, there is gunfire, an explosion, and a lengthy monologue by a character named Mr. God.

WARNING: Owing to a typographical error, the *Times* review of this play omitted the word "horrible."

WARNING: When the curtain rises, you may be startled by the sight of a former movie star's ravaged face.

WARNING: In Act III, there is full frontal nudity, but not involving the actor you would like to see naked.

WARNING: During this afternoon's performance, there will be a chatty women's group from Great Neck seated directly behind you.

WARNING: People who do not find plays about incurable bone diseases entertaining should probably go home right now.

WARNING: The lead actor in tonight's play is a veteran of the Royal Shakespeare Company who always showers the first five rows with spittle.

WARNING: In interviews, the composer of tonight's long-delayed musical has referred to it as both "a pet project" and "a labor of love."

WARNING: Any audience members you may hear laughing this evening have been paid handsomely to do so.

WARNING: Tonight's play is being produced despite explicit instructions in the dead playwright's will to "burn all remaining copies to a crisp."

WARNING: The role usually played by Sir Ian McKellen will be performed tonight by the actor who played Isaac on *The Love Boat.*

WARNING: This play has a title that is very similar to that of another play currently running on Broadway, which is the one you meant to buy tickets for.

WARNING: In order to enjoy this play, it is necessary to have some knowledge of Basque dialects.

WARNING: Tom Stoppard found the play you are about to see "confusing."

WARNING: Tonight's play is performed without an intermission and you will be stuck here forever.

2002

LYNN CARAGANIS

✳   ✳   ✳

I Loved the Garish Days

I am not going to pretend that hordes of my contemporaries urged me to write this memoir.

My first important party was on a Saturday in February, 1936. I was employed making hats at the Irving Hulder Company at that time— my first job. I left work at six on Friday. I had heard about a retail shop around Thirty-third Street that was undergoing liquidation and I hurried over there to get myself some nice material for a dress. I remember I saw a rat in that shop running along the wall, which was a surprise, considering the racket and confusion of the sale. I found some taffetas, which I have always loved, and I was especially attracted to the black taffeta—but my mother would never have let me go in black, since I was only seventeen. The styles in those days were for a straight, elegant nipped-in look—so there was really no use for taffeta anyway. I noticed that the style of those days was captured perfectly in *The Great Ziegfeld*, on that actress with the lovely little nose, Myrna Loy.

With difficulty I resisted the emerald-green taffeta and settled on some nice yellow satin—not too bright. I got four yards for three dollars and fifty cents. I looked carefully at the cashier to see if she was dreading liquidation, but I saw no sign of it. Yet she looked too old to get another job. Possibly she was able to retire.

When everyone had gone to bed, I cleared the newspapers off the table and I laid out my fabric. I always sew without a pattern—merely take a good long stare before I cut. I worked till one or two that morning and I had a nice dress in time for the party. The bodice was perfectly plain and loose-fitting, which was the style, in addition to its being rather low. It was snug around the hips and hung four inches above the floor. The aim was to present yourself as a pristine goddess while artlessly showing your bosom. I wore my mother's seed-pearl necklace.

We lived at Seventieth Street and I took a taxicab downtown. The driver complained about the cold. I was wearing an old fur stole of my mother's—the wearing of furs now seems to me criminal. This cabdriver was from Canarsie, Brooklyn, and told me about his Italian bride who hadn't arrived in this country. He wasn't Italian, but he liked Italians. When we pulled up to the place and I was still inside, a man dashed out and claimed the cab. The driver said, "Hold your horses, Jake." I let him keep the change, for luck.

I left my stole with an old lady who sat dozing by the coatroom in a frilly white apron. I then went directly to the ladies' dressing room, simply to display a nice compact, I'm afraid. The way our hair was then—flat waves jammed down on your head—nothing could dislodge it. In the midst of all those dressed-up women my outfit began to look less striking than it had at home. But I guess I powdered away undaunted.

There was a narrow, long hallway paneled in oak and I made my way along this with a shoal of other women, chatting in pairs or solitary, like myself. I had a black satin evening bag over my shoulder on a chain.

The room where the party was going on had dark walls and was lighted up with chandeliers. There was a long buffet table on one side, but there were waiters, too, to bring your drinks. One came to me right away and I took a glass from him, but I had promised not to drink. A group of five young men stood in conversation perhaps twelve feet away, and one of them kept looking up at me. I would glance away and look around the room. Soon he came over to me. If I had to describe his looks, I would say he was between handsome and plain. He was dark and medium-sized. I thought he was fairly attractive.

"Well, *you're* young," he said to me. "Did your mother let you out?"

I was determined to make the fellow understand how clumsy I found these remarks, so I stared at him and then said slowly, "Did my mother let me out?"

He brushed ashes off his shirtfront and then said, "Yes," falsely jaunty. "Want a drink? Oh, I see you've got one."

"How old might *you* be, then?" I said.

"Sorry," he said in a vague, formal voice. "I've just seen someone," and he hurried away.

I might as well say I had no more interesting conversations that evening. I ate salmon and a type of scalloped potatoes with pimento. I remember I satisfied myself that I was the tallest woman there. A red-haired man had an argument with a red-haired woman near the middle of the room, which drew the party together for the few minutes till they both rushed out. One man had a beard—a great curiosity for those times—and someone pointed out Cordell Hull.

At midnight I went home in a cab. I was pleased overall, and that was my first party. I describe it at length because it was my first, and parties are what I have loved most my whole life. I worked at the

Irving Hulder Company until April that year and left it when I could, because I had no interest in hats. I then went to work at Lazarus's, and within a year I was sent by them to Europe.

I hope no one is offended by my irreverent use of Cardinal Newman's hymn lyrics. He used "garish" sarcastically. I don't. I would say there are only too few garish days, then and now. Too many wars—too few garish days. I sympathize with that rat I mentioned, who ran out into the bright lights to "mix" and be seen.

1982

RICH COHEN

* * *

Gimme No Static

When I heard that the explosion of Flight 800, from New York to Paris, might have been caused by a buildup of static electricity on one of the plane's fuel tanks, I said to myself, "I knew it!" Probably I'm not the only one who has feared and hated static electricity since youth, not the only one for whom a trip from sofa to light switch is a time of dead reckoning. When people try to tell me the good things about static electricity—how they can rub their feet on a shag rug and then shock friends or animals—I tell them this: You cannot control static electricity. You can only work with it for a time, the way FDR worked with Stalin. But sooner or later, it will get you, too.

I could come up with a scientific explanation of static electricity, something sketched on a blackboard about polarity and electrons, but why should I? If you don't believe in static electricity, just go ahead and run your fingers along a television screen. That pleasant crackle is the enemy. And once you touch it you, too, are the enemy.

You're carrying that spark with you the way Rosemary was hauling around Satan's baby.

Besides, if you ask a scientist about static, all he'll do is give you some mumbo jumbo about its being an impersonal force of nature. It reminds me of the gangster in *The Godfather* saying it's "just business." Yeah, right! It's as personal as hell. Static holds a grudge. I sometimes think static is following me down the highway of life. One time, I crossed a room and reached to switch off the lights, and a veil of sparks leaped out and hugged my hand. For a moment, my hand was entirely blue. It was like a hand you see across a dark room, attached to someone else, floating. It was not even my hand. It was her hand now. Static's hand.

Why do some people court static electricity? Why do they rub their feet on floors until their fingertips dance like live wires? I have no idea, though I have to admit that sometimes, when I have nothing better to do, I fool static electricity into thinking she's got me. It's easy: just put on a turtleneck. Even a mock turtleneck. It's like trapping a lizard in a jar. Then, when I'm good and ready, I stand before a mirror in a dark room and rub my head. The charge fizzes up and out of my hair like carbonation in a glass. But I don't congratulate myself too much for this piece of bravery. I know the difference between a house pet and a wild animal.

In summer, when the thermometer goes above ninety and kids fill the trees with houses, I forget all about static electricity. It's as if it never happened. And then, right around this time of year, I feel the familiar charge on a pair of socks fresh out of the dryer, and think, You bastards. (Most of you know static electricity as static cling. Don't be fooled. Static cling is just one of the far-flung provinces of static electricity, a face the beast takes in daylight. It's an alias!) It comes back the way the Kellengers—a group of red-haired bullies who lived in my town, a bully for every grade, every jurisdiction—came back from camp each fall.

How, then, should we deal with static in our everyday lives? Well, let's start with static on airplanes, for what is an airplane if not a mile-high microcosm of America as a whole? For one thing, if you want to inflate a balloon on an airplane you'd better have a good reason. And even if you have a great reason you'd better not rub that balloon on your head and stick it to the ceiling. And if a representative of the airline can ask "Did you pack your own bags?" why can't he ask "When you last did a load of laundry, did you use Bounce, or a similar antistatic guard?" And surely a pilot can come on the P.A. system and tell passengers to keep their shoes on. The last thing we need is people walking up and down carpeted aisles in their socks. Another thing: no sweaters. Everyone knows about sweaters and static, how sweaters are to static as Qadaffi is to terrorism. If you must wear a sweater while traveling, wear a sweater vest—which, to make them more appealing to young people, we should call muscle sweaters.

Who knows? Maybe someone will one day get hit by a jolt of static big enough to transform him into a superhero. Staticman: cape, helmet, slipper socks. Probably not, though; static will very likely remain the bad news it is—a plague, a curse on the North. Of course, some profit by this. Some always do. The guy who invented fleece, the Hubble telescope of static attraction, must have had something up his sleeve, an agenda. Whoever this man is, I bet he lives deep underground, wears a suit made of rubber, and owns dozens of radios, all tuned to no station at all, the cool white noise of static filling every space in his bunker. When we are all shocked into submission, he will surface and take control of the world.

1997

PRUDENCE CROWTHER

✳   ✳   ✳

Hepatitis F

A man who underwent 13 laser surgeries to have a misspelled
tattoo removed from his shoulder has settled a lawsuit against
the shop where he got it, his lawyer said. . . . [The tattoo showed]
a knife stabbing into a man's back, with the words "Why Not,
Everyone Else Does." The word "Else" was spelled "Elese."

—THE TIMES

AFFIDAVIT

Joey Barstow, being duly sworn, deposes and says:

I am over the age of eighteen and work as a proofreader for Tats &
Ass, at 236 Gladstone Avenue, in New Brunswick, New Jersey. I have
been in the business since 1974 and have worked in other parlors,
including Not Just Mom, in Paterson, and Inkstain Retch, in Union

City. I learned proofreading at *Modern Fumigator*, published in Camden, where I read ad copy, and at St. Mary's Hospital in Passaic, where I used to check register marks in radiology.

On the morning of August 9, 1999, the tattooist handed me the stencil with the lettering the client wanted on his shoulder. In my defense, I should say by then I could hardly see straight, on account of we'd been up all night working on a biker wedding. At the last minute, the bridesmaids, if that's what they call them, suddenly got this idea they would get wraparound ankle tattoos with the date and the interstate-highway number of the ceremony, and my eyes were falling on the floor.

Anyway, the transfer said: WHY NOT, EVERYONE ELESE DOES. They didn't show me the picture of the back-stabbing. Obviously, that would have tipped me off; you should always look at the art. But, like I said, I was wiped out and didn't think to check.

You have to understand, this type of clientele has their own style, their own rules. If they want to say GOD COULDN'T B EVERYWHERE SO HE MADE BUDWEISER on their rear ends, you don't fix it, you don't spell it out. So I looked at the paper, and without the art I figured "Elese" was the client's way of spelling Elise, his old lady, the way they will spell Porsche "Portia," or whatever. It's not like I just read over it. In fact, I asked the client if instead he meant maybe ELESE DOES EVERYONE—AND WHY NOT? or something. I mean, this isn't Princeton.

Of course, that wasn't what the customer wanted, so Bobby—he's the artist—went ahead with the original. And when the swelling went down and the redness went away, the guy came back ballistic as a hornet. I was crashing in the back on the electrolysis couch—someone's back-hair appointment had been canceled—when they woke me up. In the old days, you would just tattoo in the delete-and-close-up sign: ELESE.

It's a look, and people used to understand that. You still even see "stet" on an old bicep once in a while. Now, never. Anyhow, I tried to sell the guy on fixing it, but he was too mad, and if it's anyone's fault I guess it would be mine. Like I say, though, I was under pressure.

Further deponent sayeth not.

2002

LARRY DOYLE

❋ ❋ ❋

Life without Leann

By the time you receive this, it will have been more than five hundred days and nearly seventy-five weeks since Leann and I broke up, and, while I cannot proclaim our long ordeal ended, I am pleased to report some encouraging developments in that direction.

LEANN WATCHER OF THE WEEK ... Kudos (and a two-year subscription to this newsletter) for Mike, of Evanston, Ill., who so eloquently and informatively captures a brief encounter he had with Leann on Jan. 6.

"Leann has lost some weight," Mike writes, "but she is no less beautiful for it. She says she has been exercising, taking classes, doing this, doing that. It appeared to me that she was struggling to fill some void. Your name didn't come up, but it wasn't so much what she said as what she didn't say."

. . .

THE STRUGGLE CONTINUES ... If only it could all be such good news. But unfortunately, operation: terrible mistake has not been the success I anticipated, and I'm afraid a new strategy may be required.

As you may recall (LWL #57), the operation's objectives were to: (1) apply societal pressure; (2) foster emotional uncertainty; (3) precipitate reevaluation; and ideally (4) achieve reconciliation.

The following conversation starter was suggested:

LEANN, I WAS SO SORRY TO HEAR ABOUT YOU AND LARRY. YOU MAKE SUCH A WONDERFUL COUPLE. SO I DON'T MIND TELLING YOU, I THINK YOU ARE MAKING A TERRIBLE MISTAKE. THIS IS MY OWN PERSONAL OPINION ON THE MATTER.

Unfortunately, a number of well-meaning individuals took this suggestion rather more literally than intended, and repeated it verbatim to Leann, creating a cumulative effect other than the one desired.

I have now received word through an intermediary that Leann requests I "call off the zombies." I will honor her wishes, as always, though I must emphasize that I cannot be held responsible for the behavior of individuals acting on their own initiative.

LEANN ANONYMOUS ... In our first meeting at Gatsby's, the bartender, Mark, graciously accommodated us by closing off the back room and supplying extra folding chairs. All in attendance praised the wisdom of moving these mutual support sessions from my apartment, which some had complained was not neutral territory, and which had become quite cramped in any case. (On a related matter, Mark told me privately that, while he appreciates our patronage, he'd prefer that in the future we try not to monopolize the jukebox, or at least play a variety of songs. He says that if he doesn't see some improvement the Hank Williams selections will have to go.)

We ordered a round, and at Tom's suggestion dispensed with the reading of the minutes. We proceeded immediately to old business, resuming debate on Leann's eyes and whether they are a turbulent sea green or a sand-flecked moon blue. It appeared there could be no middle ground on the issue, until Dick stood up and declared, "To paraphrase Elton John, 'Who cares if they're blue or if they're green, those are the sweetest eyes I've ever seen.' "

The motion to adopt Dick's language carried unanimously, and we collected more change for the jukebox.

We ordered another round, and the conversation turned naturally to the rest of Leann: her quirky perky nose, her funny sunny smile, the perfect curve of her neck, her soft shoulders, and so on, until petty jealousies precluded further discussion.

Soon thereafter, we took a break to order more refreshments, and then it was time to welcome new members. A stubby and not particularly attractive man, who had been spotted with Leann as recently as mid-November, stood up in the back of the room.

"My name is Harry," he said, "and I love Leann."

Harry then related his long, sad tale, the details of which were all too familiar, ending with that same old refrain.

"She met this guy," he said. "She says she's deliriously happy."

"Deliriously happy, eh?" Gunther said slowly, staring into his beer. "He's *doomed*."

Those of us who could still laugh did so.

"Really?" Harry said, cheering considerably. "So you think there's a chance I can win her back?"

This question prompted extensive debate, leading to the inevitable threats of violence and ceasing only when Quentin moved that we change the name of our group from Lovers of Leann to Victims of Leann. The motion was soundly defeated, and we voted to adjourn.

Elmo closed the meeting by singing "Oh, Leann," including a new verse that had recently come to him in a dream:

Oh, Leann,

I love you,

Love you still,

I love you,

I love you,

I love you still,

I always will.

LEANN ALERT ... My special friend Jane, who has been so supportive during this difficult time, has suggested there is a need for a group addressing the concerns of the lovers of the Lovers of Leann. Anybody who knows somebody who might be interested in such a group should have them write to Leann Anon at this address.

THIS WEEK'S LEANN CHALLENGE ... Leann is what she eats, but how well do you know what she eats? Everybody knows Leann likes horseradish on her hamburgers, but how many of you know what *kind* of horseradish? (Here's a hint: She received a case of it for Christmas.)

The answer to last week's challenge: From left to right.

LEANN'S MAILBAG ... The mail ran heavy this week with entries to the "Candid Leann" photo contest, and it's obvious I need to remind everyone that the rules clearly stipulate that Leann must be the only person shown in the photograph.

In consideration of those who may wish to resubmit, I've decided to extend the deadline two weeks, until Jan. 29. And remember, entries cannot be returned.

One of our foreign correspondents, Miles, writes from Windsor, Ontario, "I'm going to be in the States in the near future, and I was hoping to finally meet this Leann I've heard so much about.

Do you have her phone number or an address where I can write her directly?"

No need for that, Miles. Just send your correspondence to Leann in care of this newsletter, and I'll make sure she gets it.

And finally, Reggie, of Buffalo Grove, Ill., writes in and asks:

"Larry, isn't it time you got on with your life? It's been nearly two years [sic] since Leann broke up with you [sic], and I hate to be the one to tell you, pal, but it's over. O-V-E-R [sic]."

"But listen," Reggie continues, "there are a lot of other chicks in the sea, my friend, and they're yours for the picking. Go for it!"

Well, Reggie, I don't quite know how to answer that. It's difficult to determine exactly what it is you're driving at, since I'm afraid I do not share your bitter perspective or your particular gift for playground aphorisms. So please understand when I suggest this: You know nothing about love.

But thanks for the letter, Reg. Your "Larry Loves Leann" T-shirt is in the mail.

1990

CRITICAL THINKING

GLENN EICHLER

✳ ✳ ✳

The Magical Grasp of Antiques

On weekends, my wife and I enjoy browsing in antique stores. We get up early and drive out into the country, two, three hours away, our eyes peeled for quaint and sleepy storefronts sporting that magic word, "Antiques." Cracked wooden doorknobs, rusted ice tongs, stained handkerchiefs—that's our meat. If it's old, no longer of any use, and (fingers crossed!) damaged, we love it. My friends chuckle when I tell them that the secret behind our long and successful marriage is antiquing. But when I get yet another phone call from an old buddy with the news that he and his wife have packed it in, and that if I want to reach him I'd better call his cell phone because the voice mail in his motel doesn't work—well, who's chuckling then? I have to admit that it's me, and often I never hear from that buddy again. Which is fine—it leaves me more time for antiquing.

Weekends weren't always like this. Like other young couples, we had our period of adjustment, and I won't lie: at first, I didn't realize that Sunday could mean anything more than waking at noon, mixing up a batch of my famous mimosas, and then slowly savoring the entire pitcher along with the rest of last night's pizza before turning to the TV and the first of the day's sporting events. It took marriage to help me discover the big wide world outside my four walls—a world filled with gritty, hardscrabble towns built by mill and farm and factory laborers, who, luckily for us antique lovers, have now all gone somewhere else. Retired to their summer places, no doubt. But the towns they left behind connect me to them as surely as if they were here sifting through these old ski poles with me. Yesterday's general store is today's catacomb of treasure, the food and clothes and medicine that once packed its shelves replaced by the crates of broken clothespins and dented license plates that give my Sundays shape and meaning. Sometimes when I'm standing in one of these stores, perhaps admiring a worn Victrola, I'll think, If only these walls could talk. They'd tell the tale of an America built by determination, rock-solid values, and plain old hard work. And if this record player had a tone arm, it, too, would probably make some kind of sound.

How to describe the sensation of walking into an antique store? That first moment, so pregnant with possibility, when you exchange the tiresome sunlight and fresh air of the street outside for the musky, dark, crowded aisles where pleasure awaits? There's the initial blindness, of course, and the stumble over the uneven floorboards and perhaps a sharp howl of pain as the hand you put out to steady yourself ends up in a basket of awls. But then your eyes adjust and you see the riches laid out before you: the headless dolls, the nibless pens, the shadeless lamps. And the zithers. Dear God, the zithers.

By then, my wife has usually already found the iron tractor seats and is pawing eagerly through them for new additions to her collection. But my methodology is different. I like to pick up the first item I see and just reflect on its intrinsic beauty and its place in the long parade of American history. On this day, it's a coffee cup with no handle and a logo reading "Frank's Auto Service." Wow. Frank's Auto Service. Who was Frank? Was that his first name or his last name? Or perhaps his name was Franks. Maybe he was known as Jimmy Franks or Ted Franks or Good Ol' Charlie Franks. Well liked, sure, but his incompetence as an auto mechanic was a favorite topic for the local wags. And when he took delivery of the truckload of promotional coffee cups that he thought would save his failing garage and, upon examining them, discovered that an apostrophe had been added and "Franks Auto Service" had become "Frank's Auto Service," no doubt he hurled the cup against the wall of his shop in frustration, snapping off the handle. Or maybe he inadvertently threw it at a customer, watching in horror as it broke in two against her skull. Ouch.

Was it a local housewife, who kept pet chickens and delighted friends and neighbors with her gifts of fresh eggs? Mrs. Tucker had done nothing to deserve such an assault; the worst you could say about her was that she sometimes dragged her husband along on frivolous trips in pursuit of a new hen. Mr. Tucker, a hardworking insurance actuary, had his own hobby, making decorative leather belts; truth be told, he resented these pointless expeditions, which took him away from his basket of awls. "If you want more chickens, why don't you hatch a few of those eggs instead of giving them all away!" he'd thunder in his mind, while outwardly expressing his enthusiasm for whatever odorous fowl his wife happened to be admiring. For all I know, Mr. Tucker had a severe allergy to chicken dander, which he had kept secret for years rather than separate his wife from her birds. You see, he loved her, which was why, when he noticed the pinging in her car on the way back from the hatchery, he had suggested that she get it looked at.

She had ignored his instructions to bring the car to the town's most reliable garage, which was also the busiest, going instead to Charlie Franks, because she hated waiting in lines. You could say that Mrs. Tucker never would have been in the path of that fateful cup if she had only listened to her husband. Maybe, when he arrived home that night to find her nursing a lump on her forehead, he was even tempted to say as much. But when she fell facedown in her oatmeal the next morning, dead of a freak intracerebral hematoma, did it really matter that the whole thing was in a sense her own fault?

Two weeks later they hanged poor Charlie Franks. Between the Franks family and the Tucker family, a total of fourteen children lost a parent, and though Mr. Tucker and Mrs. Franks might have fallen in love, married, and made their families whole again, they didn't. What's more, Mr. Tucker never could bring himself to fix his wife's car. He simply sold it—he no longer needed two. Not for a few years, anyway, until his eldest daughter got her driver's license, and she'd probably want something a little "kickier" than a station wagon full of guano. I turn the cup in my hand, pondering life's larger questions.

Of course, it's quite possible that Charlie's cups were printed correctly, or were printed incorrectly but Charlie, having no stronger an understanding of punctuation than the printer, never noticed. We can only speculate. One thing's for certain, however. This cup has no handle, and there's a brown stain on the bottom that would be unappetizing to see after drinking your coffee. I do not want this cup. I look for my wife to tell her so, but she has already left the shop with her prized tractor seat wrapped in butcher paper and is in the car, leaning assertively on the horn.

As I settle in on the driver's side, I think about the large pitcher of mimosas I will make upon our return. I think about the many sporting events awaiting me on my digital video recorder and about how my wife, tired from her long day in the country and facing a meeting first thing in the morning, will probably retire early. I make a mental note to remind her to take her sleeping pill.

I look back at the store with a pang as I peel out of the parking lot, gravel flying in my wake. The day, more enchanting than I could have hoped for, is over. Next week there'll be another chance to connect with the past. But for now it is time to wrest myself, with regret, from the magical grasp of antiques.

2007

BILL FRANZEN

* * *

What the Twister Did

This morning while Daryl Eckner was equalizing my sideburns with his electric clippers, I thought I saw the ring pull from a window shade hanging down from his glasses. At first, it was just dangling down in front of his face, but it started dancing around when Daryl said to me, about the big tornado that hit us a while back, "It could have been worse." Then, just like all the other weird things I'd seen since that tornado, the ring pull was gone.

Daryl was right: it could have been a whole lot worse. Because what the big Palm Sunday twister *didn't* do, fortunately, was harm any man, woman, or child here. But that was probably only because our heroic ham-radio operators got such speedy advance warnings out around town. And the fact that we all have good, strong storm cellars didn't hurt, either. After that, we were just plain lucky, I guess, because when the big twister lifted (Dad always used to say they can take off as quickly as they land), and people came out of

hiding and started looking over the damage to their homes, property, and livestock, the old-timers in town agreed that the twister
had been pretty nasty.

It seemed nasty to me, too, even though it was my first experience with one. But there was something else about it. I mean, I
didn't have to survey what was left of Mom's and my home and
belongings or of my bicycle-repair shop in the barn for very long to
understand why people always call tornadoes mischievous. Because
you know what the big twister did? It yanked the little man off the
top of my horseshoes trophy (seven years ago, in high school, I
pitched a pretty accurate shoe) and blew him right into a small 7Up
bottle. Didn't even disturb the right arm he's got cocked back. And
you know where we finally found the bottle? Inside one of Mom's
empty hatboxes. (Ever since Dad passed on, it seems that Mom can't
collect enough empty cardboard boxes.) And that turned up in the
front seat of my Jeep, which was discovered about two-thirds of a
mile down the road from our place, sitting on top of the Metcalfs'
silo, where the dome had been.

Now, if that had been the tornado's only weird trick on us, it
wouldn't have seemed so remarkable. But there was a lot more. Take
the big Swiss Army knife I kept in my top bureau drawer. I found it
inside the grass-seed spreader, which had its T-shaped handle stuck
through one of the holes of the big birdhouse, which was still sitting undisturbed on its pole in our front yard. And all the blades
and tools on the knife were flipped out—same as in the poster they
used to have taped up in the window at the hardware store—minus
the fish-scaler/hook-disgorger, which was gone completely. The
next week, when the insurance agent was going around the place
with me, *that* showed up, with the starter rope from the lawnmower
wrapped around it, inside the banjo Dad made for me, from a locally
grown gourd, when I was born.

The twister didn't pick on just me and Mom, though. It was to blame for similar "jokes" all over town. Frank Nisswa, the half-Sioux whose farm is on the opposite side of town from us, said the tornado sucked all the water out of his well and carried his china cabinet eight hundred yards before setting it down again in his cornfield, without breaking a single cup or dish. And Frank told me that inside, sitting on top of a stack of dinner plates, he found the vise that had been clamped to his workbench. Yvette Kenner, one of those brave ham-radio operators I mentioned before, said that she and her boyfriend and her twins came out of their storm cellar expecting the very worst, but all they found was their electronic fun organ's bossa-nova beat playing and their parakeet plucked clean of feathers but otherwise OK. And Daryl Eckner himself, barber and captain of They Might Be Gods, our State Champion tug-of-war team, has told everyone over and over how he climbed out of his cellar to find that the traveling van, with the team's name painted in fancy circus lettering on both sides, which was normally parked in his backyard, had vanished. It hasn't shown up yet. According to Daryl, a spiderweb between the legs of his barbecue—only twenty feet from where the van had been sitting—hadn't been touched. All there was, he said, was the purple foil wrapping from an Easter candy stuck in the middle.

Word of what the big twister did must have gotten out fast, because a man in a red beret—some sort of carnival big shot—showed up during our cleanup. In no time, with the help of our eager ham-radio operators, he had the news out that he'd be setting up a tent where the self-service car wash used to be, and was ready to pay cash for our "tornado curiosities." Even before he got all the tent stakes in the ground he bought Chet Rittie's shotgun-with-seven-blades-of-straw-and-a-mascara-applicator-driven-into-the-stock, and Herman Malone's phone-receiver-embedded-in-the-leaf-from-a-dinner-table, and Gladys Wells' sneaker-lodged-inside-a-twenty-foot-length-of-hose.

I wonder if it was really a great idea to be pitching that easy money around a town in such disrepair, where everyone's state aid and insurance money was still two weeks away. It was tempting to me, I know, since it came right when I needed cash to get the crane to come in and take my Jeep down off the Metcalfs' silo. I didn't want to sell my horseshoe-pitcher-in-the-7Up-bottle, though. How many times is a guy—even a guy living in twister country—going to get a hold of a keepsake like that? So, several nights running, once Mom was asleep (it seems she can't sleep enough since Dad passed on), I did something I'm not proud of: I fashioned my *own* twister jokes. I figured the carnival guy wouldn't know the difference, and maybe I'd get my Jeep down.

It wasn't easy, what with half my bicycle-repair tools scattered who knows where, but after a few sleepless nights in the barn I'd assembled quite a group of "authentic" twister curiosities. There was the half-a-bowling-ball-with-the-bicycle-tire-pump-lodged-in-the-thumbhole. And the tricky ball-of-piano-wire-and-salad-forks-and-umbrella-skeleton-and-bicycle-spokes-inside-a-big-gold-fishbowl. And my favorite, which I really wished I could keep—the ice-cream-scoop-coming-out-of-bongos-with-gardening-shears-going-in. Well, the carnival man really went for them—he even whistled when he first picked up the bowling-ball thing. And I hired the crane for a hundred and seventy-five dollars *and* kept my man-in-the-bottle.

But about two months after the big twister, I put him in one of Mom's empty shoeboxes that still had the white tissue in it and buried it. I didn't need it anymore to know how weird things could be after a tornado, because even though our town was pretty much back together, I couldn't walk down Center Street without, for a moment, seeing some kind of twister-curiosity mirage, like a lampshade on a fire hydrant, or the float ball from a toilet tank drifting across a big puddle. And once I even thought I saw Mom's rocker, which we never did find, hooked upside down on the town-hall clock. I even planned how I would wait for the hand to lower to twenty after the hour and catch the thing when it slid off. But it disappeared at ten past. The worst time had to be when I was driving home in my rescued Jeep, with the annoying new whine it makes over thirty, to share some homemade soup with Mom and finish replacing the shingles. I glanced up at the top of the Metcalfs' silo, where the new dome was under way, and for just a moment I saw myself on the lookout up there in my Jeep with a portable ham radio on my knees and my half-a-pair-of-binoculars around my neck.

This condition let up all last week, but this morning, in the barber chair, there was that damn ring pull swinging from Daryl Eckner's glasses. It didn't last long, though, and next thing I knew Daryl was going on and on about the upcoming dance that's supposed to raise money for our tug-of-war team's new van. "We're all bouncing back now, huh?" Daryl said, spinning me around to look at myself in the mirror. And I saw a largemouth bass on my head—until Daryl spun me back a hundred and eighty degrees from the mirror, and I realized it was just the old prize-winner that had always been mounted on Daryl's wall. And tonight, while reorganizing the hall closet, I came across the fancy Sunday bonnet Mom used to wear to church before she started sleeping through the bells. I almost yanked the long peacock feather from under the hatband, but then I realized that that was exactly where it belonged. So while I'm hoping that the ring pull was the last of my mirages, I'm beginning to wonder now if I'll ever again see anything the way I used to.

1984

IAN FRAZIER

Lamentations of the Father

Of the beasts of the field, and of the fishes of the sea, and of all foods that are acceptable in my sight you may eat, but not in the living room. Of the hoofed animals, broiled or ground into burgers, you may eat, but not in the living room. Of the cloven-hoofed animal, plain or with cheese, you may eat, but not in the living room. Of the cereal grains, of the corn and of the wheat and of the oats, and of all the cereals that are of bright color and unknown provenance you may eat, but not in the living room. Of the quiescently frozen dessert and of all frozen after-meal treats you may eat, but absolutely not in the living room. Of the juices and other beverages, yes, even of those in sippy-cups, you may drink, but not in the living room, neither may you carry such therein. Indeed, when you reach the place where the living room carpet begins, of any food or beverage there you may not eat, neither may you drink.

But if you are sick, and are lying down and watching something, then may you eat in the living room.

And if you are seated in your high chair, or in a chair such as a greater person might use, keep your legs and feet below you as they were. Neither raise up your knees, nor place your feet upon the table, for that is an abomination to me. Yes, even when you have an interesting bandage to show, your feet upon the table are an abomination, and worthy of rebuke. Drink your milk as it is given you, neither use on it any utensils, nor fork, nor knife, nor spoon, for that is not what they are for; if you will dip your blocks in the milk, and lick it off, you will be sent away. When you have drunk, let the empty cup then remain upon the table, and do not bite it upon its edge and by your teeth hold it to your face in order to make noises in it sounding like a duck; for you will be sent away.

When you chew your food, keep your mouth closed until you have swallowed, and do not open it to show your brother or your sister what is within; I say to you, do not so, even if your brother or your sister has done the same to you. Eat your food only; do not eat that which is not food; neither seize the table between your jaws, nor use the raiment of the table to wipe your lips. I say again to you, do not touch it, but leave it as it is. And though your stick of carrot does indeed resemble a marker, draw not with it upon the table, even in pretend, for we do not do that, that is why. And though the pieces of broccoli are very like small trees, do not stand them upright to make a forest, because we do not do that, that is why. Sit just as I have told you, and do not lean to one side or the other, nor slide down until you are nearly slid away. Heed me; for if you sit like that, your hair will go into the syrup. And now behold, even as I have said, it has come to pass.

LAWS PERTAINING TO DESSERT

For we judge between the plate that is unclean and the plate that is clean, saying first, if the plate is clean, then you shall have dessert.

But of the unclean plate, the laws are these: If you have eaten most of your meat, and two bites of your peas with each bite consisting of not less than three peas each, or in total six peas, eaten where I can see, and you have also eaten enough of your potatoes to fill two forks, both forkfuls eaten where I can see, then you shall have dessert. But if you eat a lesser number of peas, and yet you eat the potatoes, still you shall not have dessert; and if you eat the peas, yet leave the potatoes uneaten, you shall not have dessert, no, not even a small portion thereof. And if you try to deceive by moving the potatoes or peas around with a fork, that it may appear you have eaten what you have not, you will fall into iniquity. And I will know, and you shall have no dessert.

ON SCREAMING

Do not scream; for it is as if you scream all the time. If you are given a plate on which two foods you do not wish to touch each other are touching each other, your voice rises up even to the ceiling, while you point to the offense with the finger of your right hand; but I say to you, scream not, only remonstrate gently with the server, that the server may correct the fault. Likewise if you receive a portion of fish from which every piece of herbal seasoning has not been scraped off, and the herbal seasoning is loathsome to you, and steeped in vileness, again I say, refrain from screaming. Though the vileness overwhelm you, and cause you a faint unto death, make not that sound from within your throat, neither cover your face, nor press your fingers to your nose. For even now I have made the fish as it should be; behold, I eat of it myself, yet do not die.

CONCERNING FACE AND HANDS

Cast your countenance upward to the light, and lift your eyes to the hills, that I may more easily wash you off. For the stains are upon you; even to the very back of your head, there is rice thereon. And in the breast pocket of your garment, and upon the tie of your shoe, rice and other fragments are distributed in a manner wonderful to see. Only hold yourself still; hold still, I say. Give each finger in its turn for my examination thereof, and also each thumb. Lo, how iniquitous they appear. What I do is as it must be; and you shall not go hence until I have done.

VARIOUS OTHER LAWS, STATUTES, AND ORDINANCES

Bite not, lest you be cast into quiet time. Neither drink of your own bathwater, nor of bathwater of any kind; nor rub your feet on bread, even if it be in the package; nor rub yourself against cars, nor against any building; nor eat sand.

Leave the cat alone, for what has the cat done, that you should so afflict it with tape? And hum not that humming in your nose as I read, nor stand between the light and the book. Indeed, you will drive me to madness. Nor forget what I said about the tape.

COMPLAINTS AND LAMENTATIONS

O my children, you are disobedient. For when I tell you what you must do, you argue and dispute hotly even to the littlest detail; and when I do not accede, you cry out, and hit and kick. Yes, and even sometimes do you spit, and shout "stupid-head" and other blasphemies, and hit and kick the wall and the molding thereof when you are sent to the corner. And though the law teaches that no one shall be sent to the corner for more minutes than he has years of age, yet I would leave you there all day, so mighty am I in anger. But upon being sent to the corner you ask straightaway, "Can I come out?" and I reply, "No, you may not come out." And again you ask, and again I give the same reply. But when you ask again a third time, then you may come out.

Hear me, O my children, for the bills they kill me. I pay and pay again, even to the twelfth time in a year, and yet again they mount higher than before. For our health, that we may be covered, I give six hundred and twenty talents twelve times in a year; but even this covers not the fifteen hundred deductible for each member of the family within a calendar year. And yet for ordinary visits we still are not covered, nor for many medicines, nor for the teeth within our mouths. Guess not at what rage is in my mind, for surely you cannot know.

For I will come to you at the first of the month and at the fifteenth of the month with the bills and a great whining and moan. And when the month of taxes comes, I will decry the wrong and unfairness of it, and mourn with wine and ashtrays, and rend my receipts. And you shall remember that I am that I am: before, after, and until you are twenty-one. Hear me then, and avoid me in my wrath, O children of me.

1997

BRUCE JAY FRIEDMAN

* * *

Let's Hear It for a Beautiful Guy

Sammy Davis is trying to get a few months off for a complete rest.
—EARL WILSON, FEBRUARY 7, 1974

I have been trying to get a few months off for a complete rest, too, but I think it's more important that Sammy Davis get one. I feel that I can scrape along and manage somehow, but Sammy Davis always looks so strained and tired. The pressure on the guy must be enormous. It must have been a terrific blow to him when he switched his allegiance to Agnew and Nixon, only to have the whole thing blow up in his face. I was angry at him, incidentally, along with a lot of other fans of his, all of us feeling he had sold us down the river. But after I had thought it over and let my temper cool a bit, I changed my mind and actually found myself standing up for him, saying I would bet anything that Agnew and Nixon had made some secret promises to Sammy about casing the situation of blacks—ones that the public still doesn't know about. Otherwise, there was no way he would have thrown in his lot with that crowd. In any case, I would forgive the guy just about anything. How can I feel any other way when I think of the pleasure he's given me over the years, dancing and clowning around and wrenching those songs out of that wiry little body? Always giving his all, no matter what the composition of the audience. Those years of struggle with the Will Mastin Trio, and then finally making it, only to find marital strife staring him in the face. None of us will ever be able to calculate what it took out of him each time he had a falling-out with Frank. Is there any doubt who Dean and Joey sided with on those occasions? You can be sure Peter Lawford didn't run over to offer Sammy any solace. And does anyone ever stop to consider the spiritual torment he must have suffered when he made the switch to Judaism? I don't even want to talk about the eye. So, if anyone in the world does, he certainly deserves a few months off for a complete rest.

Somehow, I have the feeling that if I met Sammy, I could break through his agents and that entourage of his and convince him he ought to take off with me and get the complete rest he deserves. I don't want any ten percent, I don't want any glory; I just feel I owe it to him. Sure he's got commitments, but once and for all he's got to stop and consider that it's one time around, and no one can keep up that pace of his forever.

The first thing I would do is get him out of Vegas. There is absolutely no way he can get a few months' rest in that sanatorium. I would get him away from Vegas, and I would certainly steer clear of Palm Springs. Imagine him riding down Bob Hope Drive and checking into a hotel in the Springs! For a rest? The second he walked into the lobby, it would all start. The chambermaids would ask him to do a chorus of "What Kind of Fool Am I?" right in the lobby, and, knowing Sammy and his big heart, he would probably oblige. I think I would take him to my place in New York, a studio. We would have to eat in, because if I ever showed up with Sammy Davis at the Carlton Delicatessen, where I have my breakfast, the roof would fall in. The owner would ask him for an autographed picture to hang up next to Dustin Hoffman's, and those rich young East Side girls would go to town on him. If they ever saw me walk in with Sammy Davis, that would be the end of his complete rest. They would attack him like vultures, and Sammy would be hard put to turn his back on them, because they're not broads.

We would probably wind up ordering some delicatessen from the Stage, although I'm not so sure that's a good idea; the delivery boy would recognize him, and the next thing you know, Sammy would give him a C-note, and word would get back to Alan King that Sammy had ducked into town. How would it look if he didn't drop over to the Stage and show himself? Next thing you know, the news would reach Jilly's, and if Frank was in town—well, you can imagine how much rest Sammy would get. I don't know if they're feuding these days, but you know perfectly well that, at minimum, Frank would send over a purebred Afghan. Even if they were feuding.

I think what we would probably do is lay low and order a lot of Chinese food. I have a hunch that Sammy can eat Chinese takeout food every night of the week. I know I can, and the Chinese takeout delivery guys are very discreet. So we would stay at my place. I'd give him the sleeping loft, and I'd throw some sheets on the couch downstairs for me. I would do that for Sammy to pay him back for all the joy he's given me down through the years. And I would resist the temptation to ask him to sing, even though I would flip out if he so much as started humming. Can you imagine him humming "The Candy Man"? *In my apartment?* Let's not even discuss it.

Another reason I would give him the sleeping loft is that there is no phone up there. I would try like the devil to keep him away from the phone, because I know the second he saw one he would start thinking about his commitments, and it would be impossible for the guy not to make at least one call to the Coast. So I'd just try to keep him comfortable for as long as possible, although pretty soon my friends would begin wondering what ever happened to me, and it would take all the willpower in the world not to let on that I had Sammy Davis in my loft and was giving him a complete rest.

I don't kid myself that I could keep Sammy Davis happy in my loft for a full couple of months. He would be lying on the bed, his frail muscular body looking lost in a pair of boxer shorts, and before long I would hear those fingers snapping, and I would know that the wiry little great entertainer was feeling penned up, and it would be inhuman to expect him to stay there any longer. I think that when I sensed that Sammy was straining at the leash, I would rent a car—a Ford LTD (that would be a switch for him, riding in a Middle American car)—and we would ride out to my sister and brother-in-law's place in Jersey. He would probably huddle down in the seat, but somehow I have the feeling that people in passing cars would spot him. We'd be lucky if they didn't crash into telephone poles. And if I know Sammy, whenever someone recognized him he wouldn't be able to resist taking off his shades and graciously blowing them a kiss.

The reason I would take Sammy to my sister and brother-in-law's house is not only that it's out of the way but also because they're simple people and would not hassle him—especially my brother-in-law. My sister would stand there with her hands on her hips, and when she saw me get out of the Ford with Sammy, she would cluck her tongue and say, "There goes my crazy brother again," but she would appear calm on the surface, even though she would be fainting dead away on the inside. She would say something like "Oh, my God, I didn't even clean the floors," but then Sammy would give her a big hug and a kiss, and I'm sure that he would make a call, and a few weeks later she would have a complete new dining-room set, the baby grand she always wanted, and a puppy.

She would put Sammy up in her son's room (he's away at graduate school), saying she wished she had something better, but he would say, "Honey, this is just perfect." And he would mean it, too, in a way, my nephew's bedroom being an interesting change from those $1,000-a-day suites at the Tropicana. My brother-in-law has a nice easygoing style and would be relaxing company for Sammy, except that Al does work in television and there would be a temptation on his part to talk about the time he did *The Don Rickles Show* and how different and sweet a guy Don is when you get him offstage. If I know Sammy, he would place a call to CBS—with no urging from any of us—and see to it that Al got to work on his next special. If the network couldn't do a little thing like that for him, the hell with them, he would get himself another network. Sammy's that kind of guy.

One danger is that my sister, by this time, would be going out of her mind and wouldn't be able to resist asking Sammy if she could have a few neighbors over on a Saturday night. Let's face it, it would be the thrill of a lifetime for her. I would intercede right there, because it wouldn't be fair to the guy, but if I know Sammy he would tell her, "Honey, you go right ahead." She would have a mixed group over—Italians, an Irish couple, some Jews, about twelve people tops—and she would wind up having the evening catered, which of course would lead to a commotion when she tried to pay for the stuff. No way Sammy would let her do that. He would buy out the whole delicatessen, give the delivery guy a C-note, and probably throw in an autographed glossy without being asked.

Everyone at the party would pretend to be casual, as if Sammy Davis wasn't there, but before long the Irish space salesman's wife (my sister's crazy friend, and what a flirt *she* is) would somehow manage to ask him to sing, and imagine Sammy saying no in a situation like that. Everyone would say just one song, but that bighearted son of a gun would wind up doing his entire repertoire, probably putting out every bit as much as he does when he opens at the Sands. He would do it all—"The Candy Man," "What Kind of Fool Am I?" tap-dance, play the drums with chopsticks on an end table, do some riffs on my nephew's old trumpet, and work himself into exhaustion. The sweat would be pouring out of him, and he would top the whole thing off with "This Is My Life" ("and I don't give a damn"). Of course, his agents on the Coast would pass out cold if they ever got wind of the way he was putting out for twelve nobodies in Jersey. But as for Sammy, he never did know anything about halfway measures. He either works or he doesn't, and he would use every ounce of energy in that courageous little showbiz body of his to see to it that my sister's friends—that mixed group of Italians, Irish, and Jews—had a night they'd never forget as long as they lived.

Of course, that would blow the two months of complete rest, and I would have to get him out of Jersey fast. By that time, frankly, I would be running out of options. Once in a while, I pop down to Puerto Rico for a three- or four-day holiday, but, let's face it, if I showed up in San Juan with Sammy, first thing you know, we would be hounded by broads, catching the show at the Flamboyan, and Dick Shawn would be asking Sammy to hop up onstage and do a medley from *Mr. Wonderful*. (He was really something in that show, battling Jack Carter tooth and nail, but too gracious to use his bigger name to advantage.)

Another possibility would be to take Sammy out to see a professor friend of mine who teaches modern lit at San Francisco State and would be only too happy to take us in. That would represent a complete change for Sammy, a college campus, but as soon as the school got wind he was around, I'll bet you ten to one they would ask him to speak either to a film class or the drama department or even a political-science group. And he would wind up shocking them with his expertise on the Founding Fathers and the philosophy behind the Bill of Rights. The guy reads, and I'm not talking about *The Bette Davis Story*. Anyone who sells Sammy Davis short as an intellectual is taking his life in his hands.

In the end, Sammy and I would probably end up in Vermont, where a financial-consultant friend of mine has a cabin that he never uses. He always says to me, "It's there, for God's sakes—use it." So I would take Sammy up there, away from it all, but I wouldn't tell the financial consultant who I was taking, because the second he heard it was Sammy Davis he would want to come along. Sammy and I would start out by going into town for a week's worth of supplies at the general store, and then we would hole up in the cabin. I'm not too good at mechanical things, but we would be sort of roughing it, and there wouldn't be much to do except chop some firewood, which I would take care of while Sammy was getting his complete rest.

I don't know how long we would last in Vermont. Frankly, I would worry after a while about being able to keep him entertained, even though he would be there for a complete rest. We could talk a little about Judaism, but, frankly, I would be skating on thin ice in that area, since I don't have the formal training he has or any real knowledge of theology. The Vermont woods would probably start us batting around theories about the mystery of existence, but to tell the truth, I'd be a little bit out of my depth in that department, too. He's had so much experience on panel shows, and I would just as soon not go one-on-one with him on that topic.

Let's not kid around, I would get tense after a while, and Sammy would feel it. He would be too good a guy to let on that he was bored, but pretty soon he would start snapping those fingers and batting out tunes on the back of an old *Saturday Evening Post* or something, and I think I would crack after a while and say, "Sammy, I tried my best to supply you with a couple of months of complete rest, but I'm running out of gas." He would tap me on the shoulder and say, "Don't worry about it, babe," and then, so as not to hurt my feelings, he would say he wanted to go into town to get some toothpaste. So he would drive in, with the eye and all, and I know damned well the first thing he would do is call his agents on the Coast and ask them to read him the "N.Y. to L.A." column of a few *Varieties*. Next thing you know, I would be driving him to the airport, knowing in my heart that I hadn't really succeeded. He would tell me that any time I got to the Coast or Vegas or the Springs, and I wanted anything, *anything*, just make sure to give him a ring. And the following week, I would receive a freezer and a videotape machine and a puppy.

So I think I'm just not the man to get Sammy Davis the complete rest he needs so desperately. However, I certainly think someone should. How long can he keep driving that tortured little frame of his, pouring every ounce of his strength into the entertainment of Americans? I know, I know—there's Cambodia and Watergate, and, believe me, I haven't forgotten our own disadvantaged citizens. I know all that. But when you think of all the joy that man has spread through his nightclub appearances, his albums, his autobiography, his video specials, and even his movies, which did not gross too well but were a lot better than people realized, and the things he's done not only for his friends but for a lot of causes the public doesn't know about— when you think of all that courageous little entertainer has given to this land of ours, and then you read that he's trying, repeat *trying*, to get a few months off for a complete rest and he can't, well, then, all I can say is that there's something basically rotten in the system.

1974

POLLY FROST

✳ ✳ ✳

Plan 10 from Zone R-3

"It's your mother," Dad said on the phone. He wanted me to come home immediately. Was she sick? Had they argued? "All I know," he said, "is that she's not herself."

I drove into New Mustford the next day, for the first time since last Christmas. I smiled—still the same old place, no different from when I was in high school.

Looking back, though, I can see that I was ignoring the warning signals. Old Mr. Mannheim's cornfields were nothing but dirt, with red flags dividing them into squares. And when I pulled into "Friendly Tim's" service station, Tim came out in a three-piece suit. He was carrying a smartphone. It wasn't anything like my own BlackBerry, though: it was skinny, long, and when I looked at it, I was blinded by its glare. "I don't sell gasoline anymore," Tim said.

I drove to 2725 Gesner Avenue. "It's good to see you," Dad said as we hugged. "Your mom's out stocking up on food for your visit."

At that moment, Mother pulled into the driveway. "Am I late?" she asked, opening up a smartphone identical to Tim's. "Yes. I have you down for two o'clock. I'm sorry, I was held up at the title company. Did you have a look around the place?"

I didn't know how to respond. Mom had never had a full-time job before. Dad winked at me. "I showed her the house," he said to Mom.

Mom was beaming at me. "So you're ready to make an offer?"

"For God's sake, Eileen," Dad said. "Let her change her clothes first."

Mom got a look on her face that I'd never seen before. She walked past us, into the house.

"How long has she been like this?" I asked Dad.

"Couple of weeks."

I called after her, "Can I bring in the groceries?"

Mom didn't respond.

"You did go shopping, didn't you?" Dad yelled.

She came to the door. "Of course. I picked up three foreclosures on the west side of town."

The tension between them was too much for me. I walked into town. The beauty of the summer day almost took my mind off what I'd seen at home.

As I was crossing the street, I noticed my best friend from junior high, Denise, stopped at a red light. I waved, and jumped into her car.

"This is quite a surprise," she said. "I don't have you down on my calendar. However, I do have a few minutes between appointments. Let me show you something."

"Sure." I was taken aback by her coolness. Denise had always been a sweet girl. The last time I saw her she was barely scraping by, selling her own baked goods. The economic downturn hit her hard.

But she was certainly doing better now. Her BMW convertible glided through the streets, and when her hair blew back I saw that she was wearing diamond earrings. She kept one hand on the steering wheel and the other on one of those BlackBerry-like things my mother and Tim had.

"Hey, it's great to see you doing so well!" I said, trying to break the ice.

"Whole town's doing well," she said in that same controlled tone. "No recession's going to get this little hamlet down. We know what we have to do. Keep selling real estate."

She pulled to a stop in front of an ancient shack. "Note the late-Victorian design elements," she said.

As we walked to the front door, a man swung it open and pointed a shotgun at us. "Don't come any closer," he said.

I pulled Denise away, but she shook me off and advanced toward him.

"I mean it—come any closer and I'll shoot," he said.

Denise stepped up to him, removed the gun from his hands, and threw it to the ground. "Please don't take this house away from me!" he cried. "There's no place left I can afford to rent."

"It's your responsibility," she said. "You should have bought the place when the price was low and you had some money."

This wasn't Denise. I stifled a scream and ran down the street. I cut through a vacant lot and tripped over a cement foundation. I picked myself up and tried to keep going, but there were arms around me. A voice whispered, "Don't make a sound."

I turned to face him. It was Barry, my first boyfriend. He looked like he hadn't slept for days.

"What's going on?" I asked.

He took my hand and led me to an oak tree. Beneath it was the fully clothed body of a woman. I jumped back. "Is she dead?"

Barry pointed to a kind of umbilical cord attaching her body to one of those electronic devices I'd come to fear. "Her thoughts are being transferred into the RAM of this smartphone." He kept his voice low and checked around us. "When she awakens, she won't be able to function without it."

"I don't understand."

He put his hands on my shoulders. "Aliens. They can only do one thing: take space and divide it up. My guess is they ran out of space on their planet and began dividing up the atmosphere. This went on for several light-years, then they bumped into Earth. Now they're continuing the same process here."

The weirdness seemed to be coming at me from all directions. I tore away. I needed to be with someone I could trust.

When I arrived home, my parents were on the porch. Mom was sitting on Dad's lap. Something about this gave me the creeps.

"We've been discussing your future," Dad said. "Your mom is right—you can't go on throwing money away every month on rent. We have just the place for you."

"She's already seen the house," Mom said. "Let's show her the backyard." They each took one of my hands, the way they used to when I was a kid. "Look how big it is!" Mom exclaimed. "And there are no restrictions. Wouldn't you love to look out your living-room window and see your very own mini-mall?"

"Or condo village," Dad added. "It might take a while to get some investors, but it'll give you something to look forward to."

What had the aliens done with Mom and Dad? "No, no—you can't make me buy the family home!" I shrieked. Now I knew Barry was right. I broke away and dashed to my car. I had to warn the rest of the country.

Confused, I punched 9-1-1 into my pay-as-you-go cell phone.

Finally, it was picked up. "The operator is closing a deal right now," a machine said. "But if you leave your name and number at the beep and state what kind of property you're interested in, she'll try to get back to you as soon as possible."

I drove over to Barry's place. He was packing. "We've got to get out of here," he said, throwing the last boxes into his pickup truck. "Jump in."

We headed for the freeway, but there was a roadblock at the entrance. There were hundreds of them. "Make a bid! Make a bid!" they chanted.

Barry swung the truck around. "We've got to check our financing!" he yelled to them.

"We're going to end up one of them, aren't we?" I cried, pounding the dashboard in frustration.

"I've got one more idea that might work," Barry said. "I've noticed that they're attracted to bodies of water." As soon as we pulled back into his driveway, he handed me a shovel. "Start digging," he said.

I don't know how many hours went by while we shoveled earth. We didn't see his landlord until he ran his flashlight over us.

"What do you think you're doing?"

Barry seemed unfazed. "Making an improvement," he said. He'd obviously had a lot more experience with them than I had.

His landlord seemed satisfied, and went back inside. Barry ran a hose into the ditch.

"Should I make a sign saying 'OPEN HOUSE—WATERFRONT PROPERTY'?" I said.

"All we have to do is turn on the faucet and they'll sense the possibilities," Barry said.

He was right. Before the ditch was halfway full, the entire population of the town was there.

"Prime development potential!"

"Sewers in?"

"Does it perc?"

I knew I'd never be able to get their ghoulish voices out of my head as long as I lived. But, thanks to Barry, we had a chance. I kissed him.

"Take your car and head for Bueno Pass," he said. "I'll detain them and join you in thirty minutes."

I waited in the hills above town. Seventeen years ago, Barry and I used to cut school, come up here, and smoke grass. I counted the lights in the valley below. Soon there would be hundreds more. Thousands. The area around me began to glow, like the opening of a new shopping center. Was this the dawn of their age? Was this what nighttime on Earth would be like when there wasn't a single inch of darkness left? Had the Mother Ship arrived?

I felt a touch on my neck and turned. Barry was kneeling beside me. Behind him blazed the lights of his pickup truck. I reached to embrace him. We had so many years apart to make up for. I wanted all of him. I ran my fingers down his arm and clutched his hand.

That's when I felt it, the smartphone.

"What's wrong?" Barry asked in too level a voice.

I'd backed a good five feet away. "Nothing," I said. Had they gotten him, too? I had to be certain. "God, this area up here would make a terrific suburb of New Mustford. Why don't you walk over there and take a look at the fabulous view sites?"

He took a few steps and then stopped. "You're right. It's going to grow into one of America's great cities. And it will be called Barryburg. No—Barryville."

I was out of there in a cloud of dust and gravel. I drove for hours. Sometime after midnight, I started weaving pretty badly and pulled to the side of the road. I tried to stay awake, but I was entering a dream world of overpowering beauty. People didn't have to work at jobs anymore. They invested in office condos and sat there, waiting for them to appreciate. Parking spaces, seats in stadiums, places in supermarket lines—all were for sale as timeshares. And, instead of fighting, the major powers got together and made lateral land exchanges.

Why had I struggled so hard against this? No matter what the economy was, I would have a quality lifestyle.

1987

FRANK GANNON

✳ ✳ ✳

What He Told Me

*People would rather think about Babe Ruth, Willie Mays, Hank
Aaron, and Stan Musial. Who wants to be reminded of Attila
the Hun?*

—THE MICK, MICKEY MANTLE AND HERB GLUCK

Let's begin somewhere. I don't know what "years" are, so I guess I
really couldn't tell you. Always remember that there is only one sun
in the sky and there is only one of me. So don't bother me about
what year it was. It was any year I felt like. And you *will* bow and taste
hot steel. But only if I feel like it.

So don't bother me.

At any rate, we had just crushed the descendants of the Scythians,
and we were feeling pretty good about ourselves. We were all out
there on the plain, laughing, messing around, slapping each other,
stabbing. If you want the truth, we were all about half bagged. We

were pouring whatever it was that the descendants of the Scythians used to drink over *everybody*. We were just cracking up.

It was a long time ago, but I still remember one particular descendant of a Scythian. His name was Dnargash or something, one of those Scythian names. Anyway, this guy had the worst lisp I ever heard. I don't know about you, but if there's anything that really gets on my nerves, it's a lisp.

Anyway, this is a funny story. I'm riding along, nice day, not a care in the world. Suddenly I hear this guy behind me. He's talking just like this, I swear to God. I am not making this up.

NGASHO FLAM IK WEEDELL FURESY!

Then he gets all excited:

IB FLUEW! NGASHO FLAM IK WEEDELL FURESY!

Right away I think, Cut me a break. Then I swing my horse around, bring my sword back, and his head is history. I didn't even watch the head, but I hear it went a long way. Someone told me 500 feet, but I don't know. Numbers don't mean anything to me. By that I mean numbers don't mean *anything* to me.

All I know is that I made a full, smooth swing, and I made contact. All spring I had worked on cutting down on my swing and just *meeting* the head. I had tried to stop trying to *kill* every head I saw up there.

It had paid off. It was the best year I ever had as a barbarian. I had learned patience. I was a little more mature now, and I had learned to wait on a head.

I enjoyed a great success. On top of everything else, we won the Eastern Roman Empire, which was the icing on the cake. I only wished my father could have been there to see it all, but then I remembered I had killed him a long time ago.

I slept well that winter. I had earned it.

I loved all my teammates when I was a Hun, but I guess I was closest to Thornells and Oenfig. We were an unlikely trio. Thornells's mom was one of the Kirghiz, and he talked about her often, but Oenfig's mother had been dismembered by the Kirghiz. Those two guys were as different as night and day. Me? Where did I fit in? I wouldn't know a Kirghiz from a Hungarian.

Still, the three of us hit it off almost right away. We were inseparable until Thornells got pole-axed and Oenfig got traded. I could tell a lot of stories about us three, but it's hard to think of one that you could tell in mixed company!

We were young then.

There's this one I can tell.

We had just slaughtered a lot of Teutons, I think it was. Omran, who was "one as the sun is one" at that time, told us all to take a break but be sure not to go anywhere.

That was all we needed.

We were not above bending the rules in those days, as is well known. We waited until Omran turned around. Then we hightailed it out of there and headed for the nearest town, which was some ways off. It was late, but we thought we might find an after-hours place.

We rode hard. Our horses were foaming and so was Oenfig, if I remember right.

We finally got there only to find that not only were there no private clubs, the whole place was dry!

We rode back frantically, cursing everything we could think of. It was very late and the one thing we didn't need was another fine.

We rode until we could see the campfires. Then we walked our horses up and blended into the crowd. It looked like we'd made it.

Then I heard it. That voice. I knew it instantly.

The jig was up.

It was Omran. He didn't seem real happy about our little field trip.

"Attila! I'm glad you could make it. We're not busy or anything here, so I'm glad you could find it in your schedule to drop by."

I felt like digging a hole and crawling in it, but I had tried that before. Now I knew that digging a hole and crawling into it would make Omran even crankier than he already was. And he was plenty cranky, thank you very much.

"I see you and that bum Oenfig have been gone for, oh, some long period of time."

Even though Omran was the "one as the sun is one" at that time, he was not real good with numbers. He was not a stupid man, though. He was like a lot of us back then. Born before the Depression.

Anyway, Oenfig and me were temporarily "unclean ones." We would have to ride in the back. All the way in the back. Behind the rookies, even. We would be called, by everyone, "Namd-Kark," or "without foreskin."

We looked over at Thornells and he was just smiling to himself and whistling. Like it was Sunday in the park.

Thornells, Oenfig, and me, we had a lot of laughs together. We were boys then.

When people ask me about Omran I have only one thing to say: I loved the man. We had our share of differences, but I can tell you: he was always tough but he was always fair.

Whatever else you can say about him, and it's probably plenty, he was one of a kind.

He had a very colorful way of talking. After a while we got to calling the things that he said "Omranisms." He was full of these things. Every time he opened his mouth you were liable to hear one.

"The Steppe-Land? Nobody goes there anymore. We slaughtered

everyone and took their possessions. We made the strong ones slaves."

"It's not over until we have massive carnage."

"If people don't want their cities looted and burned, there's no way you're going to make them."

Whatever else he was, and it's probably plenty, he was one of a kind.

Of course one day I looked over at Omran, and he looked a little old. So I killed him.

A lot of kids ask me questions, but I guess the question I get asked the most is, "What does it take to become the leader of a vast horde of bloodthirsty, pitiless barbarians?" I always tell them the same thing: desire. You can have everything else: shortness, ugliness, a violent disposition, semi-insanity—it doesn't matter if you don't have that thing called desire. Without that, you'll never make it as a Hun. There are plenty of other things you can be. There are a lot of short, violent doctors, for instance. It's a big world and there aren't that many barbarian hordes. Find your niche and stay there.

If you think you have what it takes, leading a horde of murderous troublemakers can be one of the most rewarding lives you can have.

Just what makes a Hun? Let's see.

Mental outlook is important, but you can't overlook the physical side. You have to be in tip-top condition if you plan to spend all your spare time swarming over the plains of eastern Europe. We have a long season, and staying in shape is a number one priority. Eat right and get plenty of rest.

Go down this list and see if you measure up.

1. You have to have a strong desire to learn the toughest
    job there is.

2. You have to take a real sincere pleasure in mayhem and carnage.
3. You can't be squeamish.
4. You should have a good throwing arm.
5. You can't be afraid of horses.

If you measure up, you may be Hun material. Maybe. Remember, again, there are lots of jobs around and not everybody can be a Hun leader. If everybody was a Hun leader, things would be a lot different, believe me.

In closing, let me say that Hun is not an easy position. But we do have protective equipment. Remember that, and never be afraid to use it.

1987

VERONICA GENG

✳ ✳ ✳

La Cosa Noshtra

(The missing chapter from Mario Puzo's Godfather)

I'll start with Connie Corleone's wedding to that despicable Carlo. Handled beautifully. Security was fantastic. And the dancing—you couldn't tell who was security and who wasn't security. My husband, Clemenza, had grown quite heavy by then, but was light on his feet. And the food—all on ice. Huge bags of ice brought in and replaced every half-hour. Invisible under the white tablecloths. The food just rested gently on these hidden beds of ice. The sun could beat down—not one single poisoning. The organization that went into it was miraculous. Some FBI came in cars, and Connie's older brother Sonny made them leave the driveway because they were blocking the union ice trucks.

Now, let me flash back here to Sicily. I'm fifteen, I'm aspiring to be an opera singer, some men come from America and talk to my parents. I listen, I hear "New York," I hear "Clemenza." So I think I'm being sent to the Metropolitan Opera to sing in *La Clemenza di*

Tito. That's a work by Mozart. *La Clemenza di Tito,* it means the clemency of the Emperor Titus. He catches his wife with somebody—the story isn't so great, but it's good music. The soprano role is Vitellia, a good role. Vitellia! But no. They say I have to marry this man Peter Clemenza. I ask who he is. They say he's a *caporegime.* I think, *caporegime*—that must be the rehearsal master, or the conductor. OK, good. But once we're married he tells me, "Never open your mouth."

It turns out *caporegime* over here means working for Vito Corleone, in the olive oil business. At first we lived in Hell's Kitchen—that means Tenth Avenue. Vito, now, he was genteel. When he came to the house, he liked just a simple, honest plate of bread, salami, and olives. Never dessert, never those vulgar cream pastries—he liked just a piece of fresh fruit. So I never had those pastries in the house. Clemenza would eat them somewhere. Slip into restaurants for extra meals—a little pasta, the veal, a glass of wine, finish with an espresso and a couple of cannoli. I had aspired to be an opera singer and the one thing an opera singer will not touch is a cannoli. The cream filling—it does something to your vocal cords, it's like a drug, it thickens the voice. The one thing you'll never see is Maria Callas and Giuseppe di Stefano wolf down a box of cannoli before going on stage to sing *Tosca.*

So not long after Connie's wedding, Vito Corleone buys oranges from a street vendor and ends up in the hospital. I feel terrible, because I had foreseen something bad would happen, but no, I'm supposed to keep my mouth shut. This young man Paulie, Vito's regular chauffeur—Paulie had been coming around complaining he was sick and could Clemenza get him off work. I could see this Paulie was faking. He said he had a bad cold. He had a handkerchief up to his nose, a big white cloth he was waving around—ridiculous, it was the size of the nightgown for *La Sonnambula.* And the coughing and the sniffling—oh, please, a travesty of Mimi in Act IV of *La*

Bohème. How exactly this led to Vito's eating a poison orange I didn't know, but obviously this Paulie was evil. So after it's too late, Clemenza sends for him. I'm hoping at least he'll take Paulie for a ride in the car, poison him, and good riddance.

All I did was knock on the garage and tell Clemenza, Paulie is here. There is a rumor about me—a complete myth—that as they got in the car, I called out, "Don't forget the cannoli!" I suspect Connie was behind this, spreading this lie. Not that she didn't have her own troubles. She couldn't send her own husband even for Chinese food.

You know what's in a cannoli? First, it's cream, heavy cream, and eggs. Like a custard. Wrapped in dough. Sometimes they put in ricotta. You buy those, you have them in a car, sun beating down—OK, they're in a box, not even a real box, a flat piece of thin cardboard folded into a box shape and tied with string. First the wax paper inside, then the string so you can carry the cannoli. Then the box gets bent or crushed, the string is tied with that one loose end so if somebody pulls it the whole thing unravels, there's no refrigeration in the car, maybe security isn't so good—by the time you get home, poison. So to anyone who believes I called out "Don't forget the cannoli!" I answer this: Clemenza and I, Catholics, we go to all the trouble of getting married and not using birth control and having children—only to poison them and ourselves with cannoli?

To tell the truth, though, as Paulie backed the car out of the driveway, I was hoping he'd run over the children and kill them. But of course you can't say this for some reason. God forbid you should utter some temperamental remark.

Then Michael. Suddenly Michael gets an overwhelming desire to eat in a restaurant. I don't know what it was—a cannoli, maybe a sfogliatelle, BOOM! He has to be sent to Sicily to recover. Then Sonny—this was 1946, 1947, postwar, you don't know what's in a cannoli at this point. Meanwhile, thanks to this whole story, I miss Pippo di Stefano's debut at La Scala. 1946.

So eventually Michael came back and married Kay, the girlfriend from New England. I always liked Kay. Educated, listened to music. A little deficient in temperament. They said Connie had temperament, but she didn't. Connie's idea of a singer was this Johnny Fontane person. He was all right, popular, God-given vocal cords, but he was no Pippo. Then they all moved to Las Vegas. Suddenly Las Vegas was someplace. These people were living in a dream world. Oh, let's all move to Las Vegas, and Fredo is gonna make a lot of money with Johnny Fontane.

I was obliged to remain here with Clemenza. We moved into Vito's old house—a big place, quiet. Later I heard that Frankie Pentangeli was out in Las Vegas, telling them Clemenza died of a heart attack, like Vito, but that was far from true. Willie Cicci knew it was no heart attack, but he was poisoned in some kind of stupid gunplay.

Have you ever really looked at a cannoli? It's wrapped—the dough is wrapped across. Like an overcoat. With this filling inside. You line these up on a plate, they're lying there. Spare me the sight of these revolting—*Mi fa schifo*. That's difficult to translate. It means, "I skeev on them."

1996

SCOTT GUTTERMAN

Gum

(*Fade in old-timey fiddle music.*)
Title: *"Something Like a Candy"*
(*Slow zoom on single shot of eight-year-old boy, in mid-chew.*)
NARRATOR: It started as an idle pursuit: a way to pass the time, to occupy the slackened jaw of street urchin and steel magnate alike. (*Hold on various stills of farmhands, factory workers, men in bowler hats.*) But even in its infancy, when America wakened to its unfurling power like a slumbering giant whose nap had been cut short by the ambulance cry of its own withered soul, when gnashing, nattering demons fought for the very plinth of this great land, when the corn was as high as an elephant's eye— even then it served as a salve to the spirit, a lulling reminder that there would still be a tomorrow, even if tomorrow never came.
FYVUSH FINKEL: I used to take my penny down to the candy store every Friday. This is in New York City, on the Lower East Side,

which could be a very rough place back then—not like it's a big picnic basket today—and if you didn't get run over by a pushcart on your way to the store, or beaten up by the Ukrainian gangs over on Cherry Street, which happened about every other day, you'd give your penny to the man behind the counter, and if he wasn't the kind of fellow to rob you blind, which most of them were, you'd get, I don't know, six or seven pieces of candy, and usually in there would be a stick of gum.

(*Hold on shots of tropical foliage, migrant laborers.*)

NARRATOR: The resin of the sapodilla tree was made to yield a chewable substance that could produce a kind of refreshment lasting all the livelong day. Mixed first with lye, then with iodine, and finally with sugar, it soon filled the mouths of schoolboys and stumblebums, of pugilists and prostitutes from Portland, Maine, to Portland, Oregon.

SUSAN SONTAG: You have to understand, gum was very much frowned upon by the rising merchant class, who saw it as a kind of repudiation of all that they had done to distance themselves from their very provincial, very backwoods sorts of backgrounds. So what you had was this tremendous excitement, this wonderful violation of the social code, whenever someone would "pop in a stick," as they'd say. It was all really very exciting, really.

(*Hold on shots of robber-baron types.*)

NARRATOR: With the rise of "gumming", came the gum lords. They were ruthless men: cold, overbearing, quick to anger, bad of breath, unfriendly, rude, and, more often than not, not nice. They would hold the burgeoning gum world by its wrapper for more than three decades. It would be more than thirty years before the world of gum would be loosed from their very sticky and unpleasant grip.

KEANU REEVES: "I intend to build me a gumworks the likes of which has not been seen east of the Mississippi, nor north of the Ohio, nor west of the Allegheny, nor south of Lake Huron. I will set it in the city of Chicago, for that is the place where I live, though not in summer, for it is too blessed hot."—Colonel Harry A. Beech-Nut.

NARRATOR: Men with names like Wrigley, Dentyne, and Bazooka would seek control of what quickly grew to be a multibillion-dollar-a-year industry (*hold on shots of bubble-popping contests, kids at candy counters*) built on the pennies of boys with names like Tommy, Frank, and Ken, and girls with names like Laura, Sandy, and Jo. Day after day, they came to stores with names like Pop's, Morry's, and the Pit Stop, to buy gum with names like Juicy Fruit, Beeman's, and Big Red.

SHELBY FOOTE: The mere fact that you could *chew* gum for so long, that it would last and last and not lose its flavor—although all gum would *eventually* lose its flavor—that fact alone made it a kind of metaphor for all that was regenerative in American life, the sense that you could go away and the place you left would *still be there*, it wouldn't be gone like some vaporous illusion—it was the same with gum, you could go out, bowl a few frames, make a phone call, get back in your car, and you'd still be chewing *the same piece of gum*. That was tremendously important in establishing the whole entire gum mystique, which is to say legend.

MARTIN SCORSESE: Sure, I saw all the gum pictures, uh, all the great, great gum-chewing heroes. Sam Spade, of course, comes to mind. *The Thin Man*, William Powell, *Cool Hand Luke*—What? They didn't? Are you sure? It's really very funny, because I always associate them with, uh, with gum.

(*Shots of clouds gathering, sound of thunderclaps.*)

NARRATOR: But a dark cloud hovered on the horizon: a bubble-gum-versus-chewing-gum conflagration that would rend the land

asunder. Brother would be set against brother, in what came to
be known as the Big Gum War.

(*Station break.*)

ANNOUNCER: The twenty-seven-part television event *Gum* will return
in a moment with Part Two: "Bubble Trouble."

1994

JACK HANDEY

JACK HANDEY

What I'd Say to the Martians

People of Mars, you say we are brutes and savages. But let me tell you one thing: if I could get loose from this cage you have me in, I would tear you guys a new Martian asshole. You say we are violent and barbaric, but has any one of you come up to my cage and extended his hand? Because, if he did, I would jerk it off and eat it right in front of him. "Mmm, that's good Martian," I would say.

You say your civilization is more advanced than ours. But who is really the more "civilized" one? You, standing there watching this cage? Or me, with my pants down, trying to urinate on you? You criticize our Earth religions, saying they have no relevance to the way we actually live. But think about this: if I could get my hands on that god of yours, I would grab his skinny neck and choke him until his big green head exploded.

We are a warlike species, you claim, and you show me films of Earth battles to prove it. But I have seen all the films about twenty times. Get some new films, or, so help me, if I ever get out of here I will empty my laser pistol into everyone I see, even pets.

Speaking of films, I could show you some films, films that portray a different, gentler side of Earth. And while you're watching the films I'd sort of slip away, because guess what: the projector is actually a thing that shoots out spinning blades! And you fell for it! Well, maybe now you wouldn't.

You point to your long tradition of living peacefully with Earth. But you know what I point to? Your stupid heads.

You say there is much your civilization could teach ours. But perhaps there is something that I could teach you—namely, how to scream like a parrot when I put your big Martian head in a vise.

You claim there are other intelligent beings in the galaxy besides earthlings and Martians. Good, then we can attack them together. And after we're through attacking them we'll attack you.

I came here in peace, seeking gold and slaves. But you have treated me like an intruder. Maybe it is not me who is the intruder but you.

No, not me. You, stupid.

You keep my body imprisoned in this cage. But I am able to transport my mind to a place far away, a happier place, where I use Martian heads for batting practice.

I admit that sometimes I think we are not so different after all. When you see one of your old ones trip and fall down, do you not point and laugh, just as we on Earth do? And I think we can agree that nothing is more admired by the people of Earth and Mars alike than a fine, high-quality cigarette. For fun, we humans like to ski down mountains covered with snow; you like to "milk" bacteria off of scum hills and pack them into your gill slits. Are we so different? Of course we are, and you will be even more different if I ever finish my homemade flamethrower.

You may kill me, either on purpose or by not making sure that all the surfaces in my cage are safe to lick. But you can't kill an idea. And that idea is: me chasing you with a big wooden mallet.

You say you will release me only if I sign a statement saying that I will not attack you. And I have agreed, the only condition being that I can sign with a long, sharp pen. And still you keep me locked up.

True, you have allowed me reading material—not the "human reproduction" magazines I requested but the works of your greatest philosopher, Zandor or Zanax or whatever his name is. I would like to discuss his ideas with him—just me, him, and one of his big, heavy books.

If you will not free me, at least deliver a message to Earth. Send my love to my wife, and also to my girlfriend. And to my children, if I have any anyplace. Ask my wife to please send me a bazooka, which is a flower we have on Earth. If my so-called friend Don asks you where the money I owe him is, please anally probe him. Do that anyway.

If you keep me imprisoned long enough, eventually I will die. Because one thing you Martians do not understand is that we humans cannot live without our freedom. So, if you see me lying lifeless in my cage, come on in, because I'm dead. Really.

Maybe one day we will not be the enemies you make us out to be. Perhaps one day a little Earth child will sit down to play with a little Martian child, or larva, or whatever they are. But, after a while, guess what happens: the little Martian tries to eat the Earth child. But guess what the Earth child has? A gun. You weren't expecting that, were you? And now the Martian child is running away, as fast as he can. Run, little Martian baby, run!

I would like to thank everyone for coming to my cage tonight to hear my speech. Donations will be gratefully accepted. (No Mars money, please.)

2005

LARRY HEINEMANN

The Fragging

Second Lieutenant Lionel Calhoun McQuade was a Citadel punk, and that's probably what killed him.

He graduated third, with honors, in the class of 1966. He accepted a direct commission in the United States Army, as had his father, General Russell Calhoun McQuade, a hero of the Battle of the Bulge. His grandfather, Lieutenant Colonel Collier Calhoun McQuade, fought with Black Jack Pershing in Mexico and France. And McQuade's great-great-grandfather, Colonel Louden Clarence McQuade, commanded a South Carolina Volunteer Infantry Regiment that fought valiantly at Gettysburg (or so the family story went), where the good colonel gave up an arm and an eye. All the McQuades were hard-drinking family men who understood the customs of respect and responsibility (*The Call*, as they referred to it) and had served honorably in our country's wars, except for the Spanish-American War (*Let us not dignify it with our participation*) and most particularly the Spanish Civil War (*Not our war; not our kind*).

That's what Lieutenant McQuade's father told him when the elder McQuade judged his son old enough to understand such things. The men who fought in Spain, the elder McQuade said, were premature anti-Fascists. The general could not bring himself to say the word "Communist" but, like Robert E. Lee, referred simply to "those people." In other words, a political embarrassment, whose services were appropriately shunned when the real war, against the Nazis, began in 1941. Not until Lionel's junior year at the Citadel did he understand that his father had been talking about the Lincoln Brigade—which Lionel came to regard as properly romantic, if militarily inept and politically naive.

The young Lieutenant McQuade arrived at the base-camp orderly room of Charlie Company, 3rd Battalion of the 51st Infantry, near the village of Ap Bo Dat, in the dry summer season during a spell of especially hot weather. In his head were all the stories told him by his father and grandfather, imagined opportunities to display his valor, and the idiot ambition to lead brave men in a desperate battle during which he would receive a wound in the extraordinary performance of his duty: nothing fatal or debilitating, mind you, just something clean and presentable—something to show his mother. McQuade's brand-new jungle fatigues and freshly polished boots pegged him for a fucking new guy, as did the twenty-four-karat-gold second-lieutenant's bar (called a butter bar) pinned to his tailored collar and the custom-embroidered white cloth nametag over his right breast pocket.

He was ushered into the company commander's office, where Captain Humphrey Eberhart sat at his paper-covered, dust-blown desk going over the morning report, trying to calculate the precise strength of his rifle company: the total manpower minus so many lately killed; minus so many convalescing at the big evacuation hospital at Cu Chi; minus so many walking wounded temporarily excused from duty; minus so many away on R and R in Bangkok, Manila, Sydney, Tokyo, and other such places; minus so many short-timers assigned to meaningless house-cat jobs awaiting their orders home; minus so many AWOL (*God knows where* they *disappeared to*), equals so many able-bodied riflemen, ready to go.

The captain was a short and fuzzy, unhappy man. Back home he had a modest fleet of tow trucks that worked the interstate from Berkeley to Davis, California, and a commission in the Army Reserve. The towing business had thrived right up to the day he got the letter calling him into active service. Now what? The captain sat in his orderly-room office, sweating his balls off. *I'm going to die.* He knew at the very least that by the time he got done with Ap Bo Dat, his tow-truck business would be in the shit can; his brother-in-law had no head for business and was money-stupid to boot. Eberhart looked down at the names on the casualty list, looked through the screened louvers of his office wall to the village women in clean white blouses washing food trays behind the mess hall, and knew that his was a fool's errand. *Who made* this *nitwit call?*

McQuade stood at attention in the middle of Eberhart's tiny screened-in office, suffocating along with everyone else in the withering, unbearable heat that boiled down through the open rafters from the roofing tin overhead. Eberhart penciled a two-digit number (87) on a pad of paper and then looked up, casually inviting McQuade to be at ease, to sit down and take a load off his feet.

Captain Eberhart was not a formal man, and McQuade's unwelcome interruption irked him to distraction. *Where do they get these guys? I don't need a God-damned rookie lieutenant. I need a couple of fearless tunnel rats and some more guys who know their way around a sniper's rifle. I need to get the hell out of here.* Pale-faced cheerleading shavetails like McQuade were a dime a dozen and, once outside the wire, were dropping like flies.

The lieutenant gave Eberhart his records and orders, which were passed immediately to First Sergeant Martin Kerby, who sighed, put the envelopes and folder on his desk, and left for lunch. The captain and the young lieutenant exchanged pleasantries, McQuade sitting properly stiff, the paper on Eberhart's desk clinging to the captain's forearms.

McQuade was to take the place of First Lieutenant Edwin Lewis, a short-timer and a cool head who had recently died after a banana-grove firefight. Eberhart's letter to Lewis's widow conveyed the archly military-rhetorical regards prescribed by Brigade Commander General Blaine Milburn for her husband's "duty to his country," but went on to say in a lengthy and heartfelt postscript that Lewis was that rare officer who actually knew what he was doing, that the whole company honestly looked up to him and keenly felt his loss, and that Ed Lewis's death was the result of astonishing chance, against which nothing can prevail. The captain looked at his new platoon leader and pondered the abyss. He told one of the clerks to show McQuade the hooch he was to share with First Lieutenant John Povey.

Lieutenant McQuade was to take over the third platoon, temporarily commanded by Staff Sergeant Floyd Deal, a very confused young man who had been promoted from the ranks after several acts of "extraordinary courage" and "willful disregard for his own safety." So said the Silver Star citation and promotion orders. Deal was proficient and adroit, but distinctly not command material. As far as the third platoon was concerned, Deal had gone berserk one evening about a month back, shot up a bunch of people, and that was that. Everybody went berserk sooner or later.

When McQuade entered the tent-covered structure that was to be his home, his hoochmate was on his knees, pouring sweat and banging on a straightened box nail with a brick, finishing the floor of rickety shipping-pallet struts covered with lumber from ammunition boxes scrounged from the artillery down the road. Lieutenant John Povey was a handy guy, a University of Wyoming ROTC slob. He was basically a grunt with a master's degree in petroleum engineering who had a knack for repairing air conditioners—and, by the way, a commission as a first lieutenant in the United States Army.

The hooch maid, Le Thi Kim (a woman from the nearby village, the mother of three), stood aside under the canvas awning and watched Povey over the low sandbag wall with intense interest. These Americans, so tall, so well fed, were always busy. They were noisy, they smelled funny, they ate too much, and everything came in cans. Where were their pigs? Their chickens? Why did they not eat rice? Where were their women? What on earth were they doing here? These questions baffled everyone she knew. At least the French wore good-looking hats and loved to sing. The Americans? They had all this "stuff." Four years before, Thi Kim's husband had gotten fed up once and for all with the vicious caprices and arrogant stupidities of the Saigon government and joined the National Liberation Front. In all that time she had had one letter from him.

Her father, Le Kham, the village poet and singer, had at first thought that the French had returned, but he could make nothing of this most exotic dialect. One day a young American military doctor, Captain Hilton Hayes, came to the village to look down throats, thump on backs with his fingers, listen to coughs, and dispense aspirin, while a senior medic demonstrated to the deeply offended, excruciatingly polite village women how to bathe children properly with Ivory soap.

Le Kham arrived at the pagoda where the American jeeps were parked carrying a pot of fresh tea, small cups, and gifts of fruit to welcome the visitors formally on behalf of the village. Immediately the examinations ceased, the villagers stood back, a chair suddenly appeared from the crowd in the doorway, and the old man sat down, in his cleanest peasant rags, to compose himself. Captain Hayes spoke only halting Vietnamese, and at first thought that Le Kham was pulling his leg, asking him what part of France he came from. The young doctor said that he came from Alabama, and tried not to make a face as he drank the aromatic, bitter tea through his teeth. Le Kham sipped his tea with elegant ease and, speaking slowly, explained that he had never heard of the Alabama province of France. How far was it from Paris? Was it more than a day's walk?

Oh, yes, the young doctor said, trying not to laugh out loud. You had to walk in a westerly direction quite a ways, then swim some, and then walk some more.

The old man stroked his long, thinnish chin whiskers and tried to imagine all this, until one of the young medics produced an atlas from his green canvas medical bag and showed the old man that Alabama was in the southern United States of America.

"America," the old man said, nodding his head deeply just as he did when he told his grandchildren the story of the crane and the turtle. "America," he repeated, and then launched into a story he had heard many years before about Thomas Jefferson and Abraham Lincoln: How one man lived on a hill and was rich and smart, and the other came from a small village and was a great poet, but poor; how one had invented democracy and the other had saved it. The way the old man told the story, one man had invented democracy much as the French Catholics' God of Heaven had invented Eve, and the other had saved it much as the old man tended the farm of his ancestors. Captain Hayes was left to ponder this story for the rest of his time at Ap Bo Dat, and years later, still puzzled, he could recall that whole afternoon with a staggering clarity.

Le Thi Kim stood under the canvas awning of Lieutenant Povey's tent watching him punch box nails into the floorboards with that brick, and wondered why he didn't get a hammer. It would be so much easier; but then, these Americans were always doing things the hard way. Thi Kim liked to watch the tall, robust John Povey; she thought him very handsome, and wished that her husband were home.

Lieutenant McQuade introduced himself and laid his bags on Ed Lewis's cot in the corner. He small-talked with Povey, eyeballed Thi Kim, and excused himself to fetch a drink of water. It was early in the afternoon, and God-awful hot. The lieutenant took a long drink and then, bending down on one knee, bowed his head under the spigot and let the water run over the back of his neck. He did not feel well, but went in search of his command.

The third platoon was down by the creek with the rest of the company, stripped to the waist and sweating, filling sandbags for the new bunkers under the careful and expert supervision of the brigade executive officer, Major Cecil Harsch, a man who loved nothing better than to tell other people what to do.

Major Harsch had the United States Army technical manual about proper bunker construction in the thigh pocket of his crisply ironed fatigues, and he made sure that the men finished the job with panache by patting the sandbags square, plumb, flush, and level with the flats of their shovels. Two weeks after the rains began the bunker sandbags would be as hard as rock. "Precision" and "utility" were two words the major used until he got tired of listening to himself talk. According to him, these several bunkers were going to be the pride of the Camp Bo Dat bunker line. He stood under the awning shade of his construction command post and swelled with pride in the blistering afternoon heat.

The major had never lifted a shovelful of dirt in his life, except to plant his wife's rose of Sharon bushes, so he could not understand for the life of him what was taking the men so long. It was hot, dry work, regardless of the major's teamwork-is-everything, can-do attitude, and it was made worse by the bright Southeast Asian sun and the melting afternoon heat. In the village everyone moved slowly and kept to the shade, and, as a general thing, no one but a fool was outdoors. Still, the major constantly exhorted the men to hurry up and keep at it.

The men looked at Major Harsch and thought that he should just hustle his ass right back up to brigade headquarters and let well enough alone.

Lieutenant McQuade walked down the hill toward the sandbag detail, squared his cap down over his eyes, adjusted the belt of his .45-caliber semiautomatic Colt pistol around his waist, and searched the crowd of tans for Sergeant Floyd Deal, who, he was told, had unmistakable scars.

The young sergeant had heard that a lieutenant named McQuade was soon to take over command of the platoon, so when some fucking new guy came pounding down the hillside, pushing soft dirt ahead of him at every stride, Deal stood up, dropped his cigarette, put on his jungle-fatigue shirt and steel helmet, and came to attention long before McQuade was anywhere near him. Who else could this be but the new lieutenant, come to punch his ticket? The men of the platoon looked up from their work, saw McQuade coming down the hillside, instantly took note of his clean green uniform and pasty pallor, looked around at one another, and muttered, "We're fucked." In plain sight of the wood line, not fifty meters downrange, Deal threw the young lieutenant a crackling crisp hand salute the like of which McQuade had not seen since the afternoon of his Citadel graduation in Charleston, South Carolina.

Lieutenant McQuade advised the young sergeant of his unbuttoned shirt and instructed him to have the men fall in yonder between the tents and the wingtank showers. He had taken a busy little tour for himself through the pathetic platoon tents and wished to speak to the men immediately.

Sergeant Deal buttoned his shirt and advised right back that a platoon formation in plain sight of the wood line was unwise. "A cluster fuck is bad for business, sir." A thing unheard of as far back as the platoon memory and legend would go. "Be that as it may," McQuade said, "I want to talk to the men; call them into formation." With extreme apology in his tone, Sergeant Deal turned and shouted that the third platoon was to fall in.

What?

Deal repeated himself twice.

The men of the platoon straightened their backs, moaning and groaning, but complied. Wearily they dropped their shovels and sandbags, gathered their hats and caps, their rifles and such, and walked up the hill to the tents with grumbling skepticism. Cluster fuck or no, who was this clown? For a gag, Sergeant Deal had the men formally dress-right-dress, ready, front. And, going along with the gag, in an instant the third platoon was standing tall with rifles, shotguns, and grenade launchers at sling arms.

Then Deal turned to McQuade, cranked another showy roundhouse salute, and said that the platoon was formed. Sir!

The rest of the company—the sandbag detail—stopped work long enough to watch in blunt disbelief. Pucker-assed, eager-beaver fucking new guys—that was all the explanation anyone needed.

Lieutenant McQuade ordered the platoon to stand at ease. They slacked their stance and watched the wood line, ready to drop, roll, and scatter at the first sign. No one paid any mind to the lieutenant; this was nuts. McQuade introduced himself (as if anyone wanted to know), said that he had been through the tents and could not believe the platoon's sorry state of affairs, and commenced the first of what came to be known as Lionel's Limp-Dicked Cop Lectures. He finished by announcing an inspection that evening, and then ordered the platoon to attention, dismissed them, and walked away.

The platoon could not believe their ears. *Junk on the bunk? Who is this asshole?* But the young lieutenant was not kidding in the least.

The platoon stood in formation with the sweat rolling down into their boots and said, "That's one."

The company was sent not many weeks later to Landing Zone Squirt, a run-down forward support base named for General Milburn's dog. This was not good. LZ Squirt was very near a VC supply trail and a rumored tunnel complex. Things were always busy. The first thing that morning—"early dawn," Lieutenant McQuade called it—the company gathered with practiced nonchalance at the chopper pad and waited for the lift ships.

The other officers had persuaded Lieutenant McQuade to take the embroidered white nametags from his shirts and leave his twenty-four-karat-gold collar insignia behind. By then everyone knew who he was and didn't need to be reminded morning, noon, and night.

Less than a week after their arrival at LZ Squirt, McQuade decided that the platoon's ambush patrol was not operating well enough to suit him, so one evening he insisted on taking charge. Sergeant Deal said that he would be right proud to sit at the radio there at the LZ and take the lieutenant's hourly situation reports. The lieutenant said that his call sign would be "Apple Pie Six": "Apple Pie" for "ambush patrol," "Six" because that number was always used to signify the officer in charge.

Everyone rolled his eyes.

The seven men detailed to go along gathered at the south end of the perimeter at deep dusk. Each man wore his flak jacket (a thick, greasy, and awkward zippered vest), six grenades, two fifty-round belts of ammunition for the machine gun, two Claymore anti-personnel mines, and as many canteens of water as he could carry. Specialist Fourth Class Adriane Harper carried the M-60 machine gun. Private First Class John Otaki brought his sniper's rifle with night-vision starlight scope.

Specialist Fourth Class Arthur Comstock, the platoon medic, carried his aid bag, which included, among other things, a dozen shots of quarter-grain morphine and two large bottles of government-issue drugs. Comstock gave each man a dozen amphetamines and a dozen barbiturates: uppers to cut the trail, and downers to keep them on their way. By the time the patrol got to the ambush site, everyone but McQuade had the range.

The men left the perimeter after dark, and McQuade had trouble reading the map by moonlight, so it was well past midnight by the time the patrol, hot and sweaty, reached the ambush coordinates. The lieutenant noisily supervised the placement of the Claymores and the machine gun; by turns several of the men asked him to be quiet and not stand in the road. *This is an ambush, sir.* When McQuade was satisfied that everything was done to his specifications, the men settled in for the night and looked at one another skeptically as they drank from their first canteens.

Two Viet Cong from a nearby village had followed along behind the patrol at a discreet distance. Hue Pho carried an old-fashioned bold-action Chinese SKS and three rounds; Hoang Dieu carried an RPG (rocket-propelled grenade) launcher with a single round, locked and loaded. The RPG was an anti-tank weapon, but it was very effective against ordinary infantry troops. The Vietnamese could see that this man was lost. They waited until the Americans were settled, watching the young officer with fascinated pity while he stood in the cart trail talking and pointing, arguing. What was this man doing?

Pho and Dieu moved slowly and quietly to a place twenty meters behind the patrol. Dieu decided to aim for the distinct silhouette of a tree just in front of the American officer. He would hit the tree head-high; the burning-hot magnesium shrapnel would spray the men underneath. Pho would fire his three rounds, and then the two of them would run to the left until they came to the footpath that would take them back to their spider holes, which were connected to the Hang Da tunnels. Several hours passed; the Americans became drowsy with boredom despite the amphetamines. When Pho heard the lieutenant talking in careful whispers on his radio, he motioned for Dieu to fire his one round. Dieu rose on one knee, settled the weapon on his shoulder, aimed at the tree, and squeezed the trigger. The RPG hit the tree in a brilliant splash of sparkling shrapnel. Pho immediately pulled off his three rounds, one at a time. Without waiting to see what happened, Pho picked up his three brass cartridges, and the two of them took to their heels.

In that moment of chaos the ambush patrol clicked off their Claymores and fired their weapons. Only Private First Class Franklin Giacoppo and young Sergeant Gary Lautner understood that the RPG had come from behind them, and they turned to fire. Almost immediately the firing ceased. Three men were dead. The lieutenant radioed for help. The patrol gathered its gear, packed up the corpses, and quickly moved to another location.

The men looked around at one another in the clean light of day while they drank the last of their canteen water and the dew gathered on their clothes. They waited for the medevac helicopter, the meat wagon, and said, "That's two."

Sergeant Deal later talked informally with McQuade, explaining the situation. Comstock talked with him when he gave McQuade the lindane powder for his crabs. Even John Otaki, the platoon sniper, took him aside. Calm down, lieutenant. Be cool. What are you trying to prove? All quietly and bluntly, man to man. Sergeant Lautner told him point-blank to get his head out of his ass and cut the bullshit. But McQuade came from the Citadel and could not be persuaded of anything.

The last straw came several weeks later, when the company was being flown out to Fire Base Kelly, named for the dancer—one of General Milburn's favorite Hollywood performers. Private First Class Humberto Reyes, a Tucson Chicano, sat in the helicopter doorway with his feet on the skid, armed with a shotgun. He was always the first man to hit the ground. Lieutenant McQuade, who was pep-talking the door gunner, turned to look the man full in the face and bumped Reyes out the door. Reyes tumbled head over heels, almost in slow motion, and cursed McQuade up one side and down the other in his finest pool-hall Spanish. "Fuck *you*, McQuade! God-*damn* your eyes!" and other such things. Then he howled until he was out of earshot.

Sing it, Coyote!

The pilot, the door gunner, McQuade, and the others looked down in horror as Reyes fell to earth, finally disappearing in the thick jungle canopy a thousand feet below.

The company landed at LZ Kelly. The third platoon gathered in turmoil around McQuade and Eberhart, outraged and shocked. After considerable mollifying discussion the platoon calmed down and took up their place among the bunkers, still snakebit. The men looked at one another as they laid out their gear and said, "That, my man, is three."

Young Sergeant Lautner was beside himself; he had had enough. McQuade was a menace, a fuck-up; he was getting people killed almost for spite. A shrewd look came into Lautner's eyes.

So, when next the company was back in Bo Dat for a couple days' stand-down, the third platoon decided to kill him. Solicitations were made for a bounty, and nearly everyone ponied up. Lautner held the pot.

Someone from the mail-room poker game volunteered an old-fashioned grenade; it resembled a pineapple. Private Giacoppo said he would rig it to McQuade's collapsible wood-and-canvas cot, booby-trap fashion.

Lieutenant Povey conveniently left the next afternoon for his R and R in Honolulu, where he was to meet his wife.

Lieutenant McQuade and the other company officers were invited that evening to attend a birthday-party barbecue for General Milburn at his double-wide air-conditioned trailer behind brigade headquarters. The general loved to party; the company officers would be gone most of the evening.

Giacoppo waited a good long while and then blackened his face, took the grenade, a spool of green cloth tape, and a length of notched bamboo, and headed for the ditch that bordered officers' country. The rest of the platoon smoked some grass, drank some beer, and went to bed, knowing they would not get any sleep. There was little moonlight. Slowly and by stealth Giacoppo made his way along the ditch that had lately been deepend in anticipation of the fall rains, and sneaked in among the officers' tents. At last he came to McQuade and Povey's tent. He lifted the flap and went inside on his hands and knees. It was not difficult to see which cot belonged to whom, even in that little light. Povey never hung anything up. McQuade kept all his gear neat and his personal effects in waterproof ammunition cans.

Giacoppo got down on his back under the head of McQuade's cot. This was going to be a piece of cake. Mostly by feel he taped the frag to the wooden cross leg of the cot, keeping the piece of bamboo between his teeth like a new pencil. When he had satisfied himself that the grenade was snug, he deftly pulled on the cotter pin until it was only barely attached. Then, still feeling with his fingers, he gently wedged the bamboo under the cot between the pull ring of the grenade and the musty canvas beneath McQuade's pillow.

McQuade's mother had sent him a heavy linen pillowcase, which Le Thi Kim had filled to bursting with chicken and goose feathers—of which there were plenty in the village.

Giacoppo carefully rolled away from his work. The whole thing had taken seven minutes by the clock. He silently gathered up his gear and left the hooch, making his way among the ropes and pegs along the path to the ditch and then back to the quiet platoon tents. He cleaned his face at the washstand, sat on his cot, took off his boots, checked his rifle, and stretched out. The platoon heard the squish of the soap, the splash of the water, the stretch of the cot canvas, the snap of the bootlaces through the eyelets, the tick and clack of the rifle stock, the draw and hush of breath.

Giacoppo lit a joint. The sweet, cloying bouquet of marijuana filled the tent. The platoon waited, sweating in the midnight heat.

McQuade and the other officers arrived not long after in two jeeps, drunk and loud. The general had provided steaks flown in from Bangkok, good liquor, and a USO troupe of young Filipino singers who could be counted on to be agreeable. Everyone had gotten laid.

The officers walked across the company street and in among their tents. One by one they peeled off, wished one another good night, and went to bed. When McQuade's turn came, he stopped, staggering; he was so drunk his body tingled. He told Captain Eberhart he would see him in the morning; he had several matters of platoon discipline to discuss. He stepped into his tent, walking the four paces across Povey's wobbly floor to his cot. He sat down heavily and took off his boots, not thinking a thing in the world, not even of the gorgeous young woman who had given him the blow job of his life just an hour before.

He fluffed his pillow, laid himself out, settled his head well in, and closed his eyes. And in that instant the stick of notched bamboo pushed down against the grenade's pull ring. The cotter pin and the length of bamboo fell to the floor with a slight clatter; the released spoon handle of the grenade arced through the air, making a distinct *sping* sound, and landed between the edge of Povey's floor and the knee-high wall of sandbags that surrounded each officer's tent. The fuse burned for four and a half seconds, barely time for the lieutenant thickly to ponder the odd noise beneath his cot.

McQuade never uttered a sound. The grenade went off with a flash of light quicker than the scratch of a kitchen match and a sound familiar to everyone. The convulsion was sufficient to lift the upper part of McQuade's body clear of the bedding and blow the back of his head off to the eyes. It dismantled the cot, tore the near sandbags to shreds, shattered and blackened Povey's floor, and blew holes in the tent canvas above. The shrapnel pieces, as large as lozenges, cut deeply into McQuade's back.

All the men in the company were suddenly awake and instantly alert, belly down on the dirt floors of the tents, manhandling loaded rifles and pistols and grenade launchers. *Incoming! Sappers! But that was a grenade. What the fuck?* There were calls and shouts. Only Lieutenant Lionel McQuade did not respond.

Captain Eberhart told Sergeant Deal by radio to find the lieutenant. The last place he looked was McQuade's tent, which was still thick with grenade smoke and smelled of rum and blood. Sergeant Deal turned on the light hanging down from the ridgepole. McQuade looked fine except for the blood still coming from the back of his head. In fact, blood and feathers were everywhere. The sagging muslin tent liner hung down like slaw; the hooch was a ruin.

The company officers and senior NCOs gathered, weapons in hand; they were shocked and cautious. Captain Eberhart and the others knew instantly that this was a fragging. Eberhart took First

Sergeant Martin Kerby and the mess sergeant to the orderly room, where he called brigade to report what had happened. Meanwhile, the other officers and NCOs went to roust the men. No incoming, no attack, Sergeant Deal told the third platoon and everyone else standing near. Lieutenant McQuade got fragged. Pity the poor lieutenant, the men of the platoon said among themselves.

Two dozen MPs with gun jeeps and briefcases of paperwork arrived in a shower of gravel followed by a thick cloud of road dust. In the dark of the moon, in that too-obvious way that all cops have, the MPs surrounded the enlisted men's tents. They stood casually beside their machine guns, which, the company saw plainly enough, were locked and loaded.

Everyone's weapon was locked and loaded.

The brigade provost marshal visited Lieutenant McQuade's tent. A fragging, he immediately surmised. Here were the pull ring and cotter pin of a grenade, and snippets of green cloth tape were blown all over the hooch. The minute particulars were noted for his report. Then he and the other MP officers took over Captain Eberhart's orderly room for the interviews and interrogations.

The provost called each man in the company one by one to be interviewed.

"Stand at ease, trooper."

"Yes, sir."

"Where were you when the explosion occurred?"

"I was asleep in my tent, sir."

"Did you see or hear anything?"

"No, sir. I did not see or hear anything."

"What is your opinion of Lieutenant McQuade?"

"Lieutenant McQuade arrived only four months ago, sir. Citadel, sir."

"Do you have any suspicions about who did this?"

"No, sir, I do not have any suspicions."

Then, almost slyly: "There may well be something in it for you, trooper."

"If I think of anything, if I hear anything, yes, sir, I will immediately communicate it to Captain Eberhart or yourself. Sir."

"Dismissed."

The provost didn't finish until well after breakfast. By then Graves Registration had sent a truck to fetch the lieutenant's remains. A fragging was a serious matter, best got to the bottom of as quickly as possible. The God-damn miscreant would get a general court-martial, go to the God-damn disciplinary barracks at Fort Leavenworth, and break rocks until the day he died.

The platoon agreed with everyone in the company that the death of Lieutenant McQuade was a terrible shame, and wondered out loud who could be responsible. Le Thi Kim was powerfully impressed that the young and handsome lieutenant could die in such a way. It was a story she would tell her grandchildren. She wept, thinking of her husband and the other men of the village, and then she cleaned up the mess.

Lieutenant Povey came back from Hawaii a week later, deeply refreshed. He expressed his astonishment at the death of McQuade, helped Thi Kim finish cleaning up, and repaired his floor. Four weeks later the divorce papers arrived—a neat little scheme that Povey and his wife had cooked up to get him compassionate leave. The Red Cross hastily approved it. A dramatically astonished Povey smiled as he packed his gear, snapped his fingers in the air, and said it was that easy.

Giacoppo saved the $500 bounty and took it and his other savings on R and R to the Wild West Pecos Hotel, in Bangkok, where he embarked on a culinary and sexual rampage. Given the stories Giacoppo brought back, it was regarded by everyone in the platoon as money well spent.

As the weeks and months went by, the men who knew of the matter left for home, one by one. Despite promises to the contrary, they never encountered one another again.

Floyd Deal went back to New Orleans, told no one he was a veteran, let his hair grow, got a job on an offshore oil rig, and was lost overboard during a platform fire.

Adriane Harper came to the end of his tour intact and went home one grateful young man. He spent the next couple of years smoking grass and collecting guns. Later he was convicted of manslaughter for shotgunning a Halloween prankster. Later still, he himself was killed by the New York State Police in the Attica prison riot.

John Otaki also got home in one piece. He worked as a mail carrier for the post office in Oakland, where he was well regarded for his goodhearted cheerfulness, but he went insane in 1989, after watching his sister and her family die in the collapse of Highway 880 during the World Series earthquake.

Arthur Comstock went home to medical school and took to heart that portion of the Hippocratic oath that reminds physicians to do no harm. He took up the practice of family medicine in St. Genevieve County, Missouri, where he concerned himself with home births and broken legs, school shots and strep throats, mononucleosis and the diseases of the rural poor.

Franklin Giacoppo was badly wounded in the legs. He recovered, but because of unanticipated medical complications brought on by incompetent treatment at the Cu Chi medical facility, he was given a discharge, and went back to Milwaukee to help his father run the family hardware store. He displayed his Purple Heart above the cash register to impress the customers, but would not talk of it or the war with anyone—especially his father, who was an Okinawa Marine.

Gary Lautner, whose idea the fragging had been, made enough

money importing marijuana from Mexico to put himself through law school, worked for the Illinois state's attorney in Chicago, taught law at the University of Chicago, was appointed to the federal bench in 1982, and soon after became a well-functioning alcoholic. He never married.

The day young Sergeant Lautner left the platoon, he threw his gear under the stretch canvas seat of the helicopter that had come to deliver some mail and the daily supplies, but before he stepped aboard, he looked around at the company and wondered, among other things, how many lives had been saved by the killing of McQuade.

He had no way of knowing, of course, but there were many—many, including Lautner's own.

The murder of Lieutenant Lionel Calhoun McQuade was attributed to a person or persons unknown, and never solved. The paperwork floated up the chain of command from the brigade provost to the division provost to the Criminal Investigations Division in Saigon, and finally to the Pentagon. The manila routing slip was a scribble of initials. In 1975 the folder was marked "Inactive/Unsolved" and forwarded to the National Archives in Suitland, Maryland, and the McQuade name passed from American military history.

In the fall of 1982, on a whim and overpowered by curiosity, John Povey, who then lived in Denver with his wife and three daughters, packed a bag and went to Washington, D.C., for the dedication of the Vietnam Veterans Memorial. He skipped the parade to find himself a place on the grassy slope up a ways from the brand-new, lustrous black marble. He was impressed by and grateful for it, if astonished at its spiritual simplicity. Soon the crowd gathered thickly around him. When the speeches began, a tall man with straight black hair, dressed in faded jeans and a vintage uniform field jacket, began pulling half pints of Jack Daniel's from the inside of his coat and passing them to the perfect strangers within his arm's reach. Povey and the others cracked the seals, swept the hand-sized bottles around in a mellow, sweeping toast, and drank the hard, hot liquor in obvious gulps while the speakers talked on. Later Povey and the man with straight black hair elbowed their way down to panel forty-six of the eastern wing of the memorial, which pointed directly at the Washington Monument. Povey put his hand to the marble and squeezed his fingertips into the deep-cut grooves; unexpected tears filled his eyes. There were Lewis, Eberhart, Reyes, and the rest. Lionel Calhoun McQuade's name was in among them. After a moment Povey turned to the tall man. "See this McQuade? What an asshole." With the crush of the crowd at his back and half a pint of whiskey in his stomach, it was the only word Povey could think of just at that moment.

The man looked at Povey, let his eyes wander down to where the marble panels were the highest and the crowd the thickest, and said, "He ain't the only one." Then he splashed what little was left in his bottle on the face of the memorial and rubbed it in with the flat of his hand, as if body-warm whiskey on a cold November day were the very thing to scour clean the polished black marble. The two men watched the whiskey trickle down through the deep, precise engravings. Then the tall man with straight black hair told Povey he would see him around, stepped backward into the crowd, and disappeared.

1997

GARRISON KEILLOR

✳ ✳ ✳

Around the Horne

BY BILL HORNE

Note: Bill Horne is sick. Today's column is by Ed Farr.

It's always a temptation to second-guess a team and say where it went wrong, but it's been my philosophy not to kick a man when he's down and that goes for the Flyers, not that it wouldn't be easy to fault this player or that after losing so many games this year. I know it's considered smart in some circles to criticize the Dutchman for letting the younger ballplayers "get away with murder" who some say didn't have much so-called desire, but the season is over and I say, "Next year means new opportunities for personal growth. Let's rebuild in a spirit of optimism." In the meantime, perhaps I could make some constructive comments about the past season as one who knows the team well, having worked with the fellows on a one-to-one and group basis as manager since Dutch moved up to general manager after the 4th of July doubleheader against Pierce.

First, a word to the fans. As Dutch pointed out last spring, the Flyers only needed confidence in themselves to succeed. I felt that they might've done so had the Flyer fans shown some patience, adopted a quietly supportive role, and not demanded instant victories. Instead, after a few defeats they became bitter. They booed every mistake however unwitting, in effect sending the players the message, "You are not OK. You are bums." By the time I arrived, the players were uncertain whether they could play ball at all. Since then, we have made some progress in talking out these problems. Perhaps if the fans got to know us a little better, they could join us next year in a helpful partnership for dynamic change. That is the purpose of this article.

Pitching: It was obvious to everyone that the pitching was not as hard as it should've been this year. Fans were quick to blame laziness or overweight. But after working with the pitchers in intensive group sessions we found that all suffered to some extent from what we have come to call "pitcher's block." Convinced that the ball would be hit anyway, they unconsciously "took something off it" (the pitch) in delivery. Typical was one right-hander whom I'll call "Phil":

PHIL:
They have always hit my knuckleball. At first I thought I was bringing my right leg over too far and dropping the elbow. But now I realize I'm withdrawing from the pitch—actually bringing both hands up in front of my face to avoid seeing it—and I don't get a good follow-through that way. I guess secretly I've always felt the knuckler was an old man's pitch and hesitated throwing it. The hesitation threw my timing way off. I guess the answer is to accept that I *am* thirty-nine and can't reach back for the old fastball anymore. If I do, I tend to fall off the mound.

After talking with the pitchers, we agreed that pitching less hard was their way of punishing themselves for past losses and perpetuating their self-image as "bad" pitchers. We agreed that this was childish behavior, and we tried to write a new scenario, or game plan, in which the umpire was cast in the role of persecutor and a hard pitch in the strike zone would "hurt" him.

Unfortunately, we did not include the catcher (whom I'll call "Milt") in these sessions. Milt felt that the hard pitches were aimed at him personally and unconsciously tried to "escape" from them, which resulted in many passed balls. Later, after I benched him and we had more opportunity to talk, I learned that Milt's father had forced him into a catching role when he was quite young; that Milt caught his father's pitching in the driveway for practice, and whenever the boy made a mistake his father indicated disapproval by throwing harder; that Milt interpreted this as an attack on his masculinity, which he came to feel was passive and precarious and had to be defended from a crouch and, in the case of very hard pitches, by dodging to the side. With more counseling and perhaps more protective equipment, I feel that Milt can make a real contribution next year.

Hitting: Once again, the problem was obvious to everyone: Flyer hitting was consistently weak. But rather than look for the cause of the weakness, fans merely complained that the batters didn't "stand up to the pitcher" and took too many called strikes. We wanted to get the players' view of the situation, and so we asked each one to draw a picture of the way things looked to him when he came up to bat.

The pictures were very interesting. One drawing, which was typical of the rest, showed the batter hiding in a deep hole and the opposing pitcher towering over him from the top of a nearby hill (the mound). The entire field was uphill from the batter and the bases in the far distance were hundreds of yards apart.

This drawing was entitled *Safe at Home*, which was just the clue we needed. Apparently, the batters did feel safer at home plate (perhaps by the very implication of its name) even if they were somewhat uncomfortable. One player ("Fred") expressed his feelings in a poem:

> *The baseball flies straight*
> *At me. Heavy shoes are stuck.*
> *How can I get out?*

Obviously, this player does not mind being "in the hole." He would rather be there and then be "called out" than take his chances on the base paths, where he could be "thrown out," "picked off," caught in a "squeeze," or even "stranded."

Unfortunately, I tried to meet these fears head on rather than work around them. I told the players they must "guard" home plate, which would be "wounded" by strike balls, by striking back at the pitches, and that they could prevent the bat from swinging and missing by "choking" it. This approach failed. If a hitter got one strike against him, he felt that home plate *had* been hurt and couldn't be hurt much more by two additional strikes. And the idea of rewarding base hits with positive strokes by the first-base coach—it just didn't work because the players who most needed this reinforcement never got to first base.

Next year, if the fans will help us create a less stressful environment at the ballpark, I believe it will help give the hitters a better perspective of the field and their relation to it.

Fielding: The rural setting of Hay Stadium has been, on the whole, relaxing and beneficial, but its use during the week as a feedlot and pasture has resulted in an uneven playing surface, especially demoralizing for the infielders. However, not all errors were due to bad hops. Infielders spoke of the ball having "eyes" and seeking holes through which to bounce for base hits. And, while they believed they could not reach the ball, they were also fearful of it hitting them, an apparent contradiction.

It seemed pointless to berate players for mistakes that stemmed from deep-seated attitudes, to tell them to respond to grounders logically and not emotionally, and so we instituted a program of simple infield exercises stressing body awareness. Working without a batter or ball and simply concentrating on movement, the infielders practiced graceful fielding and throwing motions, making impossible catches and throwing accurately while off balance. Some have come along faster than others, but at least toward the end of the season there was more action in the infield, more fluidity, more lateralness, and fewer instances of players standing in position and throwing a glove at the ball as it bounded by.

Ironically, as other players improved, the outfielders seemed to become distant and moody and to feel resentful toward balls hit to them. Previously, the low standard of play in the infield had given them a pleasurable feeling of superiority: "The infielders might miss grounders, but *we* don't, even if we do drop a few flies!" Now, with crisper infield play and better pitching, the outfielders were left with less to occupy their time. They tended to withdraw from the game and to feel that we were expecting too much of them.

"Jimmy":
I love baseball and I love being in the outfield. It's very relaxing. But then—bang!—there's a fly ball and everyone's yelling "It's yours, it's yours" and suddenly I'm expected to perform wonders.

Catching a high fly looks a lot easier than it really is, especially when you realize that if you do catch it, it's nothing, an "easy out," but if you drop it you're a bum. People sitting in the bleachers looking at you and yelling and throwing stuff over the fence—I'm sick of it! I'm sick of being treated like an animal in the zoo!

Perhaps, I thought, we do tend to brutalize outfielders. We speak of a good one as being "fast as a gazelle" or having "the eyes of a hawk" or "an arm like a rifle," and talk in terms of outfielding *instinct,* rather than outfielding intelligence and wit and creativity. Perhaps it is time we became more aware that each player, whatever his strengths or weaknesses on the field, has many fine attributes as a person. Perhaps we should begin by recognizing those attributes and reinforcing self-esteem rather than concentrating entirely on a player's faults.

Take "Bill," for instance. For weeks, we hassled him for his mistakes at third base, trying to force him into the mold of a Brooks Robinson or a Harmon Killebrew and giving him no credit for his friendly, outgoing attitude and his concern for others and willingness to offer helpful advice to other players even as his own game suffered. In effect, we were telling him, "You're not OK. You're just a player and not even a very good one. You bobble easy ones and you swing like an old lady. You bat ninth today, buddy." Last week, I came to a decision. I told Bill, "You are OK. You're my manager for next year, and you'll make a darn good one. You've got good ideas and you're a darn good communicator. Good luck." So Bill will handle the day-to-day decisions, and I'll be general manager and devote more time to the overall outlook of the team. Dutch has been a good general manager and we owe a lot to him, and I feel he'll make an excellent president.

1974

DAN KENNEDY

Evidently, It Was Live Then

SAL SALBERT (*Host, Producer*):
Oh, it was nuts. You think this stuff today is funny? You think the nighttime comedy programs these days are funny? [I start to answer, but he keeps talking.] We literally invented comedy television. We had one sketch back then that we did called "The Silly Italian," and what I would do was come out on stage in an Italian costume, with the hair and all, holding a jug of wine and saying, "Mama mia . . . maaa maaa mia. . . ." The crowd just howled. They loved it! Then what I would do is I would wait a minute for them to stop laughing, and then I'd give them a long one. You'd see me waiting. You could always see it in my eyes. Carl used to watch me from the wings, and he knew it was coming. I'd get that look in my eyes and then I'd give them a real good long, "Maaaaaaaaaaaaa. . . . Maaaaaaaaaaaaaaaaaaaaaaaaa. . . . Miiiiiiaaaaaaaaaaaaaaaaaaaaaaaaaaaaaaaaa!" And it was live back then! No

videotape! No computers! No editing, nothing! So if you screwed up your line, well. . . . [Shrugs and makes a "tough luck for you, buddy" face, because it was live.]

CARL "THE DOCTOR" NEGEL (*Head Writer, 1950–1954*):
My toes were always stubbed from kicking the wall in the writers' room. I kicked it every time somebody forgot a line I had written. Everybody remembers the sketch called "The Silly Italian," and when they recall it they always say, "Oh, yeah . . . that was the Mama Mia guy." Well, there were a dozen other lines Silly Italian was supposed to say, but half of the time all Sal remembered to say was the one line. So every time he didn't say, "Bella! Marinara spicy meatball!" or "Who got a pizza on my strombolli!" I kicked that damn wall. But those were the days. . . . We were the ones who came up with what your generation recognizes as TV comedy, but the difference was, when we were doing it we had one take to do it in. It was all live back then, so if the actors missed the line . . . that was it. No rewinding it to make it better. You couldn't go crying to some director with a robotic camera like today. This was live TV, my friend.

[I ask what a robotic camera is.]

[Silence.]

[I mention that *Saturday Night Live* is also a live program.]

[Carl asks Sal why I'm a wise guy, and they start repeating whatever I say, except in a high-pitched voice. As they do this, they're cracking up, and me, I'm not laughing.]

NAN BRECKENRIDGE (*Writer, Performer, 1950–1952*):
Oh, I don't remember too, too much about the material back then, but it seemed like we had a good time and made a little money. That was more than I had intended to do, so you could say the show was a success.

[I politely ask her not to be so modest.]

Oh, I don't know that I'm being modest. I just think that we did our job and that was that.

[I tell her that Carl and Sal claim it was quite a lot more than that.]

Oh, Sal this and Carl that. I distinctly remember thinking, "What is so brilliant about 'The Silly Italian'? It's base." That sketch was really the beginning of the end for me on that show.

[I tell her how Carl and Sal made fun of me when I mentioned that *Saturday Night Live* was also a live program.]

Well, Sal thinks he's the only comic to ever work live. I mean, if Sal says hello to you at Hamburger Hamlet on a Tuesday, he spends all day Wednesday and Thursday pointing out that it was live when he said hello to you and that if he had blown it, there would have been no editing that could save him from having said hello incorrectly. The live thing always gets me, because what line was Sal going to louse up so badly without the "safety net" of editing? Mama mia?

[She and I are both laughing at that one. I like Nan. Through our laughter, I add in a little comment about how when Sal and Carl were making fun of me it wasn't even that funny. I say, "They could've come up with something better than just repeating everything I said in a girlish voice."]

[I finish laughing, but Nan is laughing even harder now.]

Oh, actually . . . that's pretty funny because you do have that high-pitched voice, hon. You . . . [laughing] do almost . . . sound like . . . [laughing harder] I mean, don't take it the wrong way but. . . . [Wiping her eyes. Still laughing.] Oh, my. . . .

[Pulls herself together and behaves like a grown adult for a moment.]

After I talked to you on the phone, I called Sal and asked him if the nice lady from the magazine had called them about doing an interview, and he had to tell me that Dan was a young man's name! I said, "Well, somebody ought to tell the girl so she can change her name!"

[Starts laughing again and won't stop. Whatever.]

[Meanwhile Sal and Carl have come in from the next room, and when they realize what Nan is laughing at, they start making fun of me again. Sal says this is just like how they would laugh together in the old days. Talk turns to pitching networks the idea of a reunion show. Nan tries her hand at an imitation of me with a girl's voice and points out that if they were doing this live, they would all have to keep a straight face somehow.]

[Switch off tape recorder.]

2002

JAMAICA KINCAID

*** * ***

Girl

Wash the white clothes on Monday and put them on the stone heap; wash the color clothes on Tuesday and put them on the clothesline to dry; don't walk bare-head in the hot sun; cook pumpkin fritters in very hot sweet oil; soak your little cloths right after you take them off; when buying cotton to make yourself a nice blouse, be sure that it doesn't have gum on it, because that way it won't hold up well after a wash; soak salt fish overnight before you cook it; is it true that you sing benna in Sunday school?; always eat your food in such a way that it won't turn someone else's stomach; on Sundays try to walk like a lady and not like the slut you are so bent on becoming; don't sing benna in Sunday school; you mustn't speak to wharf-rat boys, not even to give directions; don't eat fruits on the street—flies will follow you; *but I don't sing benna on Sundays at all and never in Sunday school*; this is how to sew on a button; this is how to make a buttonhole for the button you have just sewed on;

this is how to hem a dress when you see the hem coming down and so to prevent yourself from looking like the slut I know you are so bent on becoming; this is how you iron your father's khaki shirt so that it doesn't have a crease; this is how you iron your father's khaki pants so that they don't have a crease; this is how you grow okra—far from the house, because okra tree harbors red ants; when you are growing dasheen, make sure it gets plenty of water or else it makes your throat itch when you are eating it; this is how you sweep a corner; this is how you sweep a whole house; this is how you sweep a yard; this is how you smile to someone you don't like too much; this is how you smile to someone you don't like at all; this is how you smile to someone you like completely; this is how you set a table for tea; this is how you set a table for dinner; this is how you set a table for dinner with an important guest; this is how you set a table for lunch; this is how you set a table for breakfast; this is how to behave in the presence of men who don't know you very well, and this way they won't recognize immediately the slut I have warned you against becoming; be sure to wash every day, even if it is with your own spit; don't squat down to play marbles—you are not a boy, you know; don't pick people's flowers—you might catch something; don't throw stones at blackbirds, because it might not be a blackbird at all; this is how to make a bread pudding; this is how to make doukona; this is how to make pepper pot; this is how to make a good medicine for a cold; this is how to make a good medicine to throw away a child before it even becomes a child; this is how to catch a fish; this is how to throw back a fish you don't like, and that way something bad won't fall on you; this is how to bully a man; this is how a man bullies you; this is how to love a man; and if this doesn't work there are other ways, and if they don't work don't feel too bad about giving up; this is how to spit up in the air if you feel like it, and this is how to move quick so that it doesn't fall on you; this is how to make ends meet; always squeeze bread to make sure it's fresh; but what if the baker won't let me feel the bread; *but what if the baker won't let me feel the bread?*; you mean to say that after all you are really going to be the kind of woman who the baker won't let near the bread?

1978

DAVID MAMET

✳ ✳ ✳

From Glengarry Glen Ross

The restaurant. Roma is seated alone at the booth. Lingk is at the booth next to him. Roma is talking to him.

ROMA: . . . all train compartments smell vaguely of shit. It gets so you don't mind it. That's the worst thing that I can confess. You know how long it took me to get there? A long time. When you die you're going to regret the things you don't do. You think you're queer . . . ? I'm going to tell you something: we're all queer. You think that you're a thief? So what? You get befuddled by a middle-class morality . . . ? Get shut of it. Shut it out. You cheated on your wife . . . ? You did it, live with it. (*pause*) You fuck little girls, so be it. There's an absolute morality? Maybe. And then what? If you think there is, then be that thing. Bad people go to hell? I don't think so. If you think that, act that way. A hell exists on earth? Yes. I won't live in it. That's me. You ever take a dump made you feel you'd just slept for twelve hours . . . ?

LINGK: Did I . . . ?

ROMA: Yes.

LINGK: I don't know.

ROMA: Or a piss . . . ? A great meal fades in reflection. Everything else gains. You know why? 'Cause it's only food. This shit we eat, it keeps us going. But it's only food. The great fucks that you may have had. What do you remember about them?

LINGK: What do I . . . ?

ROMA: Yes.

LINGK: Mmmm . . .

ROMA: I don't know. For me, I'm saying, what is is, it's probably not the orgasm. Some broad's forearms on your neck, something her eyes did. There was a sound she made . . . or, me, lying, in the, I'll tell you: me lying in bed; the next day she brought me café au lait. She gives me a cigarette, my balls feel like concrete. Eh? What I'm saying, what is our life? (*pause*) It's looking forward or it's looking back. And that's our life. That's it. Where is the moment? (*pause*) And what is it that we're afraid of? Loss. What else? (*pause*) The bank closes. We get sick, my wife died on a plane, the stock market collapsed . . . the house burnt down . . . what of these happen . . . ? None of 'em. We worry anyway. What does this mean? I'm not secure. How can I be secure? (*pause*) Through amassing wealth beyond all measure? No. And what's beyond all measure? That's a sickness. That's a trap. There is no measure. Only greed. How can we act? The right way, we would say, to deal with this: "There is a one-in-a-million chance that so and so will happen . . . Fuck it, it won't happen to me . . ." No. We know that's not the right way I think. (*pause*) We say the correct way to deal with this is "There is a one-in-so-and-so chance this will happen . . . God protect me. I am powerless, let it not happen to me . . ." But no to that. I say. There's something else. What is it? "If it happens, AS IT

MAY for that is not within our powers, I will deal with it, just as I do today with what draws my concern today." I say this is how we must act. I do those things which seem correct to me today. I trust myself. And if security concerns me, I do that which today I think will make me secure. And every day I do that, when that day arrives that I need a reserve, [a] odds are that I have it, and [b] the true reserve that I have is the strength that I have of acting each day without fear. (*pause*) According to the dictates of my mind. (*pause*) Stocks, bonds, objects of art, real estate. Now: what are they? (*pause*) An opportunity. To what? To make money? Perhaps. To lose money? Perhaps. To "indulge" and to "learn" about ourselves? Perhaps. So fucking what? What isn't? They're an opportunity. That's all. They're an event. A guy comes up to you, you make a call, you send in a brochure, it doesn't matter, "There're these properties I'd like for you to see." What does it mean? What you want it to mean. (*pause*) Money? (*pause*) If that's what it signifies to you. Security? (*pause*) Comfort? (*pause*) All it is is THINGS THAT HAPPEN TO YOU. (*pause*) That's all it is. How are they different? (*pause*) Some poor newly married guy gets run down by a cab. Some busboy wins the lottery. (*pause*) All it is, it's a carnival. What's special . . . what draws us? (*pause*) We're all different. (*pause*) We're not the same. (*pause*) We are not the same. (*pause*) Hmmm. (*pause, sighs*) It's been a long day. (*pause*) What are you drinking?

LINGK: Gimlet.

ROMA: Well, let's have a couple more. My name is Richard Roma, what's yours?

LINGK: Lingk. James Lingk.

ROMA: James. I'm glad to meet you. (*they shake hands*) I'm glad to meet you, James. (*pause*) I want to show you something. (*pause*) It might mean nothing to you . . . and it might not. I don't know.

I don't know anymore. (*pause. He takes out a small map and spreads it on a table*) What is that? Florida. Glengarry Highlands. Florida. "Florida. Bullshit." And maybe that's true; and that's what I said: but look here: what is this? This is a piece of land. Listen to what I'm going to tell you now . . .

1984

STEVE MARTIN

✳ ✳ ✳

The Third Millennium: So Far, So Good

For me, and I assume for most of you—since whatever I'm thinking
so too is the nation—it was difficult to know exactly what to celebrate
on Dec. 31, 1999. Do I celebrate the end of the year, the end of the 20th
century, or the end of the millennium? I chose the one remaining
option, and therefore I assume so did most of you: the end of the
day. This made for significantly reduced partying intensity. However,
waking up on Saturday, knowing that Friday was now over, I felt
compelled to write about the past 2,000 years and the changes that
would be wrought in this new age. This was indeed a challenge to
me as I desired to write the history of humankind, past, present, and
future, without bothering to do any research.

A SHORT HISTORY OF THOUGHT

It is of course impossible to offer anything but a cursory look at the
history of thought in the few paragraphs I'm allotted here.

For more elaborate study see my book *The Long History of Thought* or, for the enthusiast, *The Very Long and Heavy History of Thought, So Long You Can't Believe It.*

Before Jan. 1, 0000, thought did not exist. Yes, there were Socrates, Plato, and Aristotle, but their one-word names keep them from being taken seriously as philosophers. Think of them as the early Greek equivalent of Cher, Liberace, and Madonna: great entertainers, but their views on the nature of the universe are somehow not sticking. Of course Plato can't be faulted for naïvely thinking of the world in terms of forms and shadows; technology was not advanced enough for him to have known that the universe is composed of tiny particles called "futons." And think of poor Socrates, with his simple answer to the question "What is justice?" There was just no way for him to have foreseen a jury's $3 million payout to a McDonald's customer who spilled a cup of too-hot coffee in her lap.

Aristotelian thought dominated culture for 1,500 years and was immediately dumped when it was discovered that the center of the universe was not earth, as Aristotle had claimed, but was actually Donald Trump. Aristotle's metaphysics were then succeeded by the religious philosophy of the Roman Catholic Church, which created a fervor that resulted in the creation of many great paintings and sculptures, and inspired men to turn casual comments like "I need a little something over the sofa" into monumental works of art. In fact, it was Pope Sixtus IV who remarked to Michelangelo upon seeing the Sistine Chapel for the first time, "I said paint the ceiling, not go nuts."

The dogma of the church was challenged in the mid-17th-century by Rene Descartes' famous pronouncement "Cogito ergo sum" ("I am nervous about having to add"), and the age of rationalism began. Rationalism then gave way to empiricism, and David Hume declared that it was impossible to know if anything existed at all, though later he recanted when he stubbed his toe on a doorjamb.

Thought continued unchanged until the end of the second millennium, except for a brief moment in the early 20th century when Ludwig Wittgenstein destroyed the foundation of all philosophical thought, and people didn't know what to believe anymore, causing them to feel lost, hopeless, and fearful. This resulted in the biggest clothes-buying spree the world has ever seen.

The third millennium, now well into its second day, appears to have taken thought to new and unexpected extremes. The first of such extremes appears to be that the fundamental philosophical belief of the 1990s, the personal tattoo statement, is no longer tenable, and 200,000 indelibly inked young people will be shipped off to a special holding farm in Java. Out of concern for them, they will be kept in the dark about the fact that the fad has passed.

MORALITY THROUGH THE CENTURIES

The history of thought not only deals with philosophy but ethics and morality as well. I offer the advanced student of moral history the following summary:

Roman era: anything goes

Medieval era: nothing goes

Renaissance: anything goes

17th-century Spain: nothing goes

18th-century France: anything goes

19th-century England: nothing goes

1920s America: anything goes

1950s America: nothing goes

1990s America: anything goes

Even as rhythmic as these statistics are, it is impossible to predict the moral tenor of even the next few years, because of the Elvis factor. The Elvis factor is the tendency of an era with one consistent and rigid moral philosophy to be upset and radically altered by a simple, uneducated hillbilly with a new idea.

COMMUNICATION IN THE THIRD MILLENNIUM

Communication has changed so rapidly in the last 20 years, it's almost impossible to predict what might occur even in the next decade. E-mail, which now sends data hurtling across vast distances at the speed of light, has replaced primitive forms of communication such as smoke signals, which sent data hurtling across vast distances at the speed of light. Let's suppose that you want to say, "I am a jerk." In the 18th century, you would have to go around person to person and utter the phrase individually to each one of them. However, here in the third millennium, with our advances in telephone communication, it is possible to say "I am a jerk" to a thousand people at a time by forgetting to turn off your cell phone and having it ring during a performance of *Death of a Salesman*.

Also, there is now a sophisticated communication technique used between men and women that eases marital strain and opens wide the doors of understanding between the sexes. This new technique, developed by psychologists and sociologists, is called "listening." It will be interesting to see if the new technique lasts or whether it will disappear and be replaced by older, more traditional methods, such as "leaving the room."

ART IN THE THIRD MILLENNIUM

I sometimes wonder if a 19th-century artist could have imagined a Picasso. I wonder if Raphael didn't one day scratch out a nice Cubist doodle and toss it in the fireplace, or if Goya ever conjured up a de Kooning, dismissed it, and went on with his work. I think not. It seems logically impossible for a thought to be dreamed up before its time, even with the obvious catch that once it is thought up, it is, by definition, its time. All this means nothing for the real world except that the art of the third millennium is unknowable by us, just as the art of Picasso was unknowable to Manet, though Cézanne might have, on one odd night, dreamt it.

But it is clear—mayors aside—that art will continue. The great moments in art history occur when the hitherto unthinkable thought coalesces in the brain of someone capable of manifesting it. Yes, something is waiting out there in the misty future, with "unknown" as its caption, that we cannot, in no way, imagine. Once the new art is created, however, it is up to us to ensure its rightful place in the pantheon of art history by persecuting and denouncing it.

It is interesting to note that the current art scene, with its bend toward video works, installations, and performance, has devastated the picture-book industry. In fact, one CEO of a popular picturebook company, who used to vacation yearly in New York, Paris, and Venice, is now spending his summers at the New York, Parisian, and Venetian casinos in Las Vegas.

OUR WONDERFUL NEW MILLENNIUM

The third millennium, with its exciting parties and fireworks, puts to shame the incredibly dull first millennium and already outshines the violent second millennium with a significantly reduced statistic of accidental deaths by longbow. The parties and celebrations surrounding the birth of this newest and best millennium also point to its importance. There was no celebration at the start of the first millennium, as it was not known that it had begun, and the celebration at the end of the year 999 was muted because the rotating, mirrored party ball had not yet been invented.

We can measure the impact and value of each age by looking at a brief history of its inventions and accomplishments. It is lamentable that there have been only three millenniums, and the poor folk who lived before the "age of millenniums" thought they were having a good time but are actually condemned to hell.

Pre-first-millennium inventions: dice

First-millennium inventions: the windmill

Second-millennium inventions: eggplant parmigiana, the Chinese finger trap

Third-millennium inventions, since Jan. 1, 2000: nine bug fixes on Windows 98

MY DREAM FOR THE FUTURE

My dream is simple. It is that this millennium, nay, even this decade, will be the first in which we stop referring to centuries by the one-off method. How many schoolboys have been perplexed forever because we refer to the 1900s as the 20th? Why are the 1800s the 19th century? After all, when we are 39 years old and someone asks us our age, we don't say, "I'm starting my 40th year!" Why must we pause and recalculate every time we mention a century and have to figure out that the 17th century, even though it begins with a 16, is not really the 16th century because the 1st century, which has no "1" in front of it, actually counts as a century and the century that has a "1" in front of it is really the 2nd century?

So right now let's start calling the third millennium the second millennium. After all, doesn't this millennium start with a 2? You ask, so how will we refer to the first millennium, the one that begins with all the zeros? Easy. We will not refer to it. We will pretend it never existed. There is no point referring to an era whose biggest accomplishment was the windmill, and you know what? We'll get along fine without it. Problem solved.

A SAD NOTE

I hesitate to point out that by the end of this, the second millennium, we will all be dead. This is especially sad to me, as my life seems to be much more valuable than other people's, what with my special love of flowers and poetry.

Worse, it is discomforting to think that once I'm gone, all my things will be owned by someone else.

There will be people living in my house, wearing ridiculous hairdos, who will think of me and my age as hideously old-fashioned and moronically stupid, and who will look at our newspapers and see ads for clothes-storage shrink-wrap suction machines that will make them roar with laughter.

On the other hand, it is comforting to note that these people will also be frighteningly stupid, sitting on their "sunflower" chairs, wearing their "wigwam" slippers, and eating brain-enhancing toad power-pellets just as embarrassing as anything we ever sat on, wore, or consumed. And perhaps you and I will be a few atoms in the raindrops that fall on them and ruin their day.

A FINAL THOUGHT

When I was a boy, I calculated how old I would be in the year 2000. I was shocked to see that when the millennium arrived, I was fully 10 years younger than I expected to be. But then, I'm in show business. Some of us are beginning our lives, some are in the middle, and some are at the end (I have a proof of this statement, but it will not fit in the margins). But it is wonderful to think that if one day all of us humans, regardless of race or creed, could lay down our differences and create a human chain by circling the globe and holding hands, we would all come down with exactly the same cold.

2000

PATRICIA MARX

✳ ✳ ✳

Getting Along with the Russians

The Russians have come under attack lately for wanting to blow up the world. This is unfair. Before we can criticize the Russians, we must understand their point of view. So many times in life there are two equally valid ways to approach a problem. The French, for example, roast a turkey, seasoned with a hint of salt, in a 450-degree oven, basting frequently, perhaps with peach preserves, until it turns a golden brown. The English, on the other hand, prefer to wrap the turkey in foil and cook it all day in a slow oven. No mention of salt or peach preserves is made. Yet we cannot say the English method is "right" and the French method "wrong." Similarly, we cannot say that our interest in peace is superior to the Russians' interest in war.

Why do the Russians want to kill us? Psychologists tell us that the Russians want to bomb us because they really seek our approval. The Russians are very fond of foreigners. Catherine the Great so admired the French that she tried to change the name of Saint

Petersburg to Chez Moi. And one need only remember the beautiful and costly Russian pavilion at Expo '67—where visitors were allowed to touch the bears—to know how eager the Russians are to please. Though bombing us seems an inappropriate means to that end, it is supremely flattering. Other experts, noting that the Russians' strength lies in the military and not in the arts, remind us that it is natural to want to do what you do best.

Why haven't the Russians acted already? No one knows. Perhaps they are waiting for the right moment. Or perhaps they don't have enough time. There are a million and one things to do in a day, and sometimes even the most minor—trying to figure out whether you should use the "rug" or the "floor" attachment on the vacuum cleaner to clean a rubber welcome mat—can take hours.

But sorry as we may be for the overworked Russians, we must respond to their desire to destroy the world. We must respond, if not for the sake of mankind then for ourselves. Bottling up anger can be harmful, and eventually we will come to resent the Russians. This does not mean we need be vindictive. Two wrongs do not make a right, and supposing they did, we should not use this as an excuse to annoy the Russians. We still see them at cultural exchanges. Imagine how Andrei Gromyko felt after the Russians shot down the Korean jet and he had to attend a Thanksgiving jamboree with U.S. dignitaries. Should he have said he was sorry or would that have implied that he personally gave the orders to kill? Should he have skipped dessert?

Education, not force, is the effective way to change the Russians. If we want a three-year-old not to put his hand on a hot stove, we do not beat him unmercifully. Rather, we *teach* him that a stove is hot, by pressing his hand to the burner for a minute or two. And so we must teach the Russians. Why not distribute the works of Laurie Colwin (my favorite—*Happy All the Time*) in Russia? The Russian people will learn not only that totalitarianism is wrong and democracy is right but also that we are basically romantics who are not above poking fun at ourselves once in a while.

It is important that we not provoke the Russians. We should avoid pointing out how different Russia is from that festive little restaurant in New York, the Russian Tea Room. The Russians are very sensitive about this. Instead, let us compliment the Russians on their clever idea of making soup out of beets! Or tell them how much economic sense communism makes, with all those people living together, sharing rent, food, and utilities. Let's thank the Russians for letting us know months ahead that they planned to boycott the Olympics, sparing us the chore of making hospital corners on all those beds. Should politics come up, we might mention Ivan IV (never call him Ivan the Terrible) and say how great it was that he was able to annex western Siberia.

If our discretion and cordiality are not reciprocated and the Russians refuse to call off their plans to destroy the world, stern measures are in order.

WHAT IS TO BE DONE

1. Continue to send the Russians wheat, but package it in cartons filled with so many Styrofoam pellets that Russia becomes a big mess.

2. Enroll every Soviet citizen in the Columbia Record Club. Each citizen will receive eleven record albums at one ruble, after which he or she will be legally obligated to buy eight albums at list price over the next three years. This will cost the Russians more than 20 billion rubles. Plus no Russian groups.

3. Give them the broken headsets at the UN.

4. Call up Konstantin Chernenko while he is boating and

tell him that the next summit meeting is a come-as-you-are. Send everyone else normal invitations.

5. Send Cuba one Whitman's sampler every day so that the Cubans will like us more than the Russians. *Or* start a rumor that Cuba is giving up communism. When the Russians invade, they will be very embarrassed and will look stupid in the eyes of the world.

6. Rewrite history to show that the shroud of Turin was a Ukrainian shawl, proving that Jesus Christ was a Russian. Then write an article in *Pravda*, commenting, with wry wit, how Marxists supposedly don't believe in religion.

1985

BOBBIE ANN MASON

* * *

La Bamba Hot Line

"Hello. La Bamba Hot Line."

"Is it true that 'La Bamba' is derived from the Icelandic Younger Edda, set to music by Spanish sailors and transported via the Caribbean to America in 1665?"

"No, not even close. La Bamba Hot Line. Go ahead, please."

"When is the next Louie Louie Parade scheduled?"

"You want the Louie Louie Hot Line. This is the La Bamba Hot Line."

"Oh."

"La Bamba Hot Line."

"This is Senator Sethspeaks in Washington, on the Committee for the Investigation of Obscene Rock Lyrics."

"State your business, please."

"Uh—I was wondering, just what are the words to 'La Bamba'?"

"Do you have the record?"

"Yes, I do."

"Well, listen to it."

"But I can't tell if the words are obscene or not."

"That's your problem. La Bamba Hot Line."

"My teenage daughter has been acting funny lately. She refuses to eat, and she has frown lines on her face. She's become aggressive with her parrot and when you talk to her she just says everything is geeky. The doctor can't find anything wrong with her. What should I do?"

"I'm glad you asked. The La Bamba Hot Line has a special pamphlet dealing with problems of teenagers. Just send a self-addressed stamped envelope to La Bamba Hot Line, P.O. Box 4700. But first, I'd have a heart-to-heart with that parrot."

"Much obliged."

"Likewise, I'm sure. La Bamba Hot Line."

"This is Phil Donahue. Is it true that the La Bamba Hot Line is having a lip-sync contest?"

"Absolutely. October the ninth."

"What do I have to do to win?"

"What do you think? Perform 'La Bamba' till your eyes bug out, do it like a rockin' fool, blow the house down."

"Do you think I've got a chance?"

"Everybody has a chance in life, Mr. Donahue."

You wouldn't believe the stuff I get on the La Bamba Hot Line. I work twelve to four. It's an intensive job and can burn you out quick. Two short breaks, while all the calls stack up. They get a message, "All the La Bamba Hot Lines are temporarily busy. Please try again." It's unfair that people have to keep calling and calling, dialing till their nails split in order to get the La Bamba Hot Line. We need help! We need somebody to handle the genuine emergencies, weed out the crazies. The things people want to know: they want to know are they going to get cancer, will the plane they have a ticket on for tomorrow crash, which stores are giving double coupons this week? We try to answer what we can, but I mean we're not God. I tell them play "La Bamba" thirty-two times in a dark room, then improvise thirty-two versions, then listen to it standing on their head. I tell them to walk down the street muttering *"Yo no soy marinero / Soy capitán."* Count the number of people who recognize the lines and multiply by four, and whatever number that is, that's Ollie North's secret Swiss bank account. I mean, some things are so simple you wonder why anybody would bother calling up. We deal with a lot of that. Little kids call just to be funny, try to catch us off guard. Is your refrigerator running, that kind of thing. I'm on to them. I start screaming a wild, cacophonous sort of schizo "La Bamba." Blows them right out of the water.

But mostly it's scholars. Academic stuff. People wanting to know about roots, symbolism, the double-entendre of the *marinero/capi- tán* lines, etc. Idea stuff. I spend my mornings at the library just to stay even with these people. Man, they're sharp. One guy had a beaut—a positive beaut. The way he traced the Paul-is-dead hoax back to the lost Shakespearean sonnets, twisting it around and back through *Poor Ritchie's Almanac* straight up to the chord progressions of "La Bamba"—it was breathtaking. The switchboard was lit up like the stars in the open desert sky on a clear night while I listened and kept all those calls on hold. I was humbled right to my knees. Unfortunately, his spiel didn't get recorded and I didn't get the guy's name. But he'll call again. I'm sure he will.

Some of the ideas that come in are just junk, of course. Did Idi Amin record "La Bamba"? Of course not. But former president Jimmy Carter did. Some stuff you hear is so unbelievable. No, the *Voyager* is not carrying "La Bamba" out to the end of the universe.

Don't I wish. That's sort of my job really, to carry "La Bamba" to the end of the universe.

My boyfriend is giving me a hard time. He says I take my work too seriously. We'll be watching *Washington Week in Review* and I'll say, "Look at those guys. Talk about serious. Don't they ever get down?" He says, "All day it's your La Bamba duties, your La Bamba research, your La Bamba outfits. You go off in the morning with your La Bamba briefcase. When are we ever going to talk about us?"

He says, "This La Bamba thing is going to blow over any minute. It may be blown over by Friday. Things are that fast these days."

"Don't say that!" I cry. "Buddy Holly. 'American Pie.' The Big Bopper. Elvis. Things last longer than you think."

We're going through crisis time, I guess. But we'll work it out. I have faith in that. Right now, my work is at a critical juncture. I'm talking demographics. Market potentializing. La Bamba aerobics, theme weddings, instructional software. We were represented at the harmonic convergence. We met on the boardwalk at Atlantic City, an overflow crowd of La Bamba regulars. We played the song over and over and concentrated on fiber optics, sending our vibes out all over the universe.

The special thing is, my boyfriend can sing "La Bamba." He's not allowed to enter the lip-sync contest because it would be sort of a conflict of interest. He doesn't just lip-sync. He sings it a cappella. He sounds so sincere when he sings it. He makes up the words— he's not a purist—but they sound right; he has the right tune. That is the secret of "La Bamba," inventing it as you go along. That is the true soul of La Bamba. La Bamba lives.

1987

IAN MAXTONE-GRAHAM

✳ ✳ ✳

Fair Warning

Any woman who marries me better be ready for some fuckin'.

BRUCE MCCALL

* * *

Hitler's Secret Dairy

JUNE 25, 1933

Telepathic vibrations have relayed the electrokinetic force of my will into the minds of others! Today, E. led me out into the dooryard and presented me with a cow! Female, classically Rubenesque, black-and-white camouflage! Tomorrow, like a cowboy, I will pat her head!

JUNE 27, 1933

E. says a Brown Swiss would match my shirt, but I remind her that the Holstein is the more German animal. Only the left-handed and others in the grip of the world riboflavin trust, which I will smash, would dare argue to the contrary!

AUGUST 16, 1933

I will not refuse Destiny's mandate! The cow has had a cub

today, the two-hundredth anniversary of Frederick the Great's marriage to Elizabeth of Brunswick-Bevern! Führer, architect, artist, dairyman!

NOVEMBER 12, 1934

I confer with my milking instructor, who insists that I must have been a milkman in my previous incarnation, so quickly have I mastered the tricky Friesian Squeeze! No sign of Himmler (22:30 hrs.)! He should have finished cleaning the stalls by now.

APRIL 17, 1935

Göring *again* lets his straw make disgusting noises as he finishes up his milkshake. I am forced to decree that hereafter only E. and I are to be served milkshakes. E. begs me to hear her ukulele recital of highlights from "Die Walküre," but I am in no mood for culture festivals!

AUGUST 2, 1937

Bormann brings me a Belted Galloway heifer to inspect. It steps on von Rundstedt's nice shiny boots! Ha ha!

FEBRUARY 6, 1938

That Goebbels is a didactic little pettifogger and an advertising man! He wastes an hour of my time tonight attempting to convince me that cowboys should correctly be called horseboys. But he has his uses. Tonight he showed me a film. The Adolf Hitler Bovine Battalion has trained its entire crack herd to wag their tails in unison forty-eight times on command, in honor of my age! I insisted that Goebbels run this stirring tribute several times, once backward. E. claims that my eyes were brimming. This I will not deny!

SEPTEMBER 1, 1939

Busy day. Nevertheless showed Speer my sketches of an underground
dairy, which future difficulties may make advisable. He must design
the largest and grandest dairy in the entire history of the human and
bovine races, not omitting a Rotunda of the Germanic Bovines, large
enough that the Great Pyramid of Cheops could easily fit beneath its
ceiling! I shall call it "Lactia." It will last a thousand years. Who can
tell? With good management, perhaps even longer!

OCTOBER 23, 1939

My first public milking attempt is sabotaged by Ribbentrop's coughing
fit, which startles the cow, Irmtraud, who is high-strung. Hess
tries making a joke of this, knowing well how I despise jokes—and
jokesters who make jokes! He should clip his eyebrows. Ribbentrop
is a dandified weasel who incessantly puffs on English cigarettes, and
never gives me the little cards inside with pictures of ocean liners and
aircraft and trains. Hess leaps to light Ribbentrop's infernal smokes.
So! The two *are* in cahoots after all!

OCTOBER 24, 1939

Such incidents as yesterday's would be grist for the mills of that hack
Sunday painter Churchill and other smart-aleck cads. I have ordered
that my dairy interests and activities must henceforth be an official
secret of the Reich. E. must tell the locals that she is Frau Schicklgruber,
a lost aviatrix.

MARCH 4, 1940

The chubby hat collector Göring swears never to use a straw if he
is again permitted to drink milkshakes. E. says his hands feel like
blancmange and that he would make a poor dairyman. She says
I have fine hands for milking, as the perspiration makes an ideal
lubricant. I believe she is correct in this!

JUNE 30, 1940

Hess bursts in with a look of pure triumph, swiftly erased. When I demanded the Jerseys and Guernseys, I meant the *animals*!

AUGUST 21, 1940

Old Pétain, along with Laval, visits. The French know nothing of cows or milking. I explained to Schacht afterward that great dairy undertakings have been historically alien in all cultures with vowel-dominant languages. He was fascinated.

MARCH 12, 1941

The fatheaded scientific masterminds plead that my design for a rocket-powered milking machine is "impractical." That is what they think, is it? Is that what they think? I think "Ha ha."

MAY 15, 1941

Is the Aberdeen a beef cow or a milk cow? Tonight at supper (cheese, buttermilk, yogurt), Rosenberg and Funk answered yes. Bormann asked which I wanted it to be. Only Hess offered to find out. Perhaps I have misjudged him; a chowderhead, but a chowderhead with initiative!

MAY 16, 1941

The chowderhead went to Scotland!

JANUARY 21, 1942

A pair of silk milking gloves from Mussolini. Wrong size! How I wish to cuff that popinjay fibber-deluxe of a Duce with them!

SEPTEMBER 16, 1943

Doenitz claimed today that cottage cheese is not made from dairy products. Raeder disagreed violently. I let them argue it out.

NOVEMBER 8, 1944

E. insists the cows are saying "moo," not "boo." I have ordered recordings to be made and analyzed. It is just like those dumb walking milkbags to turn on one the moment adversity strikes! They bear watching!!

JANUARY 11, 1945

Treacheries afoot! I caught the entire herd red-handed today, all facing in the same direction, toward the west and the advancing Allied forces! Bormann failed to prove to my satisfaction that they were *not* British cattle parachuted in. I left him with orders to monitor the movements of Irmtraud, the walleyed Holstein—*or her double!*

FEBRUARY 2, 1945

I have today ordered Lactia to be converted immediately into a practice rink for the new roller-skating regiments that will soon reverse events—*if* Speer can get enough ball bearings!!

MARCH 12, 1945

Up all night designing a new kind of cow. Upon it depends the future!

APRIL 27, 1945

Midget cows on rocket-powered roller skates! Firing concentrated lactic acids! Penetrating tank armor from a range of ten thousand meters!

1983

PATRICK F. MCMANUS

✳ ✳ ✳

The Miracle of the Fish Plate

When I was a kid, my family belonged to the landed aristocracy of northern Idaho: we owned the wall we had our backs to. We were forced to the wall so often that my mother decided she might as well buy the thing to have it handy and not all the time have to be borrowing one.

Part of our standard fare in those days was something my grandmother called gruel, as in "Shut up and eat your gruel!" My theory is that if you called filet mignon "gruel" you couldn't get most people to touch it with a ten-foot pole. They would rather eat the pole. But when you call gruel "gruel," you have a dish that makes starvation look like the easy way out.

My mother shared this opinion. She preferred to call gruel "baked ham" or "roast beef" or "waffles," as in "Shut up and eat your waffles." One Christmas when we were hunched against the wall, she had the idea of thickening the gruel, carving it, and calling it "turkey." We were saved from this culinary aberration by a pheasant that blithely crashed through one of our windows to provide us with one of the finest Christmas dinners it has ever been my pleasure to partake of—*pheasant et gruel*. Mom said that God had sent us the pheasant. I figured that if He hadn't actually sent it, He had at least done His best by cursing the pheasant with poor eyesight and a bad sense of direction.

In that time and place, wild game was often looked upon as a sort of divine gift, not just by us but by many of the poor people, too. Hunting and fishing were a happy blend of sport, religion, and economics, and as a result, game was treated with both respect and reverence. In recent years, my affluence has increased to the point where I can dine out at Taco Tim's or Burger Betty's just about anytime I please, so I must admit that hunting and fishing are no longer economic necessities to me. To the contrary, they are largely the reasons I can't afford to dine out at better places, Smilin' John's Smorgasbord, for example. I still regard the pursuit of game as primarily a mystical, even religious quest. To tie into a lunker trout is to enter into communion with a different dimension, a spiritual realm, something wild and unknown and mysterious. This theory of mine was confirmed by no less an authority than a Catholic priest with whom I occasionally share fishing water.

"Me lad," he said, "whenever yourself catches any fish a-tall 'tis a miracle."

I personally would not go so far as to say that my catching a fish would fall into the category of miracles . . . except . . . well, yes, there was one time. You might call it The Miracle of the Fish Plate.

When I was nine years old and the only angler in our family, my catching a fish was a matter of considerable rejoicing on the part of not only myself but my mother, sister, and grandmother as well. There was none of that false praise one occasionally sees heaped upon a kid nowadays—"Oh, my goodness, look at the great big fish Johnny caught! Aren't you just a little man!" No, there was none of that nonsense.

"Hey," my sister, The Troll, would yell. "P. F. Worthless caught a fish!"

"Looks like it's worth about three bites," my grandmother would say by way of appraisal. "But it's a dang sight better than nothin'."

"Put it on the fish plate," my mother would order. "Maybe by Sunday he will have caught enough so we can have fish instead of 'baked ham' for dinner."

The concept of the fish plate may require some explanation. My fishing was confined to a small creek that ran through the back of our place. In those far-off times, the legal limit was twenty-one trout. Although I had heard people speak of "limiting out," I never really believed them. It was an achievement beyond comprehension, like somebody running a four-minute mile, or walking on the moon. No one had ever fished with greater persistence and dedication than I, day in and day out, and I knew that it was not humanly possible to catch a limit of twenty-one fish. Six or seven maybe, but certainly not twenty-one!

Days would go by when I would not get even a single tiny nibble. I would send a hundred worms into watery oblivion for every solid bite. But every so often, suddenly, flashing in a silvery arc above my head, would be a caught trout, usually coming to rest suspended by line from a tree branch or flopping forty feet behind me in the brush. The notion of "playing" a fish seemed nearly as ridiculous to me as "limiting out."

Thus, one by one and two by two I would accumulate little six-, seven-, and eight-inch trout over a period of several days (reluctantly releasing all fish less than six inches) until there were enough for a fish dinner. The collection place for these fish was a plate we kept for that purpose on the block of ice in the icebox. It was known as the fish plate.

I can say without any exaggeration whatsoever that our family watched the fish plate as intently as any investor ever watched a stock market ticker tape.

The summer of The Miracle of the Fish Plate was rather typical: we were living on gruel and greens; the garden was drying up for lack of rain; my mother was out of work; the wall had been mortgaged and the bank was threatening to foreclose. But good fortune can't last forever, and we soon fell on hard times. It was then that we received a letter from a wealthy relative by the name of Cousin Edna, informing us that she would be traveling in our part of the country and planned to spend a day visiting with us. That letter struck like a bolt of lightning.

The big question was, "What shall we feed Cousin Edna?" Cousin Edna was a cultured person, a lady who in her whole life had never once sat vis-à-vis a bowl of gruel. Certainly, we would not want her to get the impression we were impoverished. After all, we had a reputation to maintain befitting the landed aristocracy of northern Idaho.

After long deliberation, my mother fastened a hard cold eye on me, which I can tell you is just about as disgusting as it sounds. "All we can do is have fish for dinner," she said. "How's the fish plate?"

"It's got two six-inchers on it," I said.

"Pooh!" my grandmother said. "There's no way he's gonna catch enough trout before Cousin Edna gets here. The boy's just slow. And he's got no patience and is just too damn noisy to catch fish. Why his grandfather used to go to the crick and be back in an hour with a bucketful of the nicest trout you could have ever laid eyes on."

As you may have guessed, my grandfather was not one of the country's great conservationists. Although he died before my time, his ghost hovered about, needling me about my angling skills. My grandmother attributed his great fishing success to his patience and silence. Personally, I figured he probably used half a stick of dynamite as a lure.

"Don't tell me we have to depend on P. F. Worthless!" my sister wailed. "We'll be humiliated!"

"I'll catch all the fish we need," I yelled.

"Shut up," Mom said, soothingly. "If worse comes to worst, we'll let Cousin Edna eat the two fish we have and the rest of us will pretend we prefer 'baked ham.' "

"It ain't gonna wash," Gram said. "The best we can hope for is another deranged pheasant."

The gauntlet had been hurled in my face. It was up to me to save the family pride, or die trying.

I dug my worms with special care, selecting only those that showed qualities of endurance, courage, and a willingness to sacrifice themselves to a great cause. By that time of year, I had fished the creek so thoroughly that I had cataloged almost every fish in it, knew them all on a first name basis, and was familiar with their every whim and preference. They, on the other hand, knew all my tricks. It would not be easy enticing them to take a hook but I was determined to do it.

And it was not easy. I knew where a nice eight-inch brookie was holed up under a sunken stump. In the grim cold light of first dawn, when he would not be expecting me, I crawled through the wet brush and stinging nettles just above his hideout. I waited, soaked, teeth chattering quietly, passing the time by studying the waves of goosebumps rippling up and down my arms. As the first rays of morning sun began to descend through the pine trees, I lowered a superb worm, one blessed not only with dauntless courage but intellect as well, into the sluggish current that slid beneath the tangle of naked stump roots. I knew that I could not retrieve the hook without snagging it unless the point was covered by the mouth of a trout. Never was a finer bait presented so naturally, with such finesse. The line slackened, the hook drifting with the currents in the labyrinth of roots. A slight tremor came up the line. I whipped the rod back and the fat little eight-incher came flashing out from under the stump. He threw the hook and landed on the bank ten feet from me. I lunged for him, had him in my grasp. He slipped loose and landed in the water, where he circled frantically in an effort to get his bearings. I plunged in after him hoping to capitalize on his momentary confusion. Unfortunately, the water was much deeper than I expected and closed over my head like the clap of doom. As I dogpaddled my way into the shallows, I realized that filling the fish plate might be even more difficult than I had anticipated the chore would be.

Over the next two days I went up and down the creek like a purse seiner. My total take was two small fish, and Cousin Edna was arriving on the following day. I had become a nine-year-old existentialist, abandoning all faith and hope, driving myself on armed only with simple defiance of despair.

First the fish had abandoned me, then God, and now, on the final day, even the sun had slipped behind the mountains, no doubt sniggering to itself. Before me lay the bleakest, shallowest, most sterile part of the creek. Never in my whole life had I caught a fish there, mostly because it would have been pointless to even try. The water rippled over a bed of white gravel without a single place of concealment for even the smallest trout. Well, possibly there was one place. A small log was buried in the gravel diagonally to the current, and I noticed that at the downstream tip of the log there appeared to be a slight pooling of water. I eased into the stream and crept up to the butt end of the log, whereupon I perceived that the gravel had been washed from under it to form a narrow trough of dark, still water. I lowered my last worm, a pale, haggard, well-traveled fellow, into this trough and let it drift along the log, bumping over gravel, into limbs and knots, until it stopped. "Snagged!" I thought. Furious, I hauled back. My rod doubled over but the hook didn't come loose. Instead, the line began to cut a slow arc through the water, picked up speed, and then, exploding out onto the gravel bar, came what seemed to be a monstrous brook trout.

I cannot tell you how long the ensuing battle lasted because at my first glimpse of the fish, time ceased to exist, and the trout and I became a single pulsating spirit suspended in infinity. When at last we emerged into our separate identities, it was as victor and vanquished. In the dying light, the trout lay clamped between my aching knees on a white gravel beach, and I killed him with a sharp blow of a rock to the back of the head.

As he quivered into stillness, I was filled with unknown joy, unfamiliar sorrow. And I knew. I *knew*. Without the slightest doubt, I knew that under that same log, waiting in that watery darkness, was his twin. Gently, I removed the hook from those great jaws, repairing the tatters of the heroic worm, threading them as best I could onto the hook, and made my way back to the log for a repeat performance. When you have a miracle going for you, you never want to waste any of it.

The dinner for Cousin Edna was a great success. When it was over and everyone had had his fill, there were still large sections of fried trout on the platter, which I suppose I need not tell you, was the humble fish plate.

"My heavens!" exclaimed Cousin Edna. "I just don't know when I've had a finer meal!"

"It's not over yet," said Gram. And then she served Cousin Edna a heaping bowl of wild strawberries that my sister had picked with her own little troll fingers.

The wild strawberries made Cousin Edna's eyes roll back in her head, they were so good. "Why, I hope you're not giving me all the strawberries," she said suddenly, noting our attentiveness.

"Land sakes," Gram said, "we have them so often we're tired of the little beggars." I looked at Gram in disbelief. It was the first time I'd ever heard her lie.

"We thought we would have some nice pudding instead," my mother said, passing around some bowls. I looked into mine.

"Hey," I said. "This looks like . . . this smells like . . ."

"Hush, dear," my mother said, her voice edged with granite. "And eat your *pudding*."

1981

GEORGE MEYER

✳   ✳   ✳

The Royal Visitor

When Prince Charles came to our house, his staff told us that he had decided to have a typical home-cooked American meal. My mom hadn't counted on this, so each of us had to whip up one all-American dish, quick-like. I chose an easy one—pork 'n' beans. But as I tossed the can in the trash, I started to feel a little guilty. After all, baked beans were pretty dull, even for us. I figured I should class them up a bit, so I removed the usual blob of pork fat and replaced it with a nice lean chunk of pork tenderloin, grilled to perfection.

We all huddled in the kitchen as the Prince dined alone. When he had finished the meal, and two cups of Yuban, his reaction was relayed to us by his personal secretary. He found the food "delight-ful." His only complaint was that the pork in the pork 'n' beans was a bit greasy.

I was furious. Ignoring everyone's pleas, I stormed into the din-ing room and confronted our "royal" visitor. I really let him have it.

"You've got a helluva nerve, buddy! You come into our house and start giving orders like you're the Queen of England or something. Who died and made you king? Awwwwwwwwww, so the pork wasn't up to your 'royal standards'—boo-hoo! That's the saddest story ever told!

"I've got news for you, pal. Most people never even see any pork in their pork 'n' beans! The most they can hope for is a hunk of pork fat! So if 'Your Majesty' didn't find it 'acceptable' that's just too damn bad. Because that's the best we have to offer, and we aren't about to apologize for it!"

The Prince was stunned. Clearly, no one had ever dared speak to him in this manner. For a moment, his jaw worked soundlessly in his crimson face. Then he sprang out of his chair and got me in a headlock. I tried to bend his fingers back, but he was much stronger than I'd imagined. He tightened the grip on my windpipe until my head swam and I passed out.

When I came to, I was still in the headlock, only now the Prince was kneeing me in the face. Desperately, I grabbed at his hair, only to feel a stab of pain as his teeth sank into my thumb. I could feel myself starting to black out again. Why wasn't my family helping me? As I began to lose consciousness, the awful truth finally hit me.

He had bought them off with his enormous wealth!

1988

MARK O'DONNELL

✳ ✳ ✳

There Shall Be No Bottom
(A Bad Play for Worse Actors)

We hear eight bars of Handel's Water Music *or any baroque brass voluntary to indicate classy theatre is afoot. Lights come up on* Jeff, *the actor who is playing the indolent, slightly overaged young heir in this drawing room drama. He sits reading an upside-down newspaper, fitfully stealing glances off, since he expects another actor to enter.* Jeff's *main problem, we shall see in time, is a moronic tendency to misdeliver his lines, changing their meaning. He wears a secondhand smoking jacket.* Joe, *the actor who plays the Sherlock Holmes–like inspector, appears, looking menacing, he hopes. He is a smooth, ominous hero/villain, but his main problem as an actor is a tendency to skip large portions of the script. He presses an imaginary or prop doorbell several times, to no effect.*

JOE: (*Hissing stage whisper.*) Sound cue!

(*Finally he covers the error awkwardly.*)

　　Ahem . . . bing-bong!

(Jeff *jumps up promptly. He overdoes the jaunty cad act.*)

JEFF: Ah! The doorbell! That will be all, Wickersham. Inspector Billingsgate! At last you're here!

JOE: (*Crisp, formal, mysterious.*) I'm here, that is true.

JEFF: (*Sunny as only the guilty can be.*) Yes, quite here! I think it's topping of you to come to our lovely summer home, which I shall inherit in the fullness of time.

JOE: (*Doesn't give an inch.*) Do you? (*Pause.*) Where is your only sister, Fanny?

JEFF: In the garden, I expect—though I'm so indolent and destined for a bad end, I scarcely keep track of details! Do come, in? (*This last line has been oddly delivered.* JOE *eyes him hatefully, but goes to center stage.*)

JOE: Than . . . (*He crosses, sits, and elaborately crosses his legs.*) . . . Kyou.

JEFF: (*Whose back has been turned briefly.*) Have a sea . . . (*He turns, sees his error, and corrects it hastily.*) I see you're sitting, Inspector. How elegant. A drink, perhaps, or two? At once? Ha-ha?

(*Pause.*)

JOE: (*Coolly.*) You're nervous, Fenton. (*Pause. Now he makes his first attack.*) Do the words *millizend aspimoza* mean anything to you?

JEFF: (*Panicked; they clearly do have meaning.*) No! No! Why should they?

(*Pause.*)

JOE: I was just testing you. They're nonsense words, you're quite right.

(JEFF, *as Fenton, nervously leans on the fireplace mantel, imaginary or not. In any case it seems awkwardly high.* JEFF's *arms are at head level, so his attempted insouciance seems strained.*)

JEFF: (*In pain.*) Would you care for a cigarette? Or two at once, ha-ha? They're here on the mantel in this silver box . . .

(JOE, *as Billingsgate, regards* JEFF *contemptuously.*)

JOE: You make me laugh, Fenton.

JEFF: No, you make *me* laugh, Inspector!

(*There follows a brief hot uncomfortable, slightly crazed "laughing" contest.*)

BOTH: Ha-ha, ha-ha-ha, ha-ha-ha-ha—

(*It ends abruptly.*)

JOE: How little you've changed since your boyhood.

JEFF: Time is a bitter artist, Inspector. Cigarette?

JOE: (*Glowering.*) I've already said no.

JEFF: No you haven't.

JOE: (*Overlooking this.*) Have you ever known a man named Cinnamon Boris?

JEFF: (*Suavely.*) Certainly not. I've never even been to that part of town.

JOE: (*Relentless.*) But you know him well enough to borrow money of him!

JEFF: (*Confused.*) Of him?

JOE: (*Annoyed but accommodating.*) From him!

JEFF: Ahh!

(*He adopts an attitude of well-bred boredom, but then misdelivers his line like an "Is so!" schoolyard taunt.*)

Really, Inspector! . . . This IS SO fatiguing!

(*Beat. He realizes this didn't sound right, and corrects this delivery.*)

This is SO fatiguing!

JOE: You're complacence itself, aren't you? Even if the Bluebottle fortune hangs in the balance?

(*JEFF misinterprets the word* afraid *in the following line by trembling and speaking with cartoonish fearfulness.*)

JEFF: I'm afraid! . . . (*Now lackadaisical again.*) . . . I can't help you, Inspector. I think you're mistaken in your suspicion.

JOE: Do you?

JEFF: (*Breezily, automatically.*) Yes, I do. I so very do!

(*That isn't the next line, so* JOE *pointedly cues him again.*)

JOE: That's not right. So you do, do you?

(JEFF *regards him blankly. He's forgotten where they are in the script, and this throws both of them.*)

JEFF: Do I?

JOE: Do you? (*Aside.*) What's the next line? (*He covers ineptly and in a panic.*) Answer me, do you?

JEFF: (*Unhappily, also panicking.*) Yes, I do!

JOE: (*Still stuck, agonized, helpless.*) Do you?

JEFF: (*Tears and anger about to surface.*) As I've said, yes!

JOE: (*Trying to stall, a shambles.*) Do you?

JEFF: (*Resentful and near hysteria.*) Yes I do, if you want to know the truth!

JOE: (*In a tiny, miserable voice.*) Do you?

JEFF: (*Desperately takes over.*) But what's this you were about to tell me, Inspector, about my sister being in grave danger?

JOE: (*Relieved, hectic.*) Oh, that's right, thanks! (*Now, as Billingsgate.*) She is! That's right! Grave danger!

(JEFF *recoils at the news he himself has just revealed, and considering the next line, ill-advisedly puts his hands on his hips.*)

JEFF: Danger? My Fanny in danger? (*He takes one step back.*) I am taken aback! (*He turns and calls offstage.*) Fanny, enter right, quickly! (*Now he turns his hate on the Inspector, but the actor again mispronounces his line.*) You dog! You cure!

(*Fanny enters, an ingenuous bauble of a girl, played by a smart if also overaged actress named* JANE.)

JANE: Fenton, I've been dressing for simply hours! Kendall will be here at any moment! We're going to the Sophomore Ambassador's ball! Tell me, do you think the Count likes pearls on women?

JEFF: (*Frisks her from head to toe.*) Fanny, you're in no danger!

(*He turns on the Inspector angrily, in a comically overdone pivot.*)
You lied to me! And you didn't tell me the truth!

JOE: (*Implacably.*) She is in no grave danger, it is true. I did lie. I was just . . . testing you. No, it is not Fanny who is in grave danger, but her child!

JEFF: Child! Fanny!

JANE: (*With cardboard pathos.*) I am underdone!

JEFF: (*Mangling his delivery.*) Fanny, what? Have you and Kendall *been* to each other? (*He realizes his error and corrects it.*) Fanny, what have you and Kendall been to each other?

JANE: (*With painful periphrasis.*) He . . . had his way with me.

JEFF: (*Solicitously, but increasingly eager and turned on.*) You mean . . . he worked his will upon you?

JANE: (*Simply.*) He pressed the advantage.

JEFF: He led you down the path of dalliance?

JANE: He made a dishonest woman of me.

JEFF: (*Slavering.*) He enjoyed your sweet favors?

JOE: (*Intervening curtly.*) That's quite enough, Fenton.

JEFF: Sorry.

JOE: (*Significantly.*) So you mean to say you've risked the family fortune on a racehorse, just to ransom Fanny's little Charlie?

JEFF: (*Boggled.*) Uhh . . . (*Improvises.*) You read my mind, Inspector! (*With a sting.*) Like a man who has skipped many pages ahead in the script! (*He turns to deliver an entrance cue.*) But I say Hang It All to Blazes! (*Wheels again to face an expected actor, who isn't there.*) And as for you, Kendall! Uh, sorry, I thought I heard someone come in. Kendall, in fact. (*Now louder.*) Hang it all to blazes!

JANE: (*Gamely trying to cover.*) Why, I hear gravel crunching in our driveway . . . er, footpath now! (*Silent terror onstage.*) I'm sure someone is about to enter as if on cue!

JOE: (*A bad improviser, he addresses empty space with fury.*) So! You thought you were pretty clever, didn't you?

JANE: (*Again trying to help.*) Yes, er, that's right, Kendall! Hide behind the drapes like the coward you are!

JEFF: (*Actor to actor.*) Good cover!

(*Suddenly a breathless boob stumbles on, carrying the script and a clipboard. It's the stage manager,* JED, *headset and all, covering for an absent actor. He's no performer and reads tonelessly from the script.*)

JED: "I—don't ka-now . . ." Whew, sorry! Jarrod's stuck in traffic! "I"—*gasp*—"I don't know what—you're insinua—"

(*Pause as he noisily turns the page of the script and resumes.*)

   " . . . ting, Inspector!"

JANE: Kendall! Is it really you?

JED: (*Jaunty monotone.*) "I—don't—give—a—twirl—Inspector. I'm—sure—she's—no—better—than—she—should—be."

JEFF: So, Kendall! You spit in my face behind my back!

JED: (*Cheerfully, like a happy pitchman.*) "Take that, and that and that!"

(*Suddenly understands what the line means.*)

   Oh.

(*A bad fight ensues, with punches faked to the stomach met with recoiling heads and vice versa.*)

   "Take that! And that! And . . ." (*Noisily turns page again.*) ". . . that!"

JEFF: (*Unconvincingly.*) And several of these!

JOE: (*Causes the fighting to freeze with this sudden exclamation.*) What do you mean, Captain's Folly has won the race? That means the fortune is saved!

JEFF: You read *his* mind now, Inspector. (*Again with a sting and no English accent.*) Again, like a man who has skipped many pages ahead in the script!

JOE: (*The actor.*) Sorry, I sometimes have this problem with premature ejac—

JED: (*Loudly and out of it.*) "He—crosses—left—smiles—broadly—and pours—a drink—"

JANE: Oh, Fenton! And Mother!

JEFF: (*Trying to straighten the keel.*) Married? How absolutely rather!

JOE: (*Helplessly.*) Have we skipped to the end?

JED: (*Befuddled, sloppily consults script.*) What, to where it says blackout?

(*An unseen technician misunderstands and obligingly provides an instant
blackout.*)

ALL: (*In darkness, together.*) Hey!

END OF PLAY

2008

DAVID OWEN

✳ ✳ ✳

A Naturalist's Notes

People are surprised when I tell them that I, by temperament and by avocation, am a naturalist. I don't look like a naturalist. No pair of field glasses dangles from my sunburned neck (which isn't sunburned), and I don't wear hiking boots or an old bandanna, and my arms are not laden with specimen bags and notebooks and tweezers—the tools of the naturalist's trade, you are thinking, but not of mine. I don't live in a tent, not even for part of the year. I don't own a canoe or a kayak or any kind of net. The shelves in my study? I can tell you truthfully that they are not lined with large jars containing the well-preserved bodies of dead squirrels and such, or with old birds' nests, or with a dozen or so different types of ferns that are indistinguishable to you but not to me. No.

And yet a naturalist I definitely am—though of a particular type. Let me begin my explanation with a metaphor: There is a universe in a drop of water. And within that universe? Much more water, also in drop form. And within every one of those (other) drops? Yet another water-filled universe—and so on and so on, down to about a billionth of a billionth of an inch, I'd guess, at which point everything probably looks pretty much the same.

In other words, the answer to my riddle (about how I can be a naturalist without a bandanna or a kayak) is that I am a naturalist within my own home, which, for various reasons, I seldom leave. The natural world under my roof is as varied and as worthy of scientific investigation as any rain forest, or any other type of forest. Indeed, I have spent the past decade within these walls closely observing, and forming hypotheses concerning, a single domestically indigenous mammal species: *Dachshundus miniaturus*. I own two of these fascinating creatures—one "black and tan," the other brown, both "smooth"—or perhaps I should say they own me. At any rate, it is miniature dachshunds that are the objects of my naturalistic study.

For quite a few years now, my special interest has been their means of communication. Yes, my friend, you are not dreaming: miniature dachshunds—indeed, all dogs; nay, all animals—are able to communicate. They can't read aloud from even a babyish book, but they can convey complex meanings to one another and, not infrequently, to members of unrelated species, such as ours. Over the years, the patient observation of my dogs' "canine culture" has made me conversant with what I now think of as "dog language." It is almost as though an electronic apparatus of mine had suddenly detected some astonishing new radio frequency, whose existence had never before been suspected (for example, because I was listening to a different station). Allow me to share what I have learned.

My dogs—like their close genetic relatives, wolves—sleep much of the day. They do so primarily on the living-room couch, which, by now, smells strongly of them even when they are sleeping elsewhere. Hour after hour, the dogs contentedly loll near my legs or on top of my stomach, their slumber undefiled—until their exquisitely sensitive ears perceive, through the shroud of sleep, the low rumble of the battered panel truck belonging to the mailman. As the truck draws near, the dogs' ears twitch. The short hairs along their spines rise, and their tails bristle—a defensive reflex. A deep growl begins to build at the back of their throats, like an engine commencing to idle, or even to rev. As soon as the mail truck reaches the bottom of my driveway, both dogs leap across my chest and up onto the back of the couch, from which they can see (through a window) the front yard. They begin to bark furiously. Then they jump back onto my chest and down to the floor, run the length of the hallway, and hurl themselves against the front door while continuing, somehow, to bark.

To you, my dogs' fierce snarls would seem like nothing but a violent, meaningless cacophony. To me, though, this "cacophony" (as you call it) is rich with meaning, which I, after years of uncomplaining effort and reflection, am at last able to decode. Following is my translation of a recent such outburst of theirs. Using a complete dog-language lexicon of my own devising, I have rendered it into English:

"God damn it! God damn it! God damn you!!! God damn you!!! God damn! God damn it! Shit!! Shit!! Shit!!! God-God-God damn it! Crap!!! Damn!!! Damn!!! God damn! God damn!!! Fuck you! Go to Hell!!! Hell!! Go to Hell!! Son of a bitch!! Damn it! Go to Hell!!! Go to Hell!!! God damn it! Damn! God damn it to Hell!!!!" (And so on, until five or ten minutes after the mailman, himself cursing, though in his own language—as usual—had driven away, and my dogs, reluctantly, it seemed, returned to the living room and, with a couple of backward glances toward the hallway, rejoined me on the couch.)

GRACE PALEY

✳︎ ✳︎ ✳︎

Six Days: Some Rememberings

I was in jail. I had been sentenced to six days in the Women's House of Detention, a fourteen-story prison right in the middle of Greenwich Village, my own neighborhood. This happened during the American war in Vietnam, I have forgotten which important year of the famous sixties. The civil disobedience for which I was paying a small penalty probably consisted of sitting down to impede or slow some military parade.

I was surprised at the sentence. Others had been given two days or dismissed. I think the judge was particularly angry with me. After all, I was not a kid. He thought I was old enough to know better, a forty-five-year-old woman, a mother and teacher. I ought to be too busy to waste time on causes I couldn't possibly understand.

I was herded with about twenty other women, about 90 percent black and Puerto Rican, into the bullpen, an odd name for a women's holding facility. There, through someone else's lawyer, I received a note from home telling me that since I'd chosen to spend the first week of July in jail, my son would probably not go to summer camp, because I had neglected to raise the money I'd promised. I read this note and burst into tears, real running-down-the-cheek tears. It was true: thinking about other people's grown boys, I had betrayed my little son. The summer, starting that day, July 1, stood up before me day after day, steaming the city streets, the after-work crowded city pool.

I guess I attracted some attention. You—you white girl you—you never been arrested before? A black woman about a head taller than I put her arm on my shoulder. It ain't so bad. What's your time, sugar? I gotta do three years. You huh?

Six days.

Six days? What the fuck for?

I explained, sniffling, embarrassed.

You got six days for sitting down in front of a horse? Cop on the horse? Horse step on you? Jesus in hell, cops gettin' crazier and stupider and meaner. Maybe we get you out.

No, no, I said. I wasn't crying because of that. I didn't want her to think I was scared. I wasn't. She paid no attention. Shoving a couple of women aside—Don't stand in front of me, bitch. Move over. What you looking at?—she took hold of the bars of our cage, commenced to bang on them, shook them mightily, screaming, Hear me now, you motherfuckers, you grotty pigs, get this housewife out of here! She returned to comfort me. —Six days in this low-down hole for sitting in front of a horse!

Before we were distributed among our cells, we were dressed in a kind of nurse's-aide scrub uniform, blue or green, a little too large or a little too small. We had had to submit to a physical in which all our hiding places were investigated for drugs. These examinations were not too difficult, mostly because a young woman named Andrea Dworkin had fought them, refused a grosser, more painful examination some months earlier. She had been arrested protesting the war in front of the U.S. Mission to the UN. I had been there, too, but I don't think I was arrested that day. She was mocked for that determined struggle at the Women's House, as she has been for other braveries, but according to the women I questioned, certain humiliating, perhaps sadistic customs had ended—for that period at least.

My cellmate was a beautiful young woman, twenty-three years old, a prostitute who'd never been arrested before. She was nervous, but she had been given the name of an important long-termer. She explained in a businesslike way that she *was* beautiful and would need protection. She'd be okay once she found that woman. In the two days we spent together, she tried *not* to talk to the other women on our cell block. She said they were mostly street whores and addicts. She would never be on the street. Her man wouldn't allow it anyway.

I slept well for some reason, probably the hard mattress. I don't seem to mind where I am. Also, I must tell you, I could look out the window at the end of our corridor and see my children or their friends on their way to music lessons or Greenwich House pottery. Looking slantwise I could see right into Sutter's Bakery, then on the corner of Tenth Street. These were my neighbors at coffee and cake.

Sometimes the cell block was open, but not our twelve cells. Other times the reverse. Visitors came by: they were prisoners, detainees not yet sentenced. They seemed to have a strolling freedom, though several, unsentenced, unable to make bail, had been there for months. One woman peering into the cells stopped when she saw me. Grace! Hi! I knew her from the neighborhood, maybe the park, couldn't really remember her name.

What are you in for? I asked.

Oh nothing—well, a stupid drug bust. I don't even use—oh well, forget it. I've been here six weeks. They keep putting the trial off. Are you okay?

Then I complained. I had planned not to complain about anything while living among people who'd be here in these clanging cells a long time; it didn't seem right. But I said, I don't have anything to read and they took away my pen and I don't have paper.

Oh, you'll get all that eventually, she said. Keep asking.

Well, they have all my hairpins. I'm a mess.

No no, she said, you're okay. You look nice.

(A couple of years later, the war continuing, I was arrested in Washington. My hair was still quite long. I wore it in a kind of bun on top of my head. My hairpins gone, my hair straggled wildly every which way. Muriel Rukeyser, arrested that day along with about thirty other women, made the same generous sisterly remark. No no, Grace, love you with your hair down, you really ought to always wear it this way.)

The very next morning, my friend brought me *The Collected Stories of William Carlos Williams.* —These okay?

God! Okay. —Yes!

My trial is coming up tomorrow, she said. I think I'm getting off with time already done. Overdone. See you around?

That afternoon, my cellmate came for her things. —I'm moving to the fourth floor. Working in the kitchen. Couldn't be better. We were sitting outside our cells, she wanted me to know something. She'd already told me, but said it again: I still can't believe it. This creep, this guy, this cop, he waits, he just waits till he's fucked and fine, pulls his pants up, pays me, and arrests me. It's not legal. It's not. My man's so mad, he like to kill *me*, but he's not that kind of— he's not a criminal type, *my* man. She never said the word "pimp." Maybe no one did. Maybe that was our word.

I had made friends with some of the women in the cells across the aisle. How can I say "made friends"? I just sat and spoke when spoken to, I was at school. I answered questions—simple ones. Why would I do such a fool thing on purpose? How old were my children? My man any good? Then: you live around the corner? That was a good idea, Evelyn said, to have a prison in your own neighborhood, so you could keep in touch, yelling out the window. As in fact we were able to do right here and now, calling and being called from Sixth Avenue, by mothers, children, boyfriends.

About the children: One woman took me aside. Her daughter was brilliant, she was in Hunter High School, had taken a test. No, she hardly ever saw her, but she wasn't a whore—it was the drugs. Her daughter was ashamed; the grandmother, the father's mother, made the child ashamed. When she got out in six months it would be different. This made Evelyn and Rita, right across from my cell, laugh. Different, I swear. Different. Laughing. But she *could* make it, I said. Then they really laughed. Their first laugh was a bare giggle compared to these convulsive roars. Change her ways? That dumb bitch. Ha!!

Another woman, Helen, the only other white woman on the cell block, wanted to talk to me. She wanted me to know that she was not only white but Jewish. She came from Brighton Beach. Her father, he should rest in peace, thank God, was dead. Her arms were covered with puncture marks almost like sleeve patterns. But she needed to talk to me, because I was Jewish (I'd been asked by Rita and Evelyn—was I Irish? No, Jewish. Oh, they answered). She walked me to the barred window at the end of the corridor, the window that looked down on West Tenth Street. She said, How come you so friends with those black whores? You don't hardly talk to me. I said I liked them, but I liked her, too. She said, If you knew them for true, you wouldn't like them. They nothing but street whores. You know, once I was friends with them. We done a lot of things together, I knew them fifteen years, Evy and Rita maybe twenty, I been in the streets with them, side by side, Amsterdam, Lenox, West Harlem; in bad weather we covered each other. Then one day along come Malcolm X and they don't know me no more, they ain't talking to me. You too white. I ain't all that white. Twenty years. They ain't talking.

My friend Myrt called one day, that is, called from the street, called, Grace Grace. I heard and ran to the window. A policeman, the regular beat cop, was addressing her. She looked up, then walked away before I could yell my answer. Later on she told me that he'd said, I don't think Grace would appreciate you calling her name out like that.

What a mistake! For years, going to the park with my children, or simply walking down Sixth Avenue on a summer night past the Women's House, we would often have to thread our way through whole families calling up—bellowing, screaming to the third, seventh, tenth floor, to figures, shadows behind bars and screened windows, How you feeling? Here's Glena. She got big. Mami mami, you like my dress? We gettin you out baby. New lawyer come by.

And the replies, among which I was privileged to live for a few days, shouted down: —You lookin beautiful. What he say? Fuck you, James. I got a chance? Bye-bye. Come next week.

Then the guards, the heavy clanking of cell doors. Keys. Night.

I still had no pen or paper despite the great history of prison literature. I was suffering a kind of frustration, a sickness in the way claustrophobia is a sickness—this paper-and-penlessness was a terrible pain in the area of my heart, a nausea. I was surprised.

In the evening, at lights-out (a little like the army or on good days a strict, unpleasant camp), women called softly from their cells. Rita hey Rita, sing that song—come on, sister, sing. A few more importunings and then Rita in the cell diagonal to mine would begin with a ballad. A song about two women and a man. It was familiar to everyone but me. The two women were prison sweethearts. The man was her outside lover. One woman, the singer, was being paroled. The ballad told her sorrow about having been parted from him when she was sentenced, now she would leave her loved woman after three years. There were about twenty stanzas of joy and grief.

Well, I was so angry not to have pen and paper to get some of it down that I lost it all—all but the sorrowful plot. Of course she had this long song in her head, and in the next few nights she sang and chanted others, sometimes with a small chorus.

Which is how I finally understood that I didn't lack pen and paper but my own memorizing mind. It had been given away with a hundred poems, called rote learning, old-fashioned, backward, an enemy of creative thinking, a great human gift disowned.

Now there's a garden where the Women's House of Detention once stood. A green place, safely fenced in, with protected daffodils and tulips; roses bloom in it, too, sometimes into November.

The big women's warehouse and its barred blind windows have been removed from Greenwich Village's affluent throat. I was sorry when it happened; the bricks came roaring down, great trucks carried them away.

I have always agreed with Rita and Evelyn that if there are prisons, they ought to be in the neighborhood, near a subway—not way out in distant suburbs, where families have to take cars, buses, ferries, trains, and the population that considers itself innocent forgets, denies, chooses to never know that there is a whole huge country of the bad and the unlucky and the self-hurters, a country with a population greater than that of many nations in our world.

1994

CHARLES PORTIS

✳ ✳ ✳

I Don't Talk Service No More

Neap's face is not very clear to me.
It drifts just out of range. He said he could
feel his house going down while we were
talking on the phone

Once you slip past that nurses' station in the east wing of D-3, you can get into the library at night easy enough if you have the keys. They keep the phone locked up in a desk drawer there but if you have the keys you can get it out and make all the long-distance calls you want to for free, and smoke all the cigarettes you want to, as long as you open a window and don't let the smoke pile up so thick inside that it sets off the smoke alarm. You don't want to set that thing to chirping. The library is a small room. There are three walls of paperback westerns and one wall of windows and one desk.

I called up Neap down in Orange, Texas, and he said, "I live in a bog now." I hadn't seen him in forty-odd years and I woke him up in the middle of the night and that was the first thing out of his mouth. "My house is sinking. I live in a bog now." I told him I had been thinking about the Fox Company Raid and thought I would give him a ring. We called it the Fox Company Raid, but it wasn't a company raid or even a platoon raid, it was just a squad of us, with three or four extra guys carrying pump shotguns for trench work. Neap said he didn't remember me. Then he said he did remember me, but not very well. He said, "I don't talk service no more."

We had been in reserve and had gone back up on the line to relieve some kind of pacifist division. Those boys had something like "Live and Let Live" on their shoulder patches. When they went out on patrol at night, they faked it. They would go out about a hundred yards and lie down in the paddies, and doze off, too, like some of the night nurses on D-3. When they came back, they would say they had been all the way over to the Chinese outposts but had failed to engage the enemy. They failed night after night. Right behind the line the mortar guys sat around in their mortar pits and played cards all day. I don't believe they even had aiming stakes set up around their pits. They hated to fire those tubes because the Chinese would fire right back.

It was a different story when we took over. The first thing we did was go all the way over to the Chinese main line. On the first dark night we left our trenches and crossed the paddies and slipped past their outposts and went up the mountainside and crawled into their trench line before they knew what was up. We shot up the place pretty good and blew two bunkers, or tried to, and got out of there fast with three live prisoners. One was a young officer. Those trenches had a sour smell. There was a lot of noise. The Chinese fired off yellow flares and red flares, and they hollered and sprayed pistol bullets with their burp guns and threw those wooden potato-masher grenades with the cast-iron heads. The air was damp and some of them didn't go off. Their fuses weren't very good. Their grenade fuses would sputter and go out. We were in and out of there before they knew what had hit them. It could happen to anybody. They were good soldiers and just happened to get caught by surprise, by sixteen boys from Fox Company. You think of Chinese soldiers as boiling all around you like fire ants, but once you get into their trench line, not even the Chinese army can put up a front wider than one man.

Neap said, "I don't talk service no more," but he didn't hang up on me. Sometimes they do, it being so late at night when I call. Mostly they're glad to hear from me and we'll sit in the dark and talk service for a long time. I sit here in the dark at the library desk smoking my Camels and I think they sit in the dark too, on the edges of their beds with their bare feet on the floor.

I told Neap service was the only thing I did talk, and that I had the keys now and was talking service coast to coast every night. He said his house was in bad shape. His wife had something wrong with her too. I didn't care about that stuff. His wife wasn't on the Fox Company Raid. I didn't care whether his house was level or not but you like to be polite and I asked him if his house was sinking even all around. He said no, it was settling bad at the back, to where they couldn't get through the back door, and the front was all lifted up in the air, to where they had to use a little stepladder to get up on their front porch.

You were supposed to get a week of meritorious R and R in Hong Kong if you brought in a live prisoner. We dragged three live prisoners all the way back from the Chinese main line of resistance and one was an officer and I never got one day of R and R in Hong Kong. Sergeant Zim was the only one who ever did get it that I know of. On the regular kind of R and R you went to Kyoto, which was all right, but it wasn't meritorious R and R. I asked Neap if he knew of anyone besides Zim who got meritorious R and R in Hong Kong. He said he didn't even know Zim got it.

He asked me if I was in a nut ward. I asked him how many guys he could name who went on the Fox Company Raid, not counting him and me and Zim. All he could come up with was Dill, Vick, Bogue, Ball, and Sipe. I gave him eight more names real fast, and the towns and states they came from. "Now who's the nut? Who's soft in the head now, Neap? Who knows more about the Fox Company Raid, you or me?" I didn't say that to him because you try to be polite when you can. I didn't have to say it. You could tell I had rattled him pretty good, the way I whipped off all those names.

He asked me how much disability money I was drawing down. I told him and he said it was a hell of a note that guys in the nut ward were drawing down more money than he was on Social Security. I told him Dill was dead, and Gott. He said yeah, but Dill was on Okinawa in 1945, in the other war, and was older than us. He told me a little story about Dill. I had heard it before. Dill was talking to the captain outside the command-post bunker, telling him about the time on Okinawa he had guided a flamethrower tank across open ground, to burn a Jap field gun out of a cave. Dill said, "They was a whole bunch of far come out of that thang in a hurry, Skipper." Neap laughed over the phone. He said, "I still laugh every time I think about that. 'They was a whoooole bunch of far come out of that thang in a hurry, Skipper.' The way he said it, you know, Dill."

Neap thought I must be having a lot of trouble tracking people down. I haven't had any trouble to speak of. Except for me and Foy and Rust, who are far from home, and Sipe, who is a fugitive from justice, everybody else went back home and stayed there. They left home just that one time. Neap was surprised to hear that Sipe was on the lam, at his age. How fast could Sipe be moving these days, at his age? Neap said it was Dill and Sipe who grabbed those prisoners and that Zim had nothing to do with it. I told him Zim had something to do with getting us over there and back. He said yeah, Zim was all right, but he didn't do no more in that stinking trench line than we did, and so how come he got meritorious R and R in Hong Kong and we didn't? I couldn't answer that question. I can't find anyone who knows the answer to that. I told him I hadn't called up Zim yet, over in Niles, Michigan. I wanted to have the squad pretty much accounted for before I made my report to him. Neap said, "Tell Zim I'm living on a mud flat." I told him he was the last one I had to call up before Zim. I put Neap at the bottom of my list because I couldn't remember much about him.

I can still see the faces of those boys who went on the Fox Company Raid, except that Neap's face is not very clear to me. It drifts just out of range. He said he could feel his house going down while we were talking there on the phone. He said his house was going down fast now, and with him and his wife in it. It sounded to me like the Neaps were going all the way down.

He asked me how it was here. He wanted to know how it was in this place and I told him it wasn't so bad. It's not so bad here if you have the keys. For a long time I didn't have the keys.

1996

PADGETT POWELL

✳ ✳ ✳

Scarliotti and the Sinkhole

In the Pic 'N' Save Green Room, grits were free. Scarliotti, as he liked to call himself, though his real name was Rod, Scarliotti ate free grits in the Green Room. To Rod, grits were virtually sacramental; to Scarliotti they were a joke, and if he could not eat them for free in a crummy joint so down in the world it had to use free grits as a promotional gimmick, he wouldn't eat them. Scarliotti had learned that when he was Rod, treating grits as good food, *he* had been a joke, so he became Scarliotti. He wanted his other new name, his new given name, to come from the province of martial arts. Numchuks Scarliotti was strong but a little obvious. He was looking for something more refined, a name that would not start a fight but would prevent one from starting. He also thought a name from the emergency room might do: Triage Scarliotti, maybe. But he had to be careful there. Not many people knew what terms in the emergency room meant. Suture Scarliotti, maybe. Edema Scarliotti.

Lavage Scarliotti. No, he liked the martial-arts idea better. With his new name he would be a new man, one who would never eat grits with a straight face again.

There were many things he never intended to do with a straight face again. One of them was ride Tomos, a Yugoslavian moped that would go about twenty miles per hour flat out, and get clipped in the head by a mirror on a truck pulling a horse trailer and wake up with a head wound with horseshit in it in the hospital. Another was to be grateful that at least Tomos had not been hurt. Now, his collection of a quarter million dollars in damages imminent, he didn't give a shit about a motorized bicycle. He wasn't riding that and he wasn't seriously eating grits anymore. He was going to take a cab the rest of his life and eat grits only if they were free. He would never again be on the side of the road and never pay for grits, and it might just be *Mister* Scarliotti. Deal with that.

The horse Yankees who clipped him were in a world of hurt and he wanted them to be. They were the kind of yahoos who leave Ohio and find a tract of land that was orange groves until 1985 and now is plowed out and called a horse farm and buy it and fence it and call themselves horse breeders. And somehow they breed Arabian horses, and somehow it is Arabs behind it all. Somehow Minute Maid, which is really Coca-Cola, leaves, and Kuwait and Ohio are here. And the Yankees are joking and laughing about grits at first, and then they wise up and try to fit in and start eating them every morning after learning how to cook them, which it takes them about a year to do it. And driving all over the state in diesel doolies with mirrors coming off them about as long as airplane wings, and knocking *people who live here* in the ditch.

Scarliotti is in his motorized bed in his trailer in Hague, Florida. It is only ten o'clock but the trailer is already ticking in the heat. Scarliotti swears it—the trailer—moves, kind of bends, on its own, when he is lying still in the bed, and not even moving the bed, which has an up for your head and an up for your feet and both together kind of make a sandwich out of you; hard to see the TV that way, which is on an arm just like at the hospital and controlled by a remote just like at the hospital, a remote on a thick white cord, which he doesn't understand why it isn't like a remote everybody else has at their house. When the trailer moves, Scarliotti thinks that a sinkhole might be opening up. Before his accident that would have been fine. But not now. Two hundred and fifty thousand dollars would be left topside if he went down a sinkhole today, and even if he *lived* down there, which he thought was possible, he knew he couldn't spend *that* kind of money down there. He thought about maybe asking Higgins, whom he worked for before the accident, if they could put outriggers or something on the trailer to keep it from going down. They could cable it to the big oak, but the big oak might go itself. He didn't know. He didn't know if outriggers would work or not. A trailer wasn't a canoe, and the dirt was not water.

There were about a hundred pills on a tray next to him he was supposed to take but he hadn't been, and now they were piled up and he had started throwing them out the back window and he hoped they didn't *grow* or something and give him away. You could get busted for anything these days. It was not like the old days.

Tomos was beside the trailer, and Scarliotti had asked his daddy to get it running, and if his daddy had, he could get to the Lil' Champ for some beer before the nurse came by. The bandages and the bald side of his head scared the clerk at the Lil' Champ, and once she undercharged him, she was so scared. He let that go, but he didn't like having done it because he liked her and she'd have to pay for it. But right now he couldn't afford to correct an error in his favor. Any day now, he'd be able to afford to correct all the errors in his favor in the world. He was going to walk in the Lil' Champ and buy the whole store and the girl with it. See how scared she got then.

He accidentally hit both buttons on the bed thing and squeezed himself into a sandwich and it made him pee in his pants before he could get it down, but he did not care. It didn't matter now if you peed in your pants in your bed. It did not matter now.

He tried to start Tomos by push-starting it, and by the time he gave up he was several hundred yards from the trailer. It was too far to walk it back and he couldn't leave it where it was so he pushed Tomos with him to the Lil' Champ. He had done this before. The girl watched him push the dead moped up and lean it against the front of the store near the paper racks and the doors so he could keep an eye on it.

Scarliotti did not greet her but veered to the cooler and got a twelve-pack of Old Mil and presented it at the counter and began digging for his money. It had gotten in his left pocket again, which was a bitch because he had to get it out with his right hand because his left couldn't since the accident. Crossing his body this way and pronating his arm to dig into his pocket threw him into a bent slumped contortion.

The girl chewed gum fast to keep from laughing at Scarliotti. She couldn't help it. Then she got a repulsive idea, but she was bored so she went ahead with it.

"Can I help you?" she asked.

Scarliotti continued to wrestle with himself, looking like a horror-movie hunchback to her. His contorting put the wounded part of his head just above the countertop between them. It was all dirty hair and scar and Formica and his grunting. She came from behind the counter and put one hand on Scarliotti's little back and pulled his twisted hand out of his pocket and slipped hers in. Scarliotti froze. She held her breath and looked at his poor forlorn moped leaning against the brick outside and hoped she could get the money without touching anything else.

Scarliotti braced his two arms on the counter and held still and then suddenly stuck his butt out into her and made a noise and she felt, as she hoped she wouldn't, a hardening the size of one of those small purple bananas they don't sell in the store but are very good, Mexicans and people eat them. She jerked her hand out with a ten-dollar bill in it.

Scarliotti put his head down on the counter and began taking deep breaths.

"Do you want to go on a date?" he asked her, his head still down as if he were weeping.

"No." She rang up the beer.

"Any day now I will be pert a millionaire."

"Good."

"Good? *Good? Shit.* A millionare."

She started chewing rapidly again. "Go ahead and be one," she said.

"You don't believe me?"

"You going to be Arnold Schwarzenegger, too?"

This stopped Scarliotti. It was a direction he didn't understand. He made a guess. "*What?* You don't think I'm strong?" Before the girl could answer, he ran over to the copy machine and picked up a corner of it and would have turned it over but it started to roll and got away and hit the magazine rack. Suddenly, inexplicably, he was sad. He did not do sad. Sad was bullshit.

"Don't think I came," he said to the girl.

"What?"

"I didn't *come.* That's *pee!*" He left the store with dignity and pushed Tomos with the beer strapped to the little luggage rack over the rear wheel to the trailer and did not look back at approaching traffic. Hit him *again,* for all he cared.

In the trailer there wasn't shit on the TV, people in costumes he couldn't tell what they were, screaming Come on down! or something. He put the beer in the freezer. He sat against the refrigerator feeling the trailer tick and bend. Shit like that wouldn't happen if his daddy would fix damn Tomos. His daddy was letting him down. He was—he had an idea something like he was letting himself down. This was preposterous. How did one do, or not to, that? Do you extend outriggers from yourself? Can a canoe in high water just grow its own outriggers? No, it can't.

A canoe in high water takes it or it goes down. End of chapter. He drank a beer and popped a handful of the pills for the nurse and knew that things were not going to change. This was it. It was foolish to believe in anything but a steady continuation of things exactly as they are at this moment. This moment was it. This was it. Shut the fuck *up*.

He was dizzy. The trailer ticked in the sun and he felt it bending and he felt himself also ticking in some kind of heat and bending. He was dizzy, agreeably. It did not feel bad. The sinkhole that he envisioned was agreeable, too. He hoped that when the trailer went down it went smoothly, like a glycerine suppository. No protest, no screaming, twisting, scraping. The sinkhole was the kind of thing he realized that other people had when they had Jesus. He didn't need Jesus. He had a *hole*, and it was a purer thing than a *man*.

He was imagining life in the hole—how cool? how dark? how wet? Bats or blind catfish? The most positive speculation he could come up with was it was going to save on air conditioning, then maybe on clothes. Maybe you could walk around naked, and what about all the things that had gone down sinkholes over the years, *houses* and shit, at your disposal maybe—he heard a noise and thought it was the nurse and jumped in bed and tried to look asleep, but when the door opened and someone came in he knew it wasn't the nurse and opened his eyes. It was his father.

"Daddy," he said.

"Son."

"You came for Tomos?"

"I'mone Tomos your butt."

"What for?" Rather than have to hear the answer, which was predictable even though he couldn't guess what it would be, Scarliotti wished he had some of those sharp star things you throw in martial arts to pin his daddy to the trailer wall and get things even before this started happening. His father was looking in the refrigerator and slammed it. He had not found the beer. If you didn't drink beer you were too stupid to know where people who do drink it keep it after a thirty-minute walk in Florida in July. Scarliotti marveled at this simple luck of his.

He looked up and saw his daddy standing too close to him, still looking for something.

"The doctor tells me you ain't following directions."

"What directions?"

"*All* directions."

Scarliotti wasn't following any directions but didn't know how anybody knew.

"You got to be *hungry* to eat as many pills as they give me."

"You got to be *sober* to eat them pills, son."

"That, too."

The headboard above Scarliotti's head rang with a loudness that made Scarliotti jerk and made his head hurt, and he thought he might have peed some more. His father had backhanded the headboard.

"If we'd ever get the money," Scarliotti said, "but that lawyer you picked I don't think knows shit—"

"He knows plenty of shit. It ain't his fault."

"It ain't my fault."

"No, not beyond getting hit by a truck."

"Oh. That's *my* fault."

"About."

Scarliotti turned on the TV and saw Adam yelling something at Dixie. Maybe it was Adam's crazy brother. This was the best way to get his father to leave. "Shhh," he said. "This is my show." Dixie had a strange accent. "Don't fix it, then."

"Fix what?" his father said.

"Tomos."

"Forget that damned thing."

"I can't," Scarliotti said to his father, looking straight at him. "I love her."

His father stood there a minute and then left. Scarliotti peeked through the curtains and saw that he was again not taking the bike to get it fixed for him.

He got a beer and put the others in the refrigerator just in time. He wanted sometimes to have a beer joint and *really* sell the coldest beer in town, not just say it. He heard another noise outside and jumped back in bed with his beer. Someone knocked on the door. That wouldn't be his father. He put the beer under the covers.

"Come in."

It was the nurse.

"Come in, *Ma*ma," Scarliotti said when he saw her.

"Afternoon, Rod."

He winced but let it go. They thought in the medical profession you had mental problems if you changed your name. They didn't know shit about mental problems, but it was no use fighting them so he let them call him Rod.

The nurse was standing beside the bed looking at the pill tray, going "Tch, tch, tch."

"I took a bunch of 'em," Scarliotti said.

The nurse was squinching her nose as if she smelled something.

"I know you want to get well, Rod," she said.

"I am well," he said.

"Not by a long shot," she said.

"I ain't going *to the moon*," he said.

The nurse looked curiously at him. "No," she said, "you're not."

Scarliotti thought he had put her in her place. He liked her but didn't like her preaching crap at him. He was well enough to spend the $250,000, and that was as well as he needed to be. It was the Yankee Arab horse breeders were sick, not well enough to pay their debts when they go running over people because they're retired and don't have shit else to do. The nurse was putting the arm pump-up thing on his arm. She had slid some of the pills around with her weird little pill knife that looked like a sandwich spreader or something. He wanted to show her his Buck knife, but would reveal the beer and the pee if he got it out of his pocket.

"It's high, again. If you have another fit, you're back in the hospital."

"I'm not having no nother fit."

Scarliotti looked at her chest. The uniform was white and ribbed, and made a starchy little tissuey noise when she moved, and excited him. He looked closely at the ribs in the material when she got near him.

"Them lines on your shirt look like . . . crab lungs," he said.

"What?"

"I don't know, like crab lungs. You know what I mean?"

"No, Rod, I don't." She rolled her eyes and he saw her. She shouldn't do that. That was what he meant when he said, and he was right, that the medical profession did not know shit about mental problems.

The nurse went over everything again, two this four that umpteen times ninety-eleven a day, which meant you'd be up at two and three and five in the morning taking pills if you bought the program, and left. He watched Barney Fife get his bullet taken back by Andy. He wanted to see Barney *keep* his bullet. Barney should be able to keep that bullet. But if Barney shot at his own foot like that, he could see it. Barney was a dumb fuck. Barney looked like he'd stayed up all night taking pills. There was another noise outside. Scarliotti had had it with people fucking with him. He listened. There was a timid knock at the door. He just lay there. Let them break in, he thought. Then, head wound or not, he would kill them.

The door opened and someone called Hello. Then: "Anyone home?"

Scarliotti waited and was not going to say anything and go ahead and lure them in and kill them, but it was a girl's voice and familiar somehow, but not the nurse, so he said, "If you can call it that."

The girl from the Lil' Champ stepped in.

"I'm down here."

She looked down the hall and saw him and came down it with a package.

"You paid for a case," she said.

"I could use a case," Scarliotti said.

"Pshew," the girl said. Even so, she was, it seemed, being mighty friendly.

"Well, let's have us one," Scarliotti said.

The girl got two beers out of the package.

"You like Andy Griffin?" he said.

"*Fith.* He's okay. Barney's funny. Floyd is creepy."

"Floyd?"

"Barber? In the chair?"

"Oh." Scarliotti had no idea what she was talking about. Goober and Gomer, he knew. The show was over anyway. He turned the set off, holding up the white remote rig to show the girl.

"They let you off to deliver that beer?"

"I'm off."

"Oh."

"On my way."

"Oh."

Scarliotti decided to go for it. "I would dog to dog you." He blushed, so he looked directly at her to cover for it, with his eyes widened.

"That's about the nastiest idea I ever heard," the girl said.

"My daddy come by here a while ago, took a *swang* at me," Scarliotti said. "Then the nurse come by and give me a raft of shit. I nearly froze the beer. Been a rough day."

"You would like to make love to me. Is that what you're saying?" Since she had touched him in the store and he had said what he said, the girl had undergone a radical change of heart about Scarliotti's repulsiveness. She did not understand it, exactly.

Scarliotti had never in his life heard anyone say, "You would like to make love to me," nor had he said it to anyone, and did not think he could, even if it meant losing a piece of ass. He stuck by his guns.

"I would dog to dog you."

"Okay."

The girl stood up and took her clothes off. Compared to magazines she was too white and puffy, but she was a girl and she was already getting in the bed. For a minute Scarliotti thought they were fighting and then it was all warm and solid and they weren't. He said "Goddamn" several times. "God*damn*." He looked at the headboard and saw what looked like a dent where his father had backhanded it and was wondering if he was wearing a ring done that or just hit it that fucking hard with his hand when the girl bit his neck. "Ow!" he said. "*Goddamn*."

"You fucker," the girl said.

"Okay," Scarliotti said, trying to be agreeable.

"*Good*," she said.

Then it was over and she no longer looked too white and soft. She was sweaty and red. Some of Scarliotti's hair had fallen out on her from the good side of his head and he hoped nothing had fallen out of the bad side. The trailer had stopped moving from their exertions. There were ten beers sweating onto a hundred pills beside the bed. The nurse and his father would not be back before the trailer could start ticking in the heat and bending on its own, unless they bend it again themselves with exertions in the bed, but all in all Scarliotti thought it would be a good enough time to have some fun without being bothered by anyone before the trailer found its way down the hole.

Scarliotti woke up and took the sweating beers in his arms and put them in the refrigerator and came back with two cold ones. "They *look* like a commercial sitting there but they don't *taste* like a commercial," he said, waking and mystifying the girl. "Women," he said, feeling suddenly very good about things, "know what they want and how to get it. Men are big fucking babies."

"How do you come to know all that?" the girl asked.

"I know."

"How many women have you had?"

"Counting you?"

"Yeah."

"Three."

"That explains how you know so much."

Scarliotti started laughing. "Heh, heh, heh . . . *heah, heahh, heahhh*—" and did not stop until he was coughing and slumped against the wall opposite the bed.

"Quailhead," he said.

"What?"

"Nothing."

"You call me quailhead?"

"No. You want to go down to the Green Room and eat free grits?"

"Eat free grits," she said flatly, with a note of suspicion.

"Yeah."

"I thought you were going be a millionaire."

"I am. Pert near. That's why I don't pay for grits."

"Well, I still pay for grits. I ain't eating no free grits."

"See? Heh, heh . . . it proves what I said. Women know what they want."

"And men are babies."

Scarliotti started the laugh again and crawled into bed with the girl.

"Be still. Shhh!"

"What?" the girl asked.

"Listen to the trailer."

"I don't hear anything—"

"Listen! Hear that?"

"No."

"It's ticking. It's moving. You ever thought of living in a sinkhole?"

"No."

"You want to go down into a sinkhole with me?"

"No."

"You want to go to the Hank show?"

"Okay."

"I mean, us all, whole thing going. Trailer and all."

"To the Hank show?"

"No, into the *sinkhole*."

Scarliotti started the uncontrollable heaving laugh again at this, and the girl reluctantly stroked the shaved side of his head to calm him. At first she barely touched it, but she began to like the moist bristly feel of Scarliotti's wounded head.

Scarliotti woke up and looked out the window and saw a dog and a turtle. The dog appeared to be licking the turtle.

"Ballhoggey wollock dube city, man. Your dog," he said to the girl, "is licking that turtle in its *face*. That turtle can *bite*, man. You better get your dog away from that turtle, man. That dog is unnaturally *friendly*, man. I don't want to even *go* into salmonella. That turtle can kill your dog from here to Sunday. It dudn' *have* to bite him, man. I *don't* want that turtle to bite your dog, man. On the *tongue* like that. I think I'd start, like, crying. I'd cry like a son of a bitch if we had to get that turtle off your dog's tongue. It would be blue and red. Your dog would be hollering and tears coming out of *its* eyes. That turtle would be squinting and biting down *hard*, man. I don't want it. I don't.

"You better get your dog, man. We'd have to kill that turtle to get it off. If it didn' cut your dog's tongue off first, man. Shit. Take a bite out of it like cheese. This round scallop space, like. God. *Get your dog*, man. I have an appointment somewhere. What time is it? I think this damn Fruit of the Loom underwear is for shit. You see this guy walking around in his underwear with his kid, going to pee, and then popping out this fresh pair of miniature BVDs for the kid just like his, and they walk down the hall real slow in the same stupid tight pants look like *panties*? *Get* your dog, man.

"Shit. Fucking turtle. What's it *doing* here, man? I mean, your *dog's* not even supposed— What time is it? *Get* the bastard, will you? I can't move my . . . legs. I don't know when it happened. Last twenty minutes after I dogged you. I'd get him myself. That dog is . . . not trained or what? Did you train him? People shouldn't let their dogs go anarchy, man. Dogs need government. Dogs are senators in their hearts when they're trained. They have, like white hair and deep voices. And do *right*. Your dog is going to get *bit*, man. Get your dog. Please get your dog. This position I'm in, I don't know how I got in it. It dudn' make sense.

"Do you ever think about J. E. B. Stuart? His name wasn't Jeb, it's initials of J. E. B. He had a orange feather in a white hat and was, like, good. Won. Fast, smart, all that, took no survivors; well, I don't know about that. Kind of kind you want on *your* side, like that. Man. It's hard to talk, say things right. If you don't get your dog I'm going to shoot—you. No, myself. *Claim* your dog out there. The window is dirty as shit. I pay a lot of money for this trailer, you think they'd wash the goddamn window. No, you wouldn't. You *know* they wouldn't wash the goddamn window. I'd shoot the *turtle*, but the window, they wouldn't *fix* it so they wouldn't *wash* it, would they? I'd shoot your fucking *dog* before I'd shoot the turtle. The turtle idn' doing shit but getting licked in the face and *taking* it."

The girl said, "I don't have a dog."

"Well, somebody does," Scarliotti said. "*Some*body sure as hell does."

1998

SIMON RICH

✳ ✳ ✳

Play Nice

IF ADULTS WERE SUBJECTED TO THE SAME INDIGNITIES AS CHILDREN . . .

PARTY

ZOE: Dad, I'm throwing a party tonight, so you'll have to stay in your room. Don't worry, though—one of my friends brought over his father for you to play with. His name is Comptroller Brooks and he's roughly your age, so I'm sure you'll have lots in common. I'll come check on you in a couple of hours. (*Leaves.*)

COMPTROLLER BROOKS: Hello.

MR. HIGGINS: Hello.

COMPTROLLER BROOKS: So . . . um . . . do you follow city politics?

MR. HIGGINS: Not really.

COMPTROLLER BROOKS: Oh.

(*Long pause.*)

(*Zoe returns.*)

Zoe: I forgot to tell you—I told my friends you two would perform for them after dinner. I'll come get you when it's time. (*Leaves.*)

Comptroller Brooks: Oh, God, what are we going to do?

Mr. Higgins: I know a dance . . . but it's pretty humiliating.

Comptroller Brooks: Just teach it to me.

CAPITOL HILL

Lobbyist: If you fail to pass this proposition, it will lead to the deaths of thousands. Any questions?

Senator: Why are you wearing a sailor suit?

Lobbyist: My children decided to dress me this way, on a whim. I told them it was an important day for me, but they wouldn't listen.

Senator: It's adorable.

Lobbyist: OK . . . but do you agree with the proposition? About the war?

Senator: Put on the cap.

GARAGE

Lou Rosenblatt: Can I drive your car? I'll give it back when I'm done.

Mrs. Herson: I'm sorry, do I know you?

Lou Rosenblatt: No, but we're the same age and we use the same garage.

Mrs. Herson: No offense, sir, but I really don't feel comfortable lending you my car. I mean, it's by far my most important possession.

Brian Herson: Mom, I'm surprised at you! What did we learn about sharing?

Mrs. Herson: You're right . . . I'm sorry. Take my Mercedes.

Lou Rosenblatt: Thank you. Can I come over to your house later? I'm lonely and I don't have any friends.

MRS. HERSON: Well ... actually ... I kind of had plans tonight.

BRIAN HERSON: Are you *excluding* him?

MRS. HERSON: No, of course not! (*Sighs.*) Here's my address, sir. The party starts at eight.

LOU ROSENBLATT: I'll show up a little early.

MRS. HERSON: What's that on your face?

LOU ROSENBLATT: Mucus. I haven't learned how to blow my nose yet, so I just go around like this all the time.

MRS. HERSON: Oh.

LOU ROSENBLATT: I'll see you soon, inside your house.

2008

GEORGE SAUNDERS

✳ ✳ ✳

Adams

I never could stomach Adams and then one day he's standing in my kitchen, in his underwear. Facing in the direction of my kids' room! So I wonk him in the back of the head and down he goes. When he stands up, I wonk him again and down he goes. Then I roll him down the stairs into the early-spring muck and am like, If you ever again, I swear to God, I don't even know what to say, you miserable fuck.

Karen got home. I pulled her aside. Upshot was: Keep the doors locked, and if he's home the kids stay inside.

But after dinner I got to thinking: Guy comes in in his shorts and I'm sitting here taking this? This is love? Love for my kids? Because what if? What if we slip up? What if a kid gets out or he gets in? No, no, no, I was thinking, not acceptable.

So I went over and said, Where is he?

To which Lynn said, Upstairs, why?

Up I went and he was standing at the mirror, still in his goddam underwear, only now he had on a shirt, and I wonked him again as he was turning. Down he went and tried to crab out of the room, but I put a foot on his back.

If you ever, I said. If you ever again.

Now we're even, he said. I came in your house and you came in mine.

Only I had pants on, I said, and mini-wonked him in the back of his head.

I am what I am, he said.

Well, that took the cake! Him admitting it! So I wonked him again, as Lynn came in, saying, Hey, Roger, hey. Roger being me. And then he rises up. Which killed me! Him rising up? Against me? And I'm about to wonk him again, but she pushes in there, like intervening. So to wonk him again I had to like shove her back, and unfortunately she slipped, and down she went, and she's sort of lying there, skirt hiked up—and he's mad! Mad! At me! Him in his underwear, facing my kids' room, and he's mad at me? Many a night I've heard assorted wonks and baps from Adams's house, with her gasping, Frank, Jesus, I Am a Woman, You're Hurting Me, the Kids Are Watching, and so on.

Because that's the kind of guy he is.

So I wonked him again, and when she crawled at me, going, Please, Please, I had to push her back down, not in a mean way but in a like stay-there way, which is when, of course, just my luck, the kids came running in—these Adams kids, I should say, are little thespians, constantly doing musicals in the backyard, etc., etc.—so they're, you know, all dramatic: Mummy, Daddy! And, OK, that was unfortunate, so I tried to leave, but they were standing there in the doorway, blocking me, like, Duh, we do not know which way to turn, we are stunned. So I shoved my way out, not rough, very gentle—I felt for them, having on more than one occasion heard Adams whaling on them, too—but one did go down, just on one knee, and I helped her up, and she tried to bite me! She did not seem to know what was what, and it hurt, and made me mad, so I went over to Adams, who was just getting up, and gave him this like proxy wonk on top of his head, in exchange for the biting.

Keep your damn, I said. Keep your goddam kids from—

Then I needed some air, so I walked around the block, but still it wasn't sitting right. Because now it begins, you know? Adams over there all pissed off, saying false things about me to those kids, which, due to what they had seen (the wonking) and what they had not seen (him in his underwear, facing my kids' room), they were probably swallowing every mistruth, and I was like, Great, now they hate me, like *I'm* the bad guy in this, and all summer it's going to be pranks, my hose slit and syrup in my gas tank, or all of a sudden our dog has a burn mark on her belly.

So I type up these like handbills, saying, Just So You Know, Your Dad Was Standing Naked in My Kitchen, Facing My Kids' Room. And I tape one inside their screen door so they'll be sure and see it when they go to softball later, then I stuff like nine in their mailbox, and on the rest I cross out "Your Dad" and put in "Frank Adams" and distribute them in mailboxes around the block.

All night it's call after call from the neighbors, saying, you know, Call the cops, Adams needs help, he's a goof, I've always hated him, maybe a few of us should go over there, let us work with you on this, do not lose your cool. That sort of thing. Which was all well and good, but then I go out for a smoke around midnight and what is he looking at, all hateful? Their houses? Don't kid yourself. He is looking at my house, with that smoldering look, and I am like, What are you looking at?

I am what I am, he says.

You fuck, I say, and rush over to wonk him, but he runs inside.

And, as far as cops, my feeling was: What am I supposed to do, wait until he's back in my house, then call the cops and hope he stays facing my kids' room, in his shorts, until they arrive?

No, sorry, that is not my way.

The next day my little guy, Brian, is standing at the back door, with his kite, and I like reach over and pop the door shut, going, Nope, nope, you know very well why not, Champ.

So there's my poor kid, kite in lap all afternoon, watching some dumb art guy on PBS saying, Shading Is One Way We Make Depth, How About Trying It Relevant to This Stump Here?

Then Monday morning I see Adams walking toward his car and again he gives me that smoldering look! Never have I received such a hateful look. And flips me the bird! As if he is the one who is right! So I rush over to wonk him, only he gets in the car and pulls away.

All day that look was in my mind, that look of hate.

And I thought, If that was me, if I had that hate level, what would I do? Well, one thing I would do is hold it in and hold it in and then one night it would overflow and I would sneak into the house of my enemy and stab him and his family in their sleep. Or shoot them. I would. You would have to. It is human nature. I am not blaming anybody.

I thought, I have to be cautious and protect my family or their blood will be on my hands.

So I came home early and went over to Adams's house when I knew nobody was home, and gathered up his rifle from the base-ment and their steak knives and also the butter knives, which could be sharpened, and also their knife sharpener, and also two letter openers and a heavy paperweight, which, if I was him and had lost all my guns and knives, I would definitely use that to bash in the head of my enemy in his sleep, as well as the heads of his family.

That night I slept better until I woke in a sweat, asking myself what I would do if someone came in and, after shoving down my wife and one of my kids, stole my guns and knives and knife sharpener as well as my paperweight. And I answered myself: What I would do is look around my house in a frenzy for something else dangerous, such as paint, such as thinner, such as household chemicals, and then either ring the house of my enemy with the toxics and set them on fire or pour some into the pool of my enemy, which would (1) rot the liner and (2) sicken the children of my enemy when they went swimming.

Then I looked in on my sleeping kids and, oh my God, nowhere are there kids as sweet as my kids, and standing there in my pajamas, thinking of Adams standing there in his underwear, then imagining my kids choking and vomiting as they struggled to get out of the pool, I thought, No, no way, I am not living like this.

So, entering through a window I had forced earlier that afternoon, I gathered up all the household chemicals, and, believe me, he had a lot, more than I did, more than he needed, thinner, paint, lye, gas, solvents, etc. I got it all in like nine Hefty bags and was just starting up the stairs with the first bag when here comes the whole damn family, falling upon me, even his kids, whipping me with coat hangers and hitting me with sharp-edged books and spraying hair spray in my eyes, the dog also nipping at me, and rolling down the stairs of their basement I thought, They are trying to kill me. Hitting my head on the concrete floor, I saw stars, and thought, No, really, they are going to kill me, and if they kill me no more little Melanie and me eating from the same popcorn bowl, no more little Brian doing that wrinkled-brow thing we do back and forth when one of us makes a bad joke, never again Karen and me lying side by side afterward, looking out the window, discussing our future plans as those yellow-beaked birds come and go on the power line. And I struggled to my feet, thinking, Forget how I got here, I am here, I must get out of here, I have to live. And I began to wonk and wonk, and once they had fallen back, with Adams and his teenage boy huddled over the littlest one, who had unfortunately flown relatively far due to a bit of a kick I had given her, I took out my lighter and fired up the bag, the bag of toxics, and made for the light at the top of the stairs, where I knew the door was, and the night was, and my freedom, and my home.

2004

CATHLEEN SCHINE

Save Our Bus Herds!

Second Avenue, once a busy commercial thoroughfare, has been all but destroyed recently, overrun by migrating herds of enormous, baying buses. These great lumbering vehicles, which travel in groups of about eight or nine, rumble through the area each morning, scattering frightened pedestrians into the shuttered doorways of newly abandoned shops.

Approximately the size of an elephant, the once solitary bus has baffled the scientific community by beginning to exhibit herding behavior. Just before dawn, the dusty caravans make their way downtown, dawdling at intersections, where they emit their eerie honking calls, nudging each other a little before resuming their long journey.

Last January, the Federal Carrier Protection Agency designated buses an endangered vehicle. Since then, Second Avenue has drawn international crowds of omnibus watchers and conveyance researchers to the spectacle of our rare and powerfully beautiful Grummans. Residents and local merchants, however, are less appreciative of the migrating herds. "They've ruined the neighborhood," said Mrs. Edna Hardee, one of a group of antibus demonstrators gathered at Seventy-ninth Street. "Just look what they've done to the ecological balance. They travel in a pack, honking and squeaking and frightening off all the smaller vehicles." Of the flocks of yellow cabs and shore jitneys that used to frequent Second Avenue, only an occasional hardy Checker now ventures into the territory. In front of Lamston's, a perambulator stands—empty.

Several shooting incidents have been reported recently. Police say they involved deer hunters from Florida invited to the area by the more reactionary members of Young Americans Against Herds (YAAH!). The hunters picked up the trail of a herd at Thirty-fourth Street and, after stalking it for twenty-five minutes in the early-morning fog, surprised seven Grumman Flxibles placidly grazing a mailbox on the southwest corner of Twenty-third Street. Shots were fired, and two of the buses fell before the rest of the startled herd escaped around the corner. ASPCA volunteers trying to pull the fallen buses to safety vied with hunters attempting to tie the Grummans onto the roofs of their station wagons.

"Poachers are a great threat to these worthy vehicles," said noted bus researcher Charles Pearly in an emotional appearance on *Good Morning America*. "There is a flourishing black market in bus pelts. Since 1981, the U.S. Bus and Wildlife Department has confiscated six million dollars' worth of merchandise manufactured from illegally slaughtered buses. Why, just last week a raid on a Queens warehouse uncovered a huge cache of powdered bus horns destined to be sold as aphrodisiacs." Dr. Pearly, professor emeritus at Cornell University's Division of Bus Sciences, is president of the Interfaith Bus Relief Corps, a nonprofit organization established in 1979 to collect tokens for starving buses. A normal bus consumes fifteen hundred pounds of tokens per day, and the natural supply has dwindled to dangerously low levels. In theory, the buses could subsist on coins alone, but because of weather conditions this year, there has been a disappointing coin crop. Also, a subspecies native to Washington, D.C., known as the "White," because of its distinctive coloration, has joined several herds of Grumman and General Motors vehicles, almost doubling the population and causing an alarming concentration in the region. Said Dr. Pearly, "Poachers just slaughter these weakened transports."

Captain Jiminy Strout, leader of the Florida hunters, responded to Dr. Pearly's charges by saying he was "only trying to help." According to Captain Strout, the hunters must step in now that man has decimated the El and the West Side Highway, the bus's natural predators.

Conservationists, outraged by the shootings, held a press conference at Loews Tower East, during which Walt Gawd, bus biologist and chairman of the Save Our Surface Transportation Protection Foundation (SOS), raised the issue of bus shooting as a sport. "How many buses are felled every year by the hunter's bullet?" he asked. "So-called sportsmen have already wiped out the double-decker, just because it was a sitting duck."

Second Avenue has long been a haven for the migrating bus; in fact, it is believed that Second Avenue was originally a pathway beaten out by prehistoric motor coaches moving south. But researchers are still not sure where these impressive vehicles come from or where they go. And although there have been several sightings of individual rogue buses charging up Third, the actual northbound route has never been identified. Even so, scientists say, they do know enough about bus behavior to predict that any disruption of herding or migration patterns would destroy the once mighty bus altogether.

"Buses been coming by here long as I remember," one gray-haired man commented. "Grummans now. And them white ones. But there used to be green ones all along here. And they didn't travel in packs, neither. No, sir. They just come along, all by themselves, one after t'other. They gone now. Gone forever."

Concerned citizens, like Judith Needleham-Stark, of the Agency for a Very Nice New York, attributed the extinction of the green city bus to officials who had them painted blue. "We warned them what would happen," Ms. Needleham-Stark recalls. "But there is so much ignorance about buses."

1982

DAVID SEDARIS

✳   ✳   ✳

A Plague of Tics

When the teacher asked if she might visit with my mother, I touched my nose eight times to the surface of my desk.

"May I take that as a 'yes'?" she asked.

According to her calculations, I had left my chair twenty-eight times that day. "You're up and down like a flea. I turn my back for two minutes and there you are with your tongue pressed against that light switch. Maybe they do that where you come from, but here in my classroom we don't leave our seats and lick things whenever we please. That is Miss Chestnut's light switch, and she likes to keep it dry. Would you like me to come over to your house and put my tongue on *your* light switches? Well, would you?"

I tried to picture her in action, but my shoe was calling. *Take me off*, it whispered. *Tap my heel against your forehead three times. Do it now, quick, no one will notice.*

"Well?" Miss Chestnut raised her faint, penciled eyebrows. "I'm asking you a question. Would you or would you not want me licking the light switches in your house?"

I slipped off my shoe, pretending to examine the imprint on the heel.

"You're going to hit yourself over the head with that shoe, aren't you?"

It wasn't "hitting," it was tapping; but still, how had she known what I was about to do?

"Heel marks all over your forehead," she said, answering my silent question.

"You should take a look in the mirror sometime. Shoes are dirty things. We wear them on our feet to protect ourselves against the soil. It's not healthy to hit ourselves over the head with shoes, is it?"

I guessed that it was not.

"Guess? This is not a game to be guessed at. I don't 'guess' that it's dangerous to run into traffic with a paper sack over my head. There's no guesswork involved. These things are facts, not riddles." She sat at her desk, continuing her lecture as she penned a brief letter. "I'd like to have a word with your mother. You do have one, don't you? I'm assuming you weren't raised by animals. Is she blind, your mother? Can she see the way you behave, or do you reserve your antics exclusively for Miss Chestnut?" She handed me the folded slip of paper. "You may go now, and on your way out the door I'm asking you please not to bathe my light switch with your germ-ridden tongue. It's had a long day; we both have."

It was a short distance from the school to our rented house, no more than six hundred and thirty-seven steps, and on a good day I could make the trip in an hour, pausing every few feet to tongue a mailbox or touch whichever single leaf or blade of grass demanded my attention. If I were to lose count of my steps, I'd have to return to the school and begin again. "Back so soon?" the janitor would ask. "You just can't get enough of this place, can you?"

He had it all wrong. I wanted to be at home more than anything, it was getting there that was the problem. I might touch the telephone pole at step three hundred and fourteen and then, fifteen paces later, worry that I hadn't touched it in exactly the right spot. It needed to be touched again. I'd let my mind wander for one brief moment and then doubt had set in, causing me to question not just the telephone pole but also the lawn ornament back at step two hundred and nineteen. I'd have to go back and lick that concrete mushroom one more time, hoping its guardian wouldn't once again rush from her house shouting, "Get your face out of my toadstool!" It might be raining or maybe I had to go to the bathroom, but running home was not an option. This was a long and complicated process that demanded an oppressive attention to detail. It wasn't that I enjoyed pressing my nose against the scalding hood of a parked car—pleasure had nothing to do with it. A person *had* to do these things because nothing was worse than the anguish of not doing them. Bypass that mailbox and my brain would never for one moment let me forget it. I might be sitting at the dinner table, daring myself not to think about it, and the thought would revisit my mind. *Don't think about it.* But it would already be too late and I knew then exactly what I had to do. Excusing myself to go to the bathroom, I'd walk out the front door and return to that mailbox, not just touching but jabbing, practically pounding on the thing because I thought I hated it so much. What I really hated, of course, was my mind. There must have been an off switch somewhere, but I was damned if I could find it.

I didn't remember things being this way back north. Our family had been transferred from Endicott, New York, to Raleigh, North Carolina. That was the word used by the people at IBM, *transferred.* A

new home was under construction, but until it was finished we were
confined to a rental property built to resemble a plantation house.
The building sat in a treeless, balding yard, its white columns prom-
ising a majesty the interior failed to deliver. The front door opened
onto a dark, narrow hallway lined with bedrooms not much larger
than the mattresses that furnished them. Our kitchen was located
on the second floor, alongside the living room, its picture window
offering a view of the cinder-block wall built to hold back the tide of
mud generated by the neighboring dirt mound.

"Our own little corner of hell," my mother said, fanning herself
with one of the shingles littering the front yard.

Depressing as it was, arriving at the front stoop of the house
meant that I had completed the first leg of that bitter-tasting journey
to my bedroom. Once home I would touch the front door seven times
with each elbow, a task made more difficult if there was someone
else around. "Why don't you try the knob," my sister Lisa would say.
"That's what the rest of us do, and it seems to work for us." Inside
the house there were switches and doorstops to be acknowledged.
My bedroom was right there off the hallway, but first I had business
to tend to. After kissing the fourth, eighth, and twelfth carpeted stair,
I wiped the cat hair off my lips and proceeded to the kitchen, where
I was commanded to stroke the burners of the stove, press my nose
against the refrigerator door, and arrange the percolator, toaster, and
blender into a straight row. After making my rounds of the living
room, it was time to kneel beside the banister and blindly jab a butter knife in the direction of my favorite electrical socket. There were
bulbs to lick and bathroom faucets to test before finally I was free
to enter my bedroom, where I would carefully align the objects on
my dresser, lick the corners of my metal desk, and lie upon my bed,
rocking back and forth and thinking of what an odd woman she
was, my third-grade teacher, Miss Chestnut. Why come here and

lick my switches when she never used the one she had? Maybe she was drunk.

Her note had asked if she might visit our home in order to discuss what she referred to as my "special problems."

"Have you been leaving your seat to lick the light switch?" my mother asked. She placed the letter upon the table and lit a cigarette.

"Once or twice," I said.

"Once or twice what? Every half hour? Every ten minutes?"

"I don't know," I lied. "Who's counting?"

"Well, your goddamned math teacher, for one. That's her *job*, to count. What, do you think she's not going to notice?"

"Notice what?" It never failed to amaze me that people might notice these things. Because my actions were so intensely private, I had always assumed they were somehow invisible. When cornered, I demanded that the witness had been mistaken.

"What do you mean, 'notice what?' I got a phone call just this afternoon from that lady up the street, that Mrs. Keening, the one with the twins. She says she caught you in her front yard, down on your hands and knees kissing the evening edition of her newspaper."

"I wasn't kissing it. I was just trying to read the headline."

"And you had to get that close? Maybe we need to get you some stronger glasses."

"Well, maybe we do," I said.

"And I suppose this Miss . . ." My mother unfolded the letter and studied the signature. "This Miss Chestnut is mistaken, too? Is that what you're trying to tell me? Maybe she has you confused with the other boy who leaves his seat to lick the pencil sharpener or touch the flag or whatever the hell it is you do the moment her back is turned?"

"That's very likely," I said. "She's old. There are spots on her hands."

"How many?" my mother asked.

On the afternoon that Miss Chestnut arrived for her visit, I was in my bedroom, rocking. Unlike the obsessive counting and touching, rocking was not a mandatory duty but a voluntary and highly pleasurable exercise. It was my hobby, and there was nothing else I would rather do. The point was not to rock oneself to sleep: This was not a step toward some greater goal. It was the goal itself. The perpetual movement freed my mind, allowing me to mull things over and construct elaborately detailed fantasies. Toss in a radio, and I was content to rock until three or four o'clock in the morning, listening to the hit parade and discovering that each and every song was about me. I might have to listen two or three hundred times to the same song, but sooner or later its private message would reveal itself. Because it was pleasant and relaxing, my rocking was bound to be tripped up, most often by my brain, which refused to allow me more than ten consecutive minutes of happiness. At the opening chords of my current favorite song, a voice would whisper, *Shouldn't you be upstairs making sure there are really one hundred and fourteen peppercorns left in that small ceramic jar? And, hey, while you're up there, you might want to check the iron and make sure it's not setting fire to the baby's bedroom.* The list of demands would grow by the moment. *What about that television antenna? Is it still set into that perfect v, or has one of your sisters destroyed its integrity. You know, I was just wondering how tightly the lid is screwed onto that mayonnaise jar. Let's have a look, shall we?*

I would be just on the edge of truly enjoying myself, this close to breaking the song's complex code, when my thoughts would get in the way. The trick was to bide my time until the record was no longer my favorite, to wait until it had slipped from its number-one position on the charts and fool my mind into believing I no longer cared.

I was coming to terms with "The Shadow of Your Smile" when Miss Chestnut arrived. She rang the bell, and I cracked open my bedroom door, watching as my mother invited her in.

"You'll have to forgive me for these boxes." My mother flicked her cigarette out the door and into the littered yard. "They're filled with crap, every last one of them, but God forbid we throw anything away. Oh no, we can't do that! My husband's saved it all: every last Green Stamp and coupon, every outgrown bathing suit and scrap of linoleum, it's all right here along with the rocks and knotted sticks he swears look just like his old department head or associate district manager or some goddamned thing." She mopped at her forehead with a wadded paper towel. "Anyway, to hell with it. You look like I need a drink, scotch all right?"

Miss Chestnut's eyes brightened. "I really shouldn't but, oh, why not?" She followed my mother up the stairs. "Just a drop with ice, no water."

I tried rocking in bed, but the sound of laughter drew me to the top of the landing, where from my vantage point behind an oversized wardrobe box, I watched the two women discuss my behavior.

"Oh, you mean the touching," my mother said. She studied the ashtray that sat before her on the table, narrowing her eyes much like a cat catching sight of a squirrel. Her look of fixed concentration suggested that nothing else mattered. Time had stopped, and she was deaf to the sounds of the rattling fan and my sisters' squabbling out in the driveway. She opened her mouth just slightly, running her tongue over her upper lip, and then she inched forward, her index finger prodding the ashtray as though it were a sleeping thing she was trying to wake. I had never seen myself in action, but a sharp, stinging sense of recognition told me that my mother's impersonation had been accurate.

"Priceless!" Miss Chestnut laughed, clasping her hands in delight. "Oh, that's very good, you've captured him perfectly. Bravo, I give you an A-plus."

"God only knows where he gets it from," my mother said. "He's probably down in his room right this minute, counting his eyelashes or gnawing at the pulls on his dresser. One, two o'clock in the morning and he'll still be at it, rattling around the house to poke the laundry hamper or press his face against the refrigerator door. The kid's wound too tight, but he'll come out of it. So, what do you say, another scotch, Katherine?"

Now she was Katherine. Another few drinks and she'd probably be joining us for our summer vacation. How easy it was for adults to bond over a second round of cocktails. I returned to my bed, cranking up the radio so as not to be distracted by the sound of their cackling. Because Miss Chestnut was here in my home, I knew it was only a matter of time before the voices would order me to enter the kitchen and make a spectacle of myself. Maybe I'd have to suck on the broom handle or stand on the table to touch the overhead light fixture, but whatever was demanded of me, I had no choice but to do it. The song that played on the radio posed no challenge whatsoever, the lyric as clear as if I'd written it myself. "Well, I think I'm going out of my head," the man sang, "yes, I think I'm going out of my head."

Following Miss Chestnut's visit, my father attempted to cure me with a series of threats. "You touch your nose to that windshield one more time and I'll guarantee you'll wish you hadn't," he said driving home from the grocery store with a lapful of rejected, out-of-state coupons. It was virtually impossible for me to ride in the passenger seat of a car and not press my nose against the windshield, and now that the activity had been forbidden, I wanted it more than anything. I tried closing my eyes, hoping that might eliminate my desire, but found myself thinking that perhaps *he* was the one who should close his eyes. So what if I wanted to touch my nose to the windshield? Who was it hurting? Why was it that he could repeatedly worry his change and bite his lower lip without the threat of punishment?

My mother smoked and Miss Chestnut massaged her waist twenty, thirty times a day—and here *I* couldn't press my nose against the windshield of a car? I opened my eyes, defiant, but when he caught me moving toward my target, my father slammed on the brakes.

"You like that, did you?" He handed me a golf towel to wipe the blood from my nose. "Did you like the feel of that?"

Like was too feeble for what I felt. I loved it. If mashed with the right amount of force, a blow to the nose can be positively narcotic. Touching objects satisfied a mental itch, but the task involved a great deal of movement: run upstairs, cross the room, remove a shoe. I soon found those same urges could be fulfilled within the confines of my own body. Punching myself in the nose was a good place to start, but the practice was dropped when I began rolling my eyes deep in their sockets, an exercise that produced quick jolts of dull, intoxicating pain.

"I know exactly what you're talking about," my mother said to Mrs. Shatz, my visiting fourth-grade teacher. "The eyes rolling every which way, it's like talking to a slot machine. Hopefully, one day he'll pay off, but until then, what do you say we have ourselves another glass of wine?"

"Hey, sport," my father said, "if you're trying to get a good look at the contents of your skull, I can tell you right now that you're wasting your time. There's nothing there to look at, and these report cards prove it."

He was right. I had my nose pressed to the door, the carpet, and the windshield but not, apparently, to the grindstone. School held no interest whatsoever. I spent my days waiting to return to the dark bedroom of our new house, where I could roll my eyes, listen to the radio, and rock in peace.

I took to violently shaking my head, startled by the feel of my brain slamming against the confines of my skull. It felt so good and took so little time; just a few quick jerks and I was satisfied for up to forty-five seconds at a time.

"Have a seat and let me get you something cool to drink." My mother would leave my fifth- and then my sixth-grade teachers standing in the breakfast nook while she stepped into the kitchen to crack open a tray of ice. "I'm guessing you're here about the head-shaking, am I right?" she'd shout. "That's my boy, all right, no flies on him." She suggested my teachers interpret my jerking head as a nod of agreement. "That's what I do, and now I've got him washing the dishes for the next five years. I ask, he yanks his head, and it's settled. Do me a favor, though, and just don't hold him after five o'clock. I need him at home to straighten up and make the beds before his father gets home."

This was part of my mother's act. She played the ringleader, blowing the whistle and charming the crowd with her jokes and exaggerated stories. When company came, she often pretended to forget the names of her six children. "Hey, George, or Agnes, whatever your name is, how about running into the bedroom and finding my cigarette lighter." She noticed my tics and habits but was never shamed or seriously bothered by any of them. Her observations would be collected and delivered as part of a routine that bore little resemblance to our lives.

"It's a real stretch, but I'm betting you're here about the tiny voices," she said, offering a glass of sherry to my visiting seventh-grade teacher. "I'm thinking of either taking him to an exorcist or buying him a doll so he can bring home some money as a ventriloquist."

It had come out of nowhere, my desperate urge to summon high-pitched noises from the back of my throat. These were not words, but sounds that satisfied an urge I'd never before realized. The sounds were delivered not in my voice but in that of a thimble-sized,

temperamental diva clinging to the base of my uvula. "Eeeeeeee—
ummmmmmmmmmmm—ahhhh—ahhh—meeeeeeee." I was a host
to these wailings but lacked the ability to control them. When I cried
out in class, the teachers would turn from their blackboards with
increasingly troubled expressions. "Is someone rubbing a balloon?
Who's making that noise?"

I tried making up excuses, but everything sounded implausible.
"There's a bee living in my throat." Or "If I don't exercise my vocal
cords every three minutes, there's a good chance I'll never swallow
again." The noisemaking didn't replace any of my earlier habits, it
was just another addition to what had become a freakish collection of
tics. Worse than the constant yelps and twitchings was the fear that
tomorrow might bring something even worse, that I would wake
up with the urge to jerk other people's heads. I might go for days
without rolling my eyes, but it would all come back the moment my
father said, "See, I knew you could quit if you just put your mind to
it. Now, if you can just keep your head still and stop making those
noises, you'll be set."

Set for what? I wondered. Often while rocking, I would imagine my career as a movie star. There I was attending the premiere
beneath a floodlit sky, a satin scarf tied just so around my throat. I
understood that most actors probably didn't interrupt a love scene
to press their noses against the camera or wail a quick "Eeeeeee—
ahhhhhhh" during a dramatic monologue, but in my case the world
would be willing to make an exception. "This is a moving and touching film," the papers would report. "An electrifying, eye-popping
performance that has audiences squealing and the critics nodding,
'Oscar, Oscar, Oscar.' "

I'd like to think that some of my nervous habits faded during
high school, but my class pictures tell a different story. "Draw in
the missing eyeballs and this one might not be so bad," my mother

would say. In group shots I was easily identified as the blur in the back row. For a time I thought that if I accompanied my habits with an outlandish wardrobe, I might be viewed as eccentric rather than just plain retarded. I was wrong. Only a confirmed idiot would wander the halls of my high school dressed in a floor-length caftan; as for the countless medallions that hung from around my neck, I might as well have worn a cowbell. They clanged and jangled with every jerk of my head, calling attention when without them I might have passed unnoticed. My oversized glasses did nothing but provide a clearer view of my rolling, twitching eyes, and the clunky platform shoes left lumps when used to discreetly tap my forehead. I was a mess.

I could be wrong, but according to my calculations, I got exactly fourteen minutes of sleep during my entire first year of college. I'd always had my own bedroom, a meticulously clean and well-ordered place where I could practice my habits in private. Now I would have a roommate, some complete stranger spoiling my routine with his God-given right to exist. The idea was mortifying, and I arrived at the university in full tilt.

"The doctors tell me that if I knock it around hard enough, there's a good chance the brain tumor will shrink to the point where they won't have to operate," I said the first time my roommate caught me jerking my head. "Meanwhile, these other specialists have me doing these eye exercises to strengthen what they call the 'corneal fibers,' whatever that means. They've got me coming and going, but what can you do, right? Anyway, you go ahead and settle in. I think I'll just test this electrical socket with a butter knife and rearrange a few of the items on my dresser. Eeeee-sy does it. That's what I always s-ahhhhhhh."

It was hard enough coming up with excuses, but the real agony came when I was forced to give up rocking.

"Gift it a rest, Romeo," my roommate moaned the first night he heard my bedsprings creak. He thought I was masturbating, and while I wanted to set the record straight, something told me I wouldn't score any points by telling him that I was simply rocking in bed, just like any other eighteen-year-old college student. It was torture to lie there doing nothing. Even with a portable radio and earphones, there was no point listening to music unless I could sway back and forth with my head on a pillow. Rocking is basically dancing in a horizontal position, and it allowed me to practice in private what I detested in public. With my jerking head, rolling eyes, and rapid stabbing gestures, I might have been a sensation if I'd left my bed and put my tics to work on the dance floor. I should have told my roommate that I was an epileptic and left it at that. He might have charged across the room every so often to ram a Popsicle stick down my throat, but so what? I was used to picking splinters out of my tongue. *What*, I wondered, *was an average person expected to do while stretched out in a darkened room?* It felt pointless to lie there motionless and imagine a brighter life. Squinting across the cramped, cinder-block cell, I realized that an entire lifetime of wishful thinking had gotten me no further than this. There would be no cheering crowds or esteemed movie directors shouting into their bullhorns. I might have to take this harsh reality lying down, but while attempting to do so, couldn't I rock back and forth just a little bit?

Having memorized my roommate's course schedule, I took to rushing back to the room between classes, rocking in fitful spurts but never really enjoying it for fear he might return at any moment. Perhaps he might feel ill or decide to cut class at the last minute. I'd hear his key in the door and jump up from my bed, mashing down my wadded hair and grabbing one of the textbooks I kept on my prop table. "I'm just studying for that pottery test," I'd say. "That's all I've been up to, just sitting in this chair reading about the history of jugs." Hard as I tried, it always wound up sounding as if I were guilty of something secretive or perverse. *He* never acted in the least bit embarrassed when caught listening to one of his many heavy-metal albums, a practice far more shameful than anything I have yet to imagine. There was no other solution: I had to think of a way to get rid of this guy.

His biggest weakness appeared to be his girlfriend, whose photograph he had tacked in a place of honor above the stereo. They'd been dating since tenth grade, and while he had gone off to college, she'd stayed behind to attend a two-year nursing school in their hometown. A history of listening to Top 40 radio had left me with a ridiculous and clichéd notion of love. I had never entertained the feeling myself but knew that it meant never having to say you're sorry. It was a many-splendored thing. Love was a rose *and* a hammer. Both blind and all-seeing, it made the world go round.

My roommate thought that he and his girlfriend were strong enough to make it through the month without seeing each other, but I wasn't so sure. "I don't know that I'd trust her around all those doctors," I said. "Love fades when left untended, especially in a hospital environment. Absence might make the heart grow fonder, but love is a two-way street. Think about it."

When my roommate went out of town, I would spend the entire weekend rocking in bed and fantasizing about his tragic car accident. I envisioned him wrapped tight as a mummy, his arms and legs suspended by pulleys. "Time is a great healer," his mother would say, packing the last of his albums into a milk crate. "Two years of bed rest and he'll be as good as new. Once he gets out of the hospital, I figure I'll set him up in the living room. He likes it there."

Sometimes I would allow him to leave in one piece, imagining his joining the army or marrying his girlfriend and moving someplace warm and sunny, like Peru or Ethiopia. The important thing was that he leave this room and never come back. I'd get rid of him and then move on to the next person, and the one after that, until it was just me, rocking and jerking in private.

Two months into the semester, my roommate broke up with his girlfriend. "And I'm going to spend every day and night sitting right here in this room until I figure out where I went wrong." He dabbed his moist eyes with the sleeve of his flannel shirt. "You and me, little buddy. It's just you and me and Jethro Tull from here on out. Say, what's with your head? The old tumor acting up again?"

"College is the best thing that can ever happen to you," my father used to say, and he was right, for it was there that I discovered drugs, drinking, and smoking. I'm unsure of the scientific aspects, but for some reason, my nervous habits faded about the same time I took up with cigarettes. Maybe it was coincidental or perhaps the tics retreated in the face of an adversary that, despite its health risks, is much more socially acceptable than crying out in tiny voices. Were I not smoking, I'd probably be on some sort of medication that would cost the same amount of money but deny me the accoutrements: the lighters I can thoughtlessly open and close, the ashtrays that provide me with a legitimate reason to leave my chair, and the cigarettes that calm me down while giving me something to do with my hands and mouth. It's as if I had been born to smoke, and until I realized it, my limbs were left to search for some alternative. Everything's fine as long as I know there's a cigarette in my immediate future. The people who ask me not to smoke in their cars have no idea what they're in for.

"Remember when you used to roll your eyes?" my sisters ask. "Remember the time you shook your head so hard, your glasses fell into the barbecue pit?"

At their mention I sometimes attempt to revisit my former tics and habits. Returning to my apartment late at night, I'll dare myself to press my nose against the doorknob or roll my eyes to achieve that once-satisfying ache. Maybe I'll start counting the napkins sandwiched in their plastic holder, but the exercise lacks its old urgency and I soon lose interest. I would no sooner rock in bed than play "Up, Up, and Away" sixty times straight on my record player. I could easily listen to something else an equal number of times while seated in a rocking chair, but the earlier, bedridden method fails to comfort me, as I've forgotten the code, the twitching trick needed to decipher the lyrics to that particular song. I remember only that at one time the story involved the citizens of Raleigh, North Carolina, being herded into a test balloon of my own design and making. It was rigged to explode once it reached the city limits, but the passengers were unaware of that fact. The sun shone on their faces as they lifted their heads toward the bright blue sky, giddy with excitement.

"Beautiful balloon!" they all said, gripping the handrails and climbing the staircase to their fiery destiny. "Wouldn't you like to ride?"

"Sorry, folks," I'd say, pressing my nose against the surface of my ticket booth. "But I've got other duties."

1997

SUSAN SHAPIRO

The Wrong Shapiro at the Right Time

"This is Michael Anderson from the *New York Times Book Review*. Are you available for a rush assignment over the weekend?" he asked.

I'd written "In Short" critiques for other *Book Review* editors but didn't recognize his name. Like the *New Yorker*, there was no masthead, as if they belonged to a secret society only insiders understood. Editors there seemed to pass around freelancers the way high school football players passed around easy cheerleaders. But in the summer of 1989, his cold call thrilled me; it meant that somebody must have told him I was good!

"I'd be honored," I said, forgetting the Hamptons weekend I'd planned. For a young Manhattanite with literary aspirations, the *Book Review* was God.

"Good. We're really under the gun. This Little, Brown hardcover showed up without warning. The pub date's in two weeks."

He was telling me more than other editors usually did. Was saying it was a "Little, Brown hardcover" a code? Did sending me a book coming out in two weeks mean the publisher submitted it late?

"Have we met before?" I asked.

"No, I just started here in July," he said.

"Really? Welcome!" I said. Good, he wouldn't know I was a *Times* neophyte since he was greener than I was.

"Becky gave me your name," he said.

Rebecca Sinkler, the editor in chief. New to book reviewing and the *Times*, I was thrilled "Becky" knew my name. How cool was that! Mr. Anderson assigned me a review of Harrison E. Salisbury's new book, *Tiananmen Diary*. Could I get him a thousand words by Monday morning?

"Of course. Thank you, sir," I said, stunned. Salisbury was a Pulitzer Prize winner! They were trusting me with a *Times* icon chronicling an important political tragedy. The massacre of Chinese students was three months before, which explained Little, Brown's rush to publish the first book. But why were they giving me—an expert on Judaism, poetry, and feminism—a long review of a prominent China book?

I'd feared my conservative Midwest doctor father was right about going to law school. But this call seemed an omen from the writing gods. Did Mr. Anderson, a Chicago native, know I was also a Midwesterner? My beloved brother's name was Michael; his name had good karma. It was a good way to meet a new mentor.

I called my parents in Michigan, shrieking: "This new editor at *Book Review* gave me a rush assignment for a major book!"

"That's wonderful, dear," my mother said. "Jack, a new editor just gave your daughter a rush assignment for the *Book Review*."

"Which book are you reviewing?" Dad asked, picking up the line.

"*Tiananmen Square*, by Pulitzer Prize winner Harrison Salisbury!"

"Do you even know where China is?" my father asked.

"Jack! That's not nice to say to your daughter! What the hell's wrong with you?" my mother yelled.

"Why would they give her a book on China?" he grumbled.

I guessed it was jealousy. My father was a history buff who'd practically memorized Salisbury's other works and tried to interest me—to no avail. I admit I'd also been wondering why they gave me a China book. Most Manhattan critics were out of town August weekends. Of the few left in the sweltering city, maybe they'd chosen me because I'd done a terrific job on other nonfiction. Plus, I'd turned around copy fast. (I wasn't the smartest so I figured I'd be the quickest.)

I quickly read the 178 pages of the tacky-looking little book: *Tiananmen Diary* in red lettering and *Thirteen Days in June* in yellow. Although I have strong reading and comprehension skills, I didn't understand Salisbury's day-to-day diary. By coincidence, he'd been in China with a camera crew, making a TV documentary on the 40th anniversary of the People's Republic. He witnessed the slaughter of Tiananmen Square students from his window at the Beijing Hotel. He described the military action, interweaving interviews with local workers, newscasts, and historical analysis. I tried to draw a time line of the events but contradictions abounded. I worried the subject and author were over my head.

Friday at 7 p.m., I rushed to the library to look up Salisbury's other books, which were more lucid. I Xeroxed pages, along with encyclopedia articles on China, and newspaper microfilm accounts of what had happened in June in Tiananmen Square.

Comparing them to Salisbury's book, I was at sea. I had a career-making assignment, yet I was choking. I couldn't call Mr. Anderson until Monday, too late to make my deadline. I phoned my dad, a night owl, like me. I blurted out my problem, expecting "I told you so." But he was pleased to help. I read the confusing passages and asked, "What does this mean?"

"Arteriosclerotic dementia, I'd guess," he said.

"What?"

"How old is Salisbury?"

"About 80," I said. "What are you talking about?"

"The onset of dementia. There's 50 different kinds. Could be Alzheimer's, strokes, alcohol. Does he drink? Don't all journalists drink?"

"Dad, don't diagnose him!" I screamed. "Just tell me what that passage means."

"It doesn't mean anything. It's mishmash. He seems old, sleep-deprived, out of it."

"Really? That's what I thought! But I was afraid I was missing something." I lit a cigarette.

"Trust your own judgment," said my father, lighting his cigarette; I heard him inhale long-distance.

"I can't write that it's a mishmash," I lamented. "I can't trash a famous 80-year-old journalist's book in the newspaper that made him famous."

"Maybe that's why they gave you the book," he said. "They figured you'd be young, malleable, and afraid to kill it."

"Dad, stop insulting me."

"I'm not insulting you."

"Look, it's the biggest assignment I've had, so I can't screw up. He's got the angle right politically, trashing China's corrupt, scared, and geriatric leadership. He's sympathetic to the students. He asked a Chinese supporter of democracy 'What's the news today?' The man replied, 'The news is that 1.1 billion hearts are dead.' "

"Use that quote and make your piece about what happened in Tiananmen Square," my father said. "Like those boring professors who use the *Book Review* as a platform for their own issues. At the end, stick in that the author was in too much of a rush."

Well, when had Dr. Disease become an expert at book reviewing? "Thanks, Daddy," I said.

Taking Dad's advice, I handed in 1,500 words on Monday, apologizing that it came out long. Mr. Anderson quoted Samuel Johnson: "I'm sorry I'm writing you a long letter, I didn't have time to write you a short one." I assumed my piece would be cut to shreds but soon I got an early copy of the *Book Review*, with 1,500 of my words, hardly any edits, and a check for $350, the most I'd made from the *Times* thus far. The clip helped me get assignments from the *Washington Post*, the *Boston Globe*, *People*, *Us Weekly*, and the *Village Voice*.

Sixteen years later, researching my mentor book, I googled the late Harrison E. Salisbury (who'd died in 1993, at 84) and stumbled on press for *Tiananmen Diary*—very negative press. The *New York Review of Books* called it "The Lost Weekend." The worst slam, in the *Nation*, was by journalist Judith Shapiro. She said the book was a mess, riddled with mistakes. I looked up this other Shapiro. Wow, she'd authored *After the Nightmare: Inside China Today*, *Son of the Revolution*, *Mao's War Against Nature*, and *Return to China*. Man, she was the ultimate Asia expert: Why hadn't the *Times* given her Salisbury's book?

Aha! In a flash, I realized they'd meant to. I filled in the blanks of what had happened in 1989, with the first assignment Michael gave me. New at the *Book Review*, he'd obviously mixed up the two female Shapiro critics. When Michael called me, he thought he was speaking to the Shapiro who was a China expert. It wasn't such a good way to meet a mentor after all.

After my 1,500-word Salisbury review ran, Michael kept giving me assignments—but at the piddly 300-word length. I didn't get another 1,000-word review for 10 years—from a different editor.

"When you gave me that first China book, did you confuse me with the China expert Judith Shapiro?" I finally asked him.

"Yes. That assignment was a big mistake," he admitted. "There was a whole interrogation about it at work. Someone had confused the two of you and gave me the wrong name. Becky threw a shit fit."

"Were you mad at me?" I asked.

"No. I actually thought it was nice that the old guy got a good *Times* review for one of his last books," he said.

PAUL SIMMS

A Prayer

Lord?

Please don't let me die in a funny way.

Like being beaten to death with a shoe. Especially not my own shoe. And, if it absolutely has to be my own shoe, I'd rather not be wearing it at the time.

Or like choking on my own fist during a bar bet.

Perhaps I should clarify a little. I do know that I'm going to die someday. (Maybe soon! That's Your call.) And I know there's nothing funny about death—at least from this side. I'm just asking to not die in a way that leads people who don't know me to e-mail one another news items about my death. For instance:

Please don't let me get so fat that paramedics have to come to my house and cut out a wall to remove me but then bang my head against a load-bearing pillar in the process, thus killing me.

Please don't let me die on or near or—perhaps worst of all—

because of a toilet. (This includes a urinal or a baseball-stadium-style urine trough, in addition to a standard commode.)

Please don't let my death in any way involve one of those giant inflatable rats that union prostesters put up outside non-union job sites. Or a blimp of any kind. Until I see some evidence to the contrary, I'm going to have to say that my dying because of just about anything inflatable would be something I'd rather avoid. A hot air balloon, I guess, would be OK, but only if I'm actually in the balloon at the time. At least that would be kind of rugged and out-doorsy. What I'm trying to say is: if someone else's hot air balloon falls out of the sky and smothers me while I'm lying in a hammock reading *Hot Air Balloon Enthusiast* magazine, I'm going to be a litle pissed.

I apologize for that language, Lord, but I'm just trying to be hon-est with You.

A vehicular accident? Fine. Bring it on. I understand that, statis-tically, there's a pretty good chance of that happening anyway. Just please don't let it involve a moped. Or a go-kart.

Also, I'd prefer not to die in a head-on collision with someone who—against all odds—has the same name as me. Or anyone named, for instance, Roger Crash. Or Ed Oncollision. Or Jennifer Safedriver. I could go on, but I think You get the point.

I'm sure You get this one a lot, but: please don't let me die dur-ing sex. Unless the technical cause of my death is a heart attack or a stroke. If I have to die during see, please don't make the cause of death any of the following: extreme dehydration, a previously undi-agnosed allergy to fruit-scented or "massage" oils, dermatological complications arising from severe rug burn, or anything involving the use or misuse of any object best described as "foreign."

Please don't let me die in a way that allows the *Post* to run a small item about my death on page 12 or 13 or so under the headline DUDE

WHERE'S MY CORPSE? Or DUMB AND DEADER. Or DEAD AND DEADER. Or J.LO'S LASTEST NUPTIALS POSTPONED DUE TO LETHAL TENT-RAISING MISHAP.

Please don't let me cut my own head off while trying to revive the lost scouting pastime of mumblety-peg.

I would have to consider any fatality involving a prolapsed anus, of course, absolutely beyond the pale. I mean, come on, Lord.

Also—and I'm not trying to split hairs with You, Lord—when I ask You to not let me die in a funny way, I also mean please don't let me die in a noteworthily ironic way. Meaning: whether my death is "ha-ha" funny or the other kind of funny, neither of those is what I'm in the market for. For instance, please don't let me go on a Sleepwalkers Anonymous Outward Bound–type retreat and sleepwalk into a canyon or gorge in the middle of the night.

And if You deem it necessary (or just amusing) to take my mind before You take my body, let's try to keep the progressive dementia noble and epically sad rather than comical. For example: please let the last face I recognize be the photograph of a long-lost high-school girlfriend and not one of the plucky toddlers from the animated show *Rugrats*. In my final moments, let me awaken—apparently lucid—in the pre-dawn hours calling out for a kiss on the forehead from a dead great-aunt rather than from the mustachioed black bartender on *The Love Boat*.

Or from the actor who played him, for that matter.

Even if I don't die in a funny way, I'd still rather not die on the same day as some other person who does die in a funny way. Because I don't want any version of the following conversation to occur between my friends:

FRIEND ONE: Did you read his obituary?

FRIEND TWO: Yeah. Nice piece.

FRIEND ONE: Very nice.

FRIEND TWO: He would have liked it.

FRIEND ONE: That he would have. That he would have.

(*Awkward silence*)

FRIEND TWO: Did you see that other obituary about the banana wholesaler who actually slipped on the—

FRIEND ONE: Yeah. You couldn't make that up!

Well, that's about it, Lord.

Actually—as long as I've got You, let me just mention a few final ways for me to die that may or may not seem funny to You, depending on Your sense of humor.

I would rather be burned beyond all recognition than burned almost beyond all recognition, especially if the pictures are going to end up on the Internet.

If some kind of rare organism eats away at my body from the inside, please let it be microscopic. Or just slightly larger than microscopic. Let's put it this way: if it's big enough to have a face, that would be too big.

Thank You for Your time, Lord.

2007

MARK SINGER

✳ ✳ ✳

My Married Life: The Whole Truth Thus Far

It is true. I have been married quite a few times. There have been more marriages than, at certain moments, I can remember. Concentrating, however, I recall them all. Damn near half a million. The entire fleet heaves into view on the warm ocean of my memory. I am proud of all my marriages. I have gulped so often from the deep cup of life's pleasures. And each time I have come away stumbling drunk. Women, I have discovered, find my marrying moods irresistible. Frankly, I think I am a pretty good catch.

My first wife was Eos, goddess of the dawn. I have never been certain how long our union lasted. This was before the Greeks could agree upon the number of days in a month. Keeping track of time was difficult. Sustaining a marriage was difficult, too. Her career got in the way. Eos, her hair the red of turning maples, was a child of the sun and the wind and the pale pink velvet morn. I, on the other hand, am basically a night person. Often, I felt like a Tuesday or a

Thursday evening out on the town. "Come, Eos," I would say. "Let us go eat Chinese and riot in Athens till the wee hours." But she would protest: Tomorrow was a workday. How could I expect her to carouse all night? How, on little or no sleep, could she possibly usher the pristine dawn across the metallic firmament? She had a point. Inevitably, other conflicts arose between us. Fortunately, there were no children. We parted amicably and then, as can happen, lost track of each other.

I remarried almost immediately. Repeatedly, in fact, I have remarried almost immediately. Some of my wives wore black mesh stockings. Several wore heavy eye makeup. Some drank. One carried a small firearm. Two studied tae kwon do, the Korean art of self-defense. Two were Korean but defenseless. A dozen—maybe fifteen at tops—lacked conspicuous physical beauty. Their hidden beauties, however, made them ravishing. I have always taken marriage seriously and have concentrated upon the one I am involved in at the moment. I have always discovered the hidden beauties.

I married no men—only women. Men, I believe, do not make decent wives. Men make good fishing buddies. Once, I was offered a lot of money to marry Judge Crater, in the hope that this would bring him back into public view. Of course, I declined. The people who were offering this money had about them an air of being up to no good.

In addition to my own marriage ceremonies, I have attended many others. I was with Tommy Manville all thirteen times he took the leap. I witnessed three of Barbara Hutton's nuptials. Mickey Rooney and I go back a long way together. To my regret, I had to miss Norman Mailer's fifth wedding, the one that took place recently and was followed by a quick divorce so that he could marry someone else. I would have been there but I was getting married that day.

I believe that all of my wives were faithful. I believe that all of my wives were faithful despite the rumors I heard about Susan and Doreen, of Provo. This was during the six-year period when I was busy marrying all of the women in Utah. The rumors about Susan and Doreen—first Susan and then, somewhat later, Doreen—made no sense to me. I made it a policy to be totally up-front with my wives. I hid nothing from them. A marriage to me was always an eyes-open proposition. It must have been a different Susan and a different Doreen, or perhaps Susan and Doreen when they had already become ex-wives.

I was married to many movie stars. Although I loved them all, I know that in a way some of these marriages were tainted by cynicism. Some of these actresses had careers that had stalled. They needed a little ink in the columns. I married them for that reason. But that was not the reason I married Ingrid Bergman. I married her for pure, unalloyed love. This was while she was married to Roberto Rossellini, the Italian filmmaker. So great was my love of Ingrid Bergman that I was willing to become Rossellini for two years. I was willing to interrupt my own important work to direct the films *Open City* and *Paisan*. I perfected my Italian. I spoke English with a convincing inflection. Ingrid Bergman was shocked when, at last, I confessed to her that I was not, technically speaking, Rossellini. He seemed not to notice.

Briefly, I married a woman who now stars in a popular television comedy series. I will call her Angela.

We met on a blind date. In fact, now that I think of it, it's a funny coincidence; Pam Dawber, who was then a total nobody but later went on to star in *Mork & Mindy*, fixed us up. Angela and I met for lunch, on a day in early spring, asparagus time. Between the cold cucumber soup and the crabmeat salad, we became engaged. Our waiter, having overheard our pledges of troth, announced that he was a minister. Angela ordered a second carafe of the house white. Before coffee, the waiter performed the ceremony in a small alcove between the coat-check room and the pay phone. We tipped him extravagantly. As we were leaving, the coat-check lady casually mentioned that the waiter had not actually been ordained. Outside, Angela said that she was feeling vexed. I said never mind, if we consider ourselves married, we're married. But we quarreled. The quarrel made us realize that perhaps our decision to marry had been made in haste. Again, of course, there were no children. I still get Christmas cards from Angela and often watch her on TV.

That was by no means my shortest marriage. One day I married an entire subway carful of gorgeous ladies. There were forty-three of them. It was an uptown B train during rush hour. Never before had I been on a subway car with that many women and no other men present. Being recently divorced, I saw no reason not to marry all of them right then and there. I officiated at these ceremonies myself and, afterward, catered the reception and took photographs. There was plenty to drink and plenty to eat—hot chafing dishes filled with sweetbreads in wine sauce, silver trays of tiny lamb chops, roast-beef carving stations at either end of the subway car. We rode together to 168th Street, the end of the line, and then all forty-three of my new wives changed to an uptown A train headed for the George Washington Bridge Terminal, where they boarded buses for New Jersey. In New Jersey, they had homes with backyards, children, and husbands. I have been told that these forty-three marriages don't count in the final standings. I couldn't disagree more. I loved these women well and wish them well. In my book, they all count.

1981

JAKE SWEARINGEN

✳ ✳ ✳

How Important Moments in My Life Would Have Been Different If I Was Shot Twice in the Stomach at Close Range

BIRTH

The doctor tells my mother to push while she also tells the nurse to get my father. My mother has been in labor for nearly forty hours. My father rushes into the room, his face a mix of pure terror and pure joy. I come out, nearly dead from blood loss. I appear on both *Oprah* and *Phil Donahue,* being the only person ever shot twice in the stomach while still in the womb.

WALKING FOR THE FIRST TIME

I stand up on shaky, little-boy legs, and then promptly fall over, a pool of my own blood spreading out from underneath me.

FIRST DAY OF SCHOOL

I walk in, nervous and scared and wishing I could go back home, and then stumble backward, clutching my stomach. "Aw, Christ! Aw, shit!" I say as I knock over a chair, looking down as dark blood seeps from between my fingers.

I make three new friends that day.

FIRST KISS

She is the girl in my business tech class from school, and we have met in the recreation room of my church. She is wearing some sort of fruity perfume, and her hair is tied back. I lean forward, and my breath is coming in shaky little gasps. Our lips touch, and then I cough twice, blood slowly leaking out of my mouth. I ask her to call an ambulance, goddamnit, I've been fucking shot. I sob quietly that I don't want to die here.

GRADUATION

I walk across the stage and shake the principal's hand while he hands me my diploma. I collapse a few steps after, and the entire auditorium where graduation is being held goes deadly quiet. All you can hear is my girlish whimpering in pain and begging for someone to just put me out of my misery, for the love of Christ.

FIRST DAY OF COLLEGE

I step into my dorm and greet my new roommate. We talk for a while, learning about each other. I then lurch backward against the wall, a look of shock and pain on my face. My legs buckle beneath me, and I slump to the ground, my eyes staring off into nothing, but suddenly I don't look to be in pain. I look peaceful and almost happy, and I whisper, right before I go, "It's not the end, is it?"

GETTING SHOT IN THE STOMACH AT CLOSE RANGE

This is actually pretty much the same.

CALVIN TRILLIN

✳   ✳   ✳

Curtain Time

"It's absolutely unconscionable," the young man said loudly, shaking a banana in front of the fruit peddler's face. "It's simply not to be believed. It's unbelievable."

Murray Tepper looked up from his newspaper to see what was happening. Tepper was sitting behind the wheel of a dark blue Chevrolet Malibu that was parked on the uptown side of Forty-third Street, between Fifth and Sixth. Across the street, an argument was going on between an intense young man in a suit and the peddler who set up a stand on Forty-third Street every day to sell apples and bananas and peaches to office workers. Tepper had seen them go at it before. The young man was complaining about the price that the peddler charged for a single banana. The peddler was defending himself in an accent that Tepper couldn't place even by continent. There had been a time when the accents of New York fruit peddlers were dependably Italian—Tepper had for years thought of "banana" as a more or less Italian word, in the way that some New Yorkers thought of "aggravation" as a more or less Yiddish word—but that time had long passed. As the young man in the suit practically pulsated with outrage, the peddler repeated a single phrase over and over again in his mysterious accent. Finally, Tepper was able to figure out what the peddler kept saying: "free-market economy, free-market economy, free-market economy. . . ."

It was six-thirty on a Tuesday evening in May, at the tag end of the second millennium. The air was mild. For ten days, there had been clear skies and spring temperatures, disappointing those New Yorkers who liked to complain every May that the weather had changed from bitterly cold winter to brutally hot summer as if God—a stern and vengeful God—had flipped a switch. Tepper was comfortable in the suit he'd worn to work that day—a garment that was in the category he sometimes referred to as "office suits," slightly worn and maybe a bit shiny at the elbows. He thought of his office suits as the equivalents of the suits a high-school teacher nearing retirement age might wear to school. In fact, Tepper thought of himself as looking a bit like a high-school teacher nearing retirement age—a medium-sized man with thin hair going gray and a face that didn't seem designed to hold an expression long.

There was plenty of light left on Forty-third Street. Tepper was reading the *New York Post*, which he still considered an evening paper, even though it had been coming out in the morning for years. The proprietors of the *Post* could publish it any time of day they wanted to; Tepper read it in the evening. People who had finished up late at the office were walking briskly toward the subway stops or Grand Central. A few of them, before going their separate ways, stopped to chat with colleagues at building entrances. The chats tended to be brief, perhaps because the entrances still smelled something like the bottom of an ashtray from a full day of smokers having ducked out of their smoke-free offices to pace up and down in front of the building, taking long, purposeful drags and exchanging nods now and then, like lifers in the exercise yard greeting people to whom they had long ago said everything they had to say.

Aside from an occasional argument over the price of fruit, Forty-third Street didn't provide much entertainment for Tepper. Forty-seventh Street between Fifth and Sixth, just a few blocks uptown, would undoubtedly be livelier. Forty-seventh Street was the diamond district, after all, and it had always fielded an interesting variety of pedestrians—Hasidic Jews taking a break from their diamond-cutting jobs, young couples on their way to buy an engagement ring from a dealer who had apparently given a very good deal to some acquaintance's brother-in-law's uncle, innocuous-looking security people on the alert for thieves who knew that any number of people walked up and down Forty-seventh Street with thousands of dollars' worth of diamonds jangling in their pockets. Tepper had, in fact, bought his wife's engagement ring on Forty-seventh Street many years before, from a man whose device for building trust was to confide in the customer about the perfidy of other dealers.

"See that one over there," Tepper's dealer had said, indicating with a quick jerk of his eyebrows a small man in the booth across the way. "Perlmutter. I saw him sell a piece of cut glass to a young couple by implying, without actually saying so in so many words, that it was a four-carat diamond that may have been—*may* have been, he wanted to emphasize; he didn't claim to have proof of this—worn by Marie of Rumania. The boy he was talking to was a yokel, a farmer. You could practically see the hay coming out of his ears. He looked like he came from Indiana or Idaho or one of them. Perlmutter had to spell 'Rumania' for him. Maybe 'Marie,' too; I don't remember.

The yokel bought the ring. A *shonda* was what that was, young man. A scandal. A disgrace to the trade and to those of us trying to make an honest living. Now, let me show you a small but elegant little stone that, to be quite frank with you . . ."

Forty-seventh Street would be livelier, Tepper thought, although the dealer who'd pointed out the wily Perlmutter was undoubtedly long gone and these days a lot of young couples probably bought their engagement rings over the Internet.

Behind Tepper, a car was coming slowly down Forty-third Street. As it passed the imposing structure occupied by the Century Club, it slowed even more, and, a few yards farther, came to a stop just behind Tepper's Chevrolet. Taking his eyes away from the paper for only an instant, Tepper shot a quick glance toward his side mirror. He could see a Mercury with New Jersey license plates—probably theatergoers from the suburbs who knew that these streets in the forties were legal for long-term metered parking after six. The New Jersey people would be hoping to find a spot, grab a bite in a sushi bar or a deli, and then walk to the theater. Good planners, people from New Jersey, Tepper thought, except for the plan they must have hatched at some point to move to New Jersey. (The possibility that anybody started out in New Jersey—that any number of people had actually been born there—was not a possibility Tepper had ever dwelled on.) He pretended to concentrate on his newspaper, although he was, in fact, still thinking of the state of New Jersey, which he envisioned as a series of vast shopping-mall parking lots, where any fool could find a spot. The Mercury's driver tapped his horn a couple of times, and then, getting no response, moved even with Tepper's Chevy. The woman who was sitting on the passenger side stuck her head out of the window and said, "Going out?"

Tepper said nothing.

"Are you going out?" the woman asked again.

Tepper did not look up, but with his right hand he reached over toward the window and wagged his index finger back and forth, in the gesture some Southern Europeans have perfected as a way of dealing with solicitations from shoeshine boys or beggars. Tepper had been able to wag his finger in the negative with some authority since 1954, when, as a young draftee who regularly reminded himself to be grateful that at least the shooting had stopped, he spent thirteen miserable months as a clerk-typist in a motor pool in Pusan and had to ward off prostitutes and beggars every time he left the base. An acquaintance had once expressed envy for the gesture as something that seemed quite cosmopolitan, but Tepper would have traded it in an instant for the ability to do the legendary New York taxi-hailing whistle that was accomplished by jamming a finger in each corner of the mouth.

He had never been able to master that whistle, despite years of patient coaching by a doorman named Hector, on West Eighty-third. Tepper had encountered Hector while looking for overnight parking spots in his own neighborhood, in the days before his wife managed to persuade him to take space for his car by the month in a multilevel garage a few blocks from their apartment. He hadn't seen anybody use the fingers-in-the-mouth whistle on the street for a long time. He hadn't tried it for a long time himself. Was it something that might simply come to him, after all these years? Now that he wasn't trying it several evenings a week under the pressure of Hector's watchful eye, might it just appear, the way a smooth golf swing sometimes comes inexplicably to duffers once the tension of their expensive lessons has ended? He was about to jam a couple of fingers in the corners of his mouth to see if the gift might have arrived unannounced when he realized that the Mercury was still idling next to him, making it necessary to remain focused on the newspaper.

"He's not going out," the woman shouted to the man at the wheel, loudly enough for Tepper to hear.

"He's not going out?" the driver shouted back, sounding incredulous. "What do you mean he's not going out?"

"He probably parks there just before six and sits there so he can tell people he's not going out," the woman shouted.

The driver gunned the motor in irritation, and the Mercury from New Jersey pulled away. Just past the entrance to the Princeton Club, it briefly stopped again, the occupants apparently having mistaken a no-parking zone in front of the post office for a legal spot. Then the driver slowly made his way toward Sixth Avenue, speeding up suddenly when a spot came open on the left and screeching to a halt a moment later as a sport-utility vehicle two cars in front of him positioned itself to go into the spot. The woman got out of the Mercury and shouted back toward Tepper. "It's your fault!" she said. "That should have been our spot! It's your fault. Making people waste time talking to you! You ought to be ashamed of yourself."

Tepper, pretending not to hear her, went back to his newspaper. He was reading a story about an office betting pool that had been held every week in a commodities-trading firm for as long as anyone in the firm could remember. A committee of the firm's partners met regularly to decide on each week's pool topic, always based on current events. The office pool had been a subject of press interest before. During the Vietnam War, some people objected to the pool's being based for several weeks in a row on casualty figures. One of the firm's partners responded by saying, "People who don't want to play hardball should get out of the game," but the casualty-figure pools were quietly dropped in favor of pools based on how many tons of explosives would be dropped on North Vietnam that week.

The commodity firm's pool was back in the news because it had been based that week on how many people would be cited for hailing a taxicab incorrectly. The mayor, Frank Ducavelli, as part of his never-ending campaign to make the city more orderly, had declared a crackdown on people who stepped out in the street to hail a taxi rather than remaining on the curb, as required by an ordinance that nobody but the mayor and his city attorney had ever heard of. Tabloid headlines didn't have the space for the mayor's entire last name. It was known that when Frank Ducavelli first became a force in the city he had hoped that headline writers might refer to him as the Duke, suggesting not only nobility but the Dodger great Duke Snider. Given the mayor's interest in order and his draconian response to anyone who disagreed with him, though, the tabloids tended to go with Il Duce. The item Tepper was reading about the weekly pool at the commodities-trading firm was headlined IL DUCE EDICT HOT COMMODITY.

The taxi drivers had objected to the enforcement of the ordinance, of course, and the mayor had called them vermin. The senior staff attorney of the New York Civil Liberties Union, Jeremy Thornton, had said that Ducavelli's attempt to enforce the ordinance was "another of the spitballs that our mayor regularly flings at the Constitution of the United States." The mayor had replied that Jeremy Thornton had a constitutional right to demonstrate that he was a reckless and irresponsible fool but that he should probably be disbarred anyway, as a public service. When a city councilman, Norm Plotkin, usually a supporter of City Hall, pointed out that someone flagging a cab from behind a line of parked cars was unlikely to be seen, he had been dismissed by Mayor Ducavelli as "stupid and imbecilic—someone who obviously has no regard whatsoever for public safety and is totally unconcerned about citizens of this city being struck down and killed in the street like dogs."

Years before, in an article about how jokes get created and

spread around, Tepper had read that commodities traders were at the heart of the joke distribution system. The article had inspired him to test a list of licensed commodities brokers for a client who was trying to sell a book of elephant jokes through the mail, and the list had done fairly well—well enough to justify its use again to sell a book of lightbulb jokes and a tape-cassette course on how to be a hit at parties. Tepper had decided that the actual trading of commodities must not require a lot of time if traders could engage in so many extracurricular activities, like organizing betting pools and distributing jokes.

Tepper could hear the drone of another car moving slowly down the street behind him. He decided to use the backhand flick if the car stopped next to him. He had perfected the backhand flick only that week—a speeded-up version of someone clearing away cobwebs while walking through a dimly lit attic. He used only his left hand. Without looking up from his newspaper, he would flick his fingers in the direction of the inquiring parker. It had taken some time to find precisely the right velocity of flicking—a movement that contained authority but lacked aggression.

The first time he had used the backhand flick—it was on Fifty-seventh Street, between Tenth and Eleventh avenues, around the dinner hour—he had obviously flicked too aggressively. The gesture had brought a fat, red-faced man out of a huge sport-utility vehicle—a vehicle so high off the ground that the fat man, before laboriously lowering himself to the pavement, hovered in the doorway like a parachutist who'd taken a moment to reconsider before deciding that he did indeed want to leap out into thin air. Once on terra firma, the fat man had stood a few inches from Tepper's window, which was closed, and shouted, "Ya jerky bastard, ya!" again and again. Tepper was interested to hear the expression "ya jerky bastard, ya"—he hadn't heard it used since the old days at Ebbets

Field—but he did recognize the need to flick his hand more subtly. Tepper hadn't replied to the fat man, and not simply because there really didn't seem to be any appropriate reply to "ya jerky bastard, ya." Tepper tried to avoid speaking to the people who wanted to park in his spot.

2001

GEORGE W. S. TROW

✳ ✳ ✳

I Embrace the New Candor

Today I have been particularly candid. I have expressed candid thoughts about the Right to Life movement and the new high-energy Golf Classics and the way some books which don't really have *that* much literary merit are sold to paperback houses for huge figures. I have expressed candid thoughts about the fact that the Academy Awards seem to have lost a lot of their meaning (especially with the way they stop the awards during the television commercials), and the fact that Helen Hayes probably isn't the First Lady of the American Theatre anymore (although she probably is still the First Lady of the American Charitable Endorsement), and the fact that my environment at the Keowa Motel, where I live, has a damp and *stagnant* side to it that is evocative of small-time crime and emotional disaffection. Also, I have issued a no-holds-barred report on my last remaining friend, Bob Mern, which will almost certainly cost me his friendship but which will, I am sure, confirm my reputation with the public at large as a man of candor.

Let's go right to the report on Bob. I have always felt that to keep the trust of the public it was necessary for me to be ruthlessly candid in matters touching on my private life and those closest to me. In the past, as the record will show, I have been almost brutal in my statements about my wife, but since our divorce opportunities for frankness in this area have lessened. I continue to have many forthright things to say about her syndicated television program, *Jean Stapleton Duff . . . In Touch* (which has been devoted, this week, to the Right to Life movement, the new high-energy Golf Classics, and the California-style casual mode in outdoor entertaining, which is another subject about which I have had candid thoughts), but that isn't the same thing. When it comes to my personal life my most candid announcements now have to do with my friend Bob Mern. The fact is that I have had to lower Bob's rating twice in the last six months. Bob began the year with a "BAA" rating ("Secure Investment–Minimum Risk"), but after a really bad first quarter during which he was almost always completely drunk, during which he passed out six different times on my bathroom floor, during which he failed to pass his driving test, and during which he was unbelievably boring, I lowered his rating to a "B" ("Some Risk"). And now, after a second quarter during which he tried to pull a really obvious aggressive-dependence number on me (making me bring him his beer on account of his limp, etc., etc., etc.), I have released a statement announcing that I will not rate him at all. Bob will have a little bit of a rough time as a result, and I will have to watch TV by myself, but I have done the honest thing. Because I *have* done and said the honest thing *time* after *time* there has arisen among the public (among the public that reads the rotogravures, among the public that buys cologne, among the public in chronic pain) a deep trust in my word. I live nourished by public confidence. This confidence has reference to me as a public figure, as an artist (I am Jack Duff, and I am the founder of the Jack Duff Dance Experience), and as a human being. Even on those days I spend in bed, even on those days I spend lying on the floor, even on those days when I eschew all muscular movement, I find that I continue to be wrapped in a pervasive health—the physical manifestation of public faith in my candor.

When I speak of "the public," I do not include so-called Important Men. It annoys Important Men that I am straightforward in my speech, because it shows them up. It galls Important Men that I don't promise special treats I can't deliver, for instance. Certain men of influence promise Aerial Tramways. I say *forget* Aerial Tramways. Other men encourage the anticipation of People Movers. I say *forget* People Movers. There will be weeping in the streets (I say), and increased incidence of interregional discourtesy, but *no People Movers*. In fact, the report I'm working on right now says that we are not likely to have reliable high-speed elevators for very much longer. My report says candidly that some of the fabulous new high-speed elevators we are installing are going to be involved in heart-wrenching mishaps, leading to an investigation, leading to new ordinances, leading to new safety-amenity parameters that will make it economically unfeasible for the high-speed-elevator manufacturers to continue in their work. In my report I foresee a generation of painful, inefficient, low-speed elevators manufactured in Asia, and then stairs. No one has to take my word for it. Private-school girls in good buildings, for instance, are free to do as they please. It is my opinion, however, that private-school girls who ignore my warning will find themselves dragging their party frocks up twenty-six floors of fire stairs; it is my opinion that they will arrive late (and tired) at the Junior Gaiety Dances; it is my opinion that no one will agree to attend the after-parties given by private-school girls who ignore my warning. I don't mean to be severe, but those girls ought to watch their step.

It is important, I feel, not to project a negative tone. There must be, always, a *constructive* side to candor. It is this constructive aspect that I seek to promote. I now urge the public to stress what I call the *Achievable Goals*. Achievable Goals—so simple an idea! I believe that through an emphasis on the *achievable* we can break the cycle of failure-fantasy-failure around which our national life has tended to carom, and regain a sense of purpose and control. So many goals *are* achievable that it seems perverse to stress goals whose realization is in doubt. I have some Achievable Goals to suggest. I suggest, for instance, that we set out now to *increase our dependence on imported oil*. This goal can be achieved almost immediately. It would be exhilarating, I think, to achieve, almost immediately, a goal with such important long-term implications.

To move on to the crucial housing field, where we have experienced setback after unpleasant setback, I suggest that we seek to *increase the stock of substandard housing*. I suggest here a Model Cities approach which could seek to dispel the pervasive air of failure engendered by the "real" Model Cities program, in which so many hopes were dashed. If a Model Cities approach were adopted we could draw up an elaborate plan in which we could set out specific figures denoting the amount by which we intended to increase the stock of substandard housing in Year One, in Year Two, etc., etc. Other Achievable Goals programs in the model district might seek to increase the use of drugs, and so on.

In the area of Social Engineering, I suggest that we *increase the amount of violence on television*. I suggest that we set up programs to increase the number of aimless people who loathe their elders, and I suggest that, whatever the cost, we guarantee to *every* Senior American the right to a drab old age. Sometimes (as now), when I think of just how much we could do, I get a little overexcited and I have to sit down for a minute and have a drink and smoke a cigarette.

Now I set for myself only those goals that I know to be completely achievable. I forgo all fantasy. In the coming quarter, I plan
to *increase the number of molds* on the wall of my sleeping space; to
increase the number of apéritifs I have before dinner; and of course I
plan to increase my dependence on imported oil, which, since it is a
broad national goal, I don't really count. The results, I know, will be
very gratifying. Sometimes, however, my candor and consistency are
so overwhelming that I have to sit down and have a drink and smoke
a cigarette. I have such a large amount of public trust now that in
some ways it is almost too much. I don't want to cut myself off from
simple human experience, after all. I don't want to surrender my
warm human qualities. The public doesn't want that, surely. So I
have decided to relent in the case of my friend Bob Mern. I think the
public will understand. I'd like Bob to come over and watch *Starsky &
Hutch* with me. I will raise Bob's rating back to a "B" ("Some Risk").
I will suppress this quarter's report and send him a notice that his
rating is "B." I wonder if he will call me back. If he doesn't, it will
be a triumph, in a way, since it is a goal of mine to receive thirty-two
percent fewer phone calls this quarter than last.

1977

JOHN UPDIKE

A Mild 'Complaint'

I do not know exactly 'what' it 'is,' but 'something' about a close and reverent 'exposure' to the work of Henry James seems to lead his commentators into a virtually 'manic' use of quotation marks. I have recently read—or, rather, 'read' until my eyelids became abraded 'beyond endurance' by incessant typographical 'pricking'—the introduction, by Alma Louise Lowe, to 'the master's' *English Hours*. The edition was 'printed in England,' so the intrusive 'marks' are 'single.' Some 'specimens':

> Because he listened 'with proper credulity' at Haddon Hall,
> he seemed to hear the 'ghostly footfalls' of Dorothy Vernon
> and Lord John Manners 'on the flags of the castle court.' On
> occasions he 'did see' ghosts 'as we see ghosts nowadays.' . . .
>
> The material he plucked while travelling accounts in a
> large measure for the 'air of reality' in James's fiction. . . .

That James, the 'master,' the celebrity so devoted to the
'art' of writing . . .

There were scores of other Americans who felt the 'pull'
of Europe. . . .

He was reminded of 'the early pages of *Oliver Twist*' as he
watched . . .

Now, what is the "point"? Are we to assume that "commonplace
expressions" such as "air of reality," "art," "pull," and "the early pages
of *Oliver Twist*," by their presumed preappearance in the "vast body"
of James's prose, have acquired a "magic," a "special sense," which
their "unadorned" use would allow to "slip through the net"? Or is it
merely that the "good" Miss Lowe wishes to demonstrate her "finger-
tip mastery" of "the material"? Thinking that it might be an "eccen-
tricity" peculiar to her, I turned to John L. Sweeney's introduction to
The Painter's Eye and "in an instant" encountered

His eye and memory were thus filled with images of a
'world' . . . long before discriminations had begun to 'bristle.' . . .
. . . what he expected of them in terms of 'subject' and
why, for example, he 'detested' Winslow Homer's . . .
We have no conclusive evidence that James eventually
'embraced' the Impressionists. We have, however, some
convincing hints that he learned to appreciate them and to
utilize their 'suggestion.'

And Morton Dauwen Zabel's introduction to *In the Cage and Other
Tales* yielded, in American typographical style, a "double harvest":

The "germ" that gave James his story . . . that the "spark" of his
tale was kindled by the "wonderment" of his "speculation" . . .

And it was thus that his "young woman," the "caged
telegraphist" . . .

Without denying that in some "instances" an "atom" of "pertinency"
may be glimpsed in this "practice," "wonderment" is nevertheless
aroused. It is not "enough" to observe that here we have a "conta-
gion" originating in the "punctuational excesses" of James's own
"later style." The "effect" is "different." In James himself, these boot-
less exclamation marks serve as a "kind of spice" to the "lavish feast"
whose most "delicious" ingredient is the host's visible relish in the
"fare" he is "setting forth." Whereas with the scholars "barnacled"
to the underside of his "stately gliding" reputation, the "marks" are
"symptomatic of" a mere "itch," if for which an appropriate cure, or
at least "implement for scratching," can be located, I will, indeed,
"be grateful."

1983

PART II

SOME
GREAT
OLD
STUFF

BRET HARTE

✳ ✳ ✳

Muck-a-Muck: A Modern Indian Novel After Cooper

CHAPTER I

It was toward the close of a bright October day. The last rays of the setting sun were reflected from one of those sylvan lakes peculiar to the Sierras of California. On the right the curling smoke of an Indian village rose between the columns of the lofty pines, while to the left the log cottage of Judge Tompkins, embowered in buckeyes, completed the enchanting picture.

Although the exterior of the cottage was humble and unpretentious, and in keeping with the wildness of the landscape, its interior gave evidence of the cultivation and refinement of its inmates. An aquarium, containing goldfishes, stood on a marble center-table at one end of the apartment, while a magnificent grand piano occupied the other. The door was covered with a yielding tapestry carpet, and the walls were adorned with paintings from the pencils of Van Dyck, Rubens, Tintoretto, Michelangelo, and the productions of the more modern Turner, Kensett, Church, and Bierstadt. Although Judge Tompkins had chosen the frontiers of civilization as his home, it was impossible for him to entirely forgo the habits and tastes of his former life. He was seated in a luxurious armchair, writing at a mahogany escritoire, while his daughter, a lovely young girl of seventeen summers, plied her crotchet-needle on an ottoman beside him. A bright fire of pine logs flickered and flamed on the ample hearth.

Genevra Octavia Tompkins was Judge Tompkins's only child. Her mother had long since died on the Plains. Reared in affluence, no pains had been spared with the daughter's education. She was a graduate of one of the principal seminaries, and spoke French with a perfect Benicia accent. Peerlessly beautiful, she was dressed in a white moiré antique robe trimmed with tulle. That simple rosebud, with which most heroines exclusively decorate their hair, was all she wore in her raven locks.

The Judge was the first to break the silence.

"Genevra, the logs which compose yonder fire seem to have been incautiously chosen. The sibilation produced by the sap, which exudes copiously therefrom, is not conducive to composition."

"True, father, but I thought it would be preferable to the constant crepitation which is apt to attend the combustion of more seasoned ligneous fragments."

The Judge looked admiringly at the intellectual features of the graceful girl, and half forgot the slight annoyances of the green wood in the musical accents of his daughter. He was smoothing her hair tenderly, when the shadow of a tall figure, which suddenly darkened the doorway, caused him to look up.

CHAPTER II

It needed but a glance at the new-comer to detect at once the form and features of the haughty aborigine,—the untaught and untrammeled son of the forest. Over one shoulder a blanket, negligently but gracefully thrown, disclosed a bare and powerful breast, decorated with a quantity of three-cent postage-stamps which he had despoiled from an Overland Mail stage a few weeks previous. A cast-off beaver of Judge Tompkins's, adorned by a simple feather, covered his erect head, from beneath which his straight locks descended. His right hand hung lightly by his side, while his left was engaged in holding on a pair of pantaloons, which the lawless grace and freedom of his lower limbs evidently could not brook.

"Why," said the Indian, in a low sweet tone,—"why does the Pale Face still follow the track of the Red Man? Why does he pursue him, even as O-kee chow, the wild cat, chases Ka-ka, the skunk? Why are the feet of Sorrel-top, the white chief, among the acorns of Muck-a-Muck, the mountain forest? Why," he repeated, quietly but firmly abstracting a silver spoon from the table,—"why do you seek to drive him from the wigwams of his fathers? His brothers are already gone to the happy hunting-grounds. Will the Pale Face seek him there?" And, averting his face from the Judge, he hastily slipped a silver cake-basket beneath his blanket, to conceal his emotion.

"Muck-a-Muck has spoken," said Genevra softly. "Let him now listen. Are the acorns of the mountain sweeter than the esculent and nutritious bean of the Pale Face miner? Does my brother prize the edible qualities of the snail above that of the crisp and oleaginous bacon? Delicious are the grasshoppers that sport on the hillside,— are they better than the dried apples of the Pale Faces? Pleasant is the gurgle of the torrent, Kish-Kish, but is it better than the cluck-cluck of old Bourbon from the old stone bottle?"

"Ugh!" said the Indian,—"ugh! good. The White Rabbit is wise. Her words fall as the snow on Tootoonolo, and the rocky heart of Muck-a-Muck is hidden. What says my brother the Gray Gopher of Dutch Flat?"

"She has spoken, Muck-a-Muck," said the Judge, gazing fondly on his daughter. "It is well. Our treaty is concluded. No, thank you,—you need not dance the Dance of Snow-shoes, or the Moccasin Dance, the Dance of Green Corn, or the Treaty Dance. I would be alone. A strange sadness overpowers me."

"I go," said the Indian. "Tell your great chief in Washington, the Sachem Andy, that the Red Man is retiring before the footsteps of the adventurous pioneer. Inform him, if you please, that westward the star of empire takes its way, that the chiefs of the Pi-Ute nation are for Reconstruction to a man, and that Klamath will poll a heavy Republican vote in the fall."

And folding his blanket more tightly around him, Muck-a-Muck withdrew.

CHAPTER III

Genevra Tompkins stood at the door of the log-cabin, looking after the retreating Overland Mail stage which conveyed her father to Virginia City. "He may never return again," sighed the young girl, as she glanced at the frightfully rolling vehicle and wildly careering horses,—"at least, with unbroken bones. Should he meet with an accident! I mind me now a fearful legend, familiar to my childhood. Can it be that the drivers on this line are privately instructed to dispatch all passengers maimed by accident, to prevent tedious litigation? No, no. But why this weight upon my heart?"

She seated herself at the piano and lightly passed her hand over the keys. Then, in a clear mezzo-soprano voice, she sang the first verse of one of the most popular Irish ballads:—

> O Arrah ma dheelish, the distant dudheen
> Lies soft in the moonlight, ma bouchal vourneen:
> The springing gossoons on the heather are still,
> And the caubeens and colleens are heard on the hill.

But as the ravishing notes of her sweet voice died upon the air, her hands sank listlessly to her side. Music could not chase away the mysterious shadow from her heart. Again she rose. Putting on a white crape bonnet, and carefully drawing a pair of lemon-colored gloves over her taper fingers, she seized her parasol and plunged into the depths of the pine forest.

CHAPTER IV

Genevra had not proceeded many miles before a weariness seized upon her fragile limbs, and she would fain seat herself upon the trunk of a prostrate pine, which she previously dusted with her handkerchief. The sun was just sinking below the horizon, and the scene was one of gorgeous and sylvan beauty. "How beautiful is nature!" murmured the innocent girl, as, reclining gracefully against the root of the tree, she gathered up her skirts and tied a handkerchief around her throat. But a low growl interrupted her meditation. Starting to her feet, her eyes met a sight which froze her blood with terror.

The only outlet to the forest was the narrow path, barely wide enough for a single person, hemmed in by trees and rocks, which she had just traversed. Down this path, in Indian file, came a monstrous grizzly, closely followed by a Californian lion, a wild cat, and a buffalo, the rear being brought up by a wild Spanish bull. The mouths of the three first animals were distended with frightful significance, the horns of the last were lowered as ominously. As Genevra was preparing to faint, she heard a low voice behind her.

"Eternally dog-gone my skin ef this ain't the puttiest chance yet!"

At the same moment, a long, shining barrel dropped lightly from behind her, and rested over her shoulder.

Genevra shuddered.

"Dern ye—don't move!"

Genevra became motionless.

The crack of a rifle rang through the woods. Three frightful yells were heard, and two sullen roars. Five animals bounded into the air and five lifeless bodies lay upon the plain. The well-aimed bullet had done its work. Entering the open throat of the grizzly it had traversed his body only to enter the throat of the California lion, and in like manner the catamount, until it passed through into the respective foreheads of the bull and the buffalo, and finally fell flattened from the rocky hillside.

Genevra turned quickly. "My preserver!" she shrieked, and fell into the arms of Natty Bumpo, the celebrated Pike Ranger of Donner Lake.

CHAPTER V

The moon rose cheerfully above Donner Lake. On its placid bosom a dug-out canoe glided rapidly, containing Natty Bumpo and Genevra Tompkins.

Both were silent. The same thought possessed each, and perhaps there was sweet companionship even in the unbroken quiet. Genevra bit the handle of her parasol, and blushed. Natty Bumpo took a fresh chew of tobacco. At length Genevra said, as if in half-spoken reverie:—

"The soft shining of the moon and the peaceful ripple of the waves seem to say to us various things of an instructive and moral tendency."

"You may bet yer pile on that, miss," said her companion gravely. "It's all the preachin' and psalm-singin' I've heern since I was a boy."

"Noble being!" said Miss Tompkins to herself, glancing at the stately Pike as he bent over his paddle to conceal his emotion. "Reared in this wild seclusion, yet he has become penetrated with visible consciousness of a Great First Cause." Then, collecting herself, she said aloud: "Methinks 'twere pleasant to glide ever thus down the stream of life, hand in hand with the one being whom the soul claims as its affinity. But what am I saying?"—and the delicate-minded girl hid her face in her hands.

A long silence ensued, which was at length broken by her companion.

"Ef you mean you're on the marry," he said thoughtfully, "I ain't in no wise partikler."

"My husband!" faltered the blushing girl; and she fell into his arms.

In ten minutes more the loving couple had landed at Judge Tompkins's.

CHAPTER VI

A year has passed away. Natty Bumpo was returning from Gold Hill, where he had been to purchase provisions. On his way to Donner Lake rumors of an Indian uprising met his ears. "Dern their pesky skins, ef they dare to touch my Jenny," he muttered between his clenched teeth.

It was dark when he reached the borders of the lake. Around a glittering fire he dimly discerned dusky figures dancing. They were in war paint. Conspicuous among them was the renowned Muck-a-Muck. But why did the fingers of Natty Bumpo tighten convulsively around his rifle?

The chief held in his hand long tufts of raven hair. The heart of the pioneer sickened as he recognized the clustering curls of Genevra. In a moment his rifle was at his shoulder, and with a sharp "ping" Muck-a-Muck leaped into the air a corpse. To knock out the brains of the remaining savages, tear the tresses from the stiffening hand of Muck-a-Muck, and dash rapidly forward to the cottage of Judge Tompkins, was the work of a moment.

He burst open the door. Why did he stand transfixed with open mouth and distended eyeballs? Was the sight too horrible to be borne? On the contrary, before him, in her peerless beauty, stood Genevra Tompkins, leaning on her father's arm.

"Ye'r not scalped, then!" gasped her lover.

"No. I have no hesitation in saying that I am not; but why this abruptness?" responded Genevra.

Bumpo could not speak, but frantically produced the silken tresses. Genevra turned her face aside.

"Why, that's her waterfall!" said the Judge.

Bumpo sank fainting to the door.

The famous Pike chieftain never recovered from the deceit, and refused to marry Genevra, who died, twenty years afterward, of a broken heart. Judge Tompkins lost his fortune in Wild Cat. The stage passes twice a week the deserted cottage at Donner Lake. Thus was the death of Muck-a-Muck avenged.

1867

MARK TWAIN

✳ ✳ ✳

1601

[*Mem.—The following is supposed to be an extract from the diary of the Pepys of that day, the same being Queen Elizabeth's cup-bearer. He is supposed to be of ancient and noble lineage; that he despises these literary canaille; that his soul consumes with wrath, to see the queen stooping to talk with such; and that the old man feels that his nobility is defiled by contact with Shakespeare, etc., and yet he has got to stay there till her Majesty chooses to dismiss him.*]

Yesternight toke her maiste ye queene a fantasie such as she sometimes hath, and had to her closet certain that doe write playes, bokes, and such like, these being my lord Bacon, his worship Sir Walter Ralegh, Mr. Ben Jonson, and ye child Francis Beaumonte, which being but sixteen, hath yet turned his hand to ye doing of ye Lattin masters into our Englishe tong, with grete discretion and much applaus. Also came with these ye famous Shaxpur. A righte straunge mixing truly of mighty blode with mean, ye more in especial since ye queenes grace was present, as likewise these following, to wit: Ye Duchess of Bilgewater, twenty-two yeres of age; ye Countesse of Granby, twenty-six; her doter, ye Lady Helen, fifteen; as also these two maides of honor, to-wit, ye Lady Margery Boothy, sixty-five, and ye Lady Alice Dilberry, turned seventy, she being two yeres ye queenes graces elder.

I being her maites cup-bearer, had no choice but to remaine and beholde rank forgot, and ye high holde converse wh ye low as uppon equal termes, a grete scandal did ye world heare thereof.

In ye heat of ye talk it befel yt one did breake wind, yielding an exceding mightie and distresfull stink, whereat all did laugh full sore, and then—

YE QUEENE.—Verily in mine eight and sixty yeres have I not heard the fellow to this fart. Meseemeth, by ye grete sound and clamour of it, it was male; yet ye belly it did lurk behinde shoulde now fall lean and flat against ye spine of him yt hath bene delivered of so stately and so wastea bulk, where as ye guts of them yt doe quiff-splitters bear, stand comely still and rounde. Prithee let ye author confess ye offspring. Will my Lady Alice testify?

LADY ALICE.—Good your grace, an' I had room for such a thun-dergust within mine ancient bowels, 'tis not in reason I coulde discharge ye same and live to thank God for yt He did choose handmaid so humble whereby to shew his power. Nay, 'tis not I yt have broughte forth this rich o'ermastering fog, this fragrant gloom, so pray you seeke ye further.

YE QUEENE.—Mayhap ye Lady Margery hath done ye companie this favor?

LADY MARGERY.—So please you madam, my limbs are feeble wh ye weighte and drouth of five and sixty winters, and it behoveth yt I be tender unto them. In ye good providence of God, an' I had

contained this wonder, forsoothe wolde I have gi'en 'ye whole evening of my sinking life to ye dribbling of it forth, with trembling
and uneasy soul, not launched it sudden in its matchless might,
taking mine own life with violence, rending my weak frame like
rotten rags. It was not I, your maisty.

YE QUEENE.—O' God's name, who hath favored us? Hath it come to
pass yta fart shall fart itself? Not such a one as this, I trow. Young
Master Beaumont—but no; 'twould have wafted him to heaven
like down of goose's boddy. 'Twas not ye little Lady Helen—nay,
ne'er blush, my child; thoul't tickle thy tender maidenhedde with
many a mousie-squeak before thou learnest to blow a harricane
like this. Wasn't you, my learned and ingenious Jonson?

JONSON.—So fell a blast hath ne'er mine ears saluted, nor yet a
stench so all-pervading and immortal. 'Twas not a novice did it,
good your maisty, but one of veteran experience—else hadde he
failed of confidence. In sooth it was not I.

YE QUEENE.—My lord Bacon?

LORD BACON.—Not from my leane entrailes hath this prodigy burst
forth, so please your grace. Naught doth so befit ye grete as grete
performance; and haply shall ye finde yt 'tis not from mediocrity
this miracle hath issued.

[*Tho' ye subjoct be but a fart, yet will this tedious sink of learning pon-
drously phillosophize. Meantime did the foul and deadly stink pervade
all places to that degree, yt never smelt I ye like, yet dare I not to leave
ye presence, albeit I was like to suffocate.*]

YE QUEENE.—What saith ye worshipful Master Shaxpur?

SHAXPUR.—In the great hand of God I stand and so proclaim mine
innocence. Though ye sinless hosts of heaven had foretold ye
coming of this most desolating breath, proclaiming it a work of
uninspired man, its quaking thunders, its firmament-clogging
rottenness his own achievement in due course of nature, yet had

not I believed it; but had said the pit itself hath furnished forth the stink, and heaven's artillery hath shook the globe in admiration of it.

[*Then was there a silence, and each did turn him toward the worshipful Sr Walter Ralegh, that browned, embattled, bloody swashbuckler, who rising up did smile, and simpering say,*]

Sr W.—Most gracious maisty, 'twas I that did it, but indeed it was so poor and frail a note, compared with such as I am wont to furnish, yt in sooth I was ashamed to call the weakling mine in so august a presence. It was nothing—less than nothing, madam—I did it but to clear my nether throat; but had I come prepared, then had I delivered something worthy. Bear with me, please your grace, till I can make amends.

[*Then delivered he himself of such a godless and rock-shivering blast that all were fain to stop their ears, and following it did come so dense and foul a stink that that which went before did seem a poor and trifling thing beside it. Then saith he, feigning that he blushed and was confused, I perceive that I am weak to-day, and cannot justice do unto my powers; and sat him down as who should say, There, it is not much yet he that hath an arse to spare, let him fellow that, an' he think he can. By God, an' I were ye queene, I would e'en tip this swaggering braggart out o' the court, and let him air his grandeurs and break his intolerable wind before ye deaf and such as suffocation pleaseth.*]

Then fell they to talk about ye manners and customs of many peoples, and Master Shaxpur spake of ye boke of ye sieur Michael de Montaine, wherein was mention of ye custom of widows of Perigord to wear uppon ye headdress, in sign of widowhood, a jewel in ye similitude of a man's member wilted and limber, whereat ye queene did laugh and say widows in England doe wear prickes too, but betwixt the thighs, and not wilted neither, till coition hath done that office for them. Master Shaxpur did likewise observe how yt ye sieur de Montaine hath also spoken of a certain emperor of such mighty prowess that he did take ten maidenheddes in ye compass of a single night, ye while his empress did entertain two and twenty lusty knights between her sheetes, yet was not satisfied; whereat ye merrie Countess Granby saith a ram is yet ye emperor's superior, sith he wil tup above a hundred yewes 'twixt sun and sun; and after, if he can have none more to shag, will masturbate until he hath enrich'd whole acres with his seed.

Then spake ye damned windmill, Sr Walter, of a people in ye uttermost parts of America, yt capulate not until they be five and thirty yeres of age, ye women being eight and twenty, and do it then but once in seven yeres.

YE QUEENE.—How doth that like my little Lady Helen? Shall we send thee thither and preserve thy belly?

LADY HELEN.—Please your highnesses grace, mine old nurse hath told me there are more ways of serving God than by locking the thighs together; yet am I willing to serve him yt way too, sith your highnesses grace hath set ye ensample.

YE QUEENE.—God' wowndes a good answer, childe.

LADY ALICE.—Mayhap 'twill weaken when ye hair sprouts below ye navel.

LADY HELEN.—Nay, it sprouted two yeres syne; I can scarce more than cover it with my hand now.

YE QUEENE.—Hear Ye that, my little Beaumonte? Have ye not a little birde about ye that stirs at hearing tell of so sweete a neste?

BEAUMONTE.—'Tis not insensible, illustrious madam; but mousing owls and bats of low degree may not aspire to bliss so whelming and ecstatic as is found in ye downy nests of birdes of Paradise.

YE QUEENE.—By ye gullet of God, 'tis a neat-turned compliment. With such a tongue as thine, lad, thou'lt spread the ivory thighs of many a willing maide in thy good time, an' thy cod-piece be as handy as thy speeche.

Then spake ye queene of how she met old Rabelais when she was turned of fifteen, and he did tell her of a man his father knew that had a double pair of bollocks, whereon a controversy followed as concerning the most just way to spell the word, ye contention running high betwixt ye learned Bacon and ye ingenious Jonson, until at last ye old Lady Margery, wearying of it all, saith, 'Gentles, what mattereth it how ye shall spell the word? I warrant Ye when ye use your bollocks ye shall not think of it; and my Lady Granby, be ye content; let the spelling be, ye shall enjoy the beating of them on your buttocks just the same, I trow. Before I had gained my fourteenth year I had learnt that them that would explore a cunt stop'd not to consider the spelling o't.'

Sʀ W.—In sooth, when a shift's turned up, delay is meet for naught but dalliance. Boccaccio hath a story of a priest that did beguile a maid into his cell, then knelt him in a corner to pray for grace to be rightly thankful for this tender maidenhead ye Lord had sent him; but ye abbot, spying through ye key-hole, did see a tuft of brownish hair with fair white flesh about it, wherefore when ye priest's prayer was done, his chance was gone, forasmuch as ye little maid had but ye one cunt, and that was already occupied to her content.

Then conversed they of religion, and ye mightie work ye old dead Luther did doe by ye grace of God. Then next about poetry, and Master Shaxpur did rede a part of his King Henry IV., ye which, it seemeth unto me, is not of ye value of an arsefull of ashes, yet they praised it bravely, one and all.

Ye same did rede a portion of his "Venus and Adonis," to their prodigious admiration, whereas I, being sleepy and fatigued withal, did deme it but paltry stuff, and was the more discomforted in that ye blody bucanier had got his wind again, and did turn his mind to farting with such villain zeal that presently I was like to choke once more. God damn this windy ruffian and all his breed. I wolde that hell mighte get him.

They talked about ye wonderful defense which old Sr. Nicholas Throgmorton did make for himself before ye judges in ye time of Mary; which was unlucky matter to broach, sith it fetched out ye quene with a 'Pity yt he, having so much wit, had yet not enough to save his doter's maidenhedde sound for her marriage-bed.' And ye quene did give ye damn'd Sr. Walter a look yt made hym wince—for she hath not forgot he was her own lover it yt olde day. There was silent uncomfortableness now; 'twas not a good turn for talk to take, sith if ye queene must find offense in a little harmless debauching, when pricks were stiff and cunts not loathe to take ye stiffness out of them, who of this company was sinless; behold, was not ye wife of Master Shaxpur four months gone with child when she stood uppe before ye altar? Was not her Grace of Bilgewater roger'd by four lords before she had a husband? Was not ye little Lady Helen born on her mother's wedding-day? And, beholde, were not ye Lady Alice and ye Lady Margery there, mouthing religion, whores from ye cradle?

In time came they to discourse of Cervantes, and of the new painter, Rubens, that is beginning to be heard of. Fine words and dainty-wrought phrases from the ladies now, one or two of them being, in other days, pupils of that poor ass, Lille, himself; and I marked how that Jonson and Shaxpur did fidget to discharge some venom of sarcasm, yet dared they not in the presence, the queene's grace being ye very flower of ye Euphuists herself. But behold, these be they yt, having a specialty, and admiring it in themselves, be jealous when a neighbor doth essaye it, nor can abide it in them long. Wherefore 'twas observable yt ye quene waxed uncontent; and in time labor'd grandiose speeche out of ye mouth of Lady Alice, who manifestly did mightily pride herself thereon, did quite exhauste ye quene's endurance, who listened till ye gaudy speeche was done, then lifted up her brows, and with vaste irony, mincing saith 'O shit!' Whereat they alle did laffe, but not ye Lady Alice, yt olde foolish bitche.

Now was Sr. Walter minded of a tale he once did hear ye ingenious Margrette of Navarre relate, about a maid, which being like to
suffer rape by an olde archbishoppe, did smartly contrive a device
to save her maidenhedde, and said to him, First, my lord, I prithee,
take out thy holy tool and piss before me; which doing, lo his member felle, and would not rise again.

1880

DANIIL KHARMS

✳ ✳ ✳

Anegdotes from the Life of Pushkin

1. Pushkin was a poet and he wrote all kinds of stuff. One day Zhukovsky came upon him, writing, and he cried out loudly, "Boy, you really are a writing guy!" From that time Pushkin really liked Zhukovsky, and began to call him simply "Zhukie."

2. As everyone knows, Pushkin never grew a beard. This bothered Pushkin a lot, and he always envied Zaharin, who on the contrary could grow a very proper one. "For him it grows, for me it doesn't grow," Pushkin often said, pointing his long fingernail at Zaharin. And always, it was the truth.

3. One day Petrushevsky's watch broke, and he called Pushkin. Pushkin came over, looked at Petrushevsky's watch, and put it back on the chair. "What do you say, brother Pushkin?" Petrushevsky asked. "No go," said Pushkin.

4. When Pushkin broke his leg, he had to go around on wheels. His friends liked to tease Pushkin and grab him by the wheels. This made Pushkin angry, and he wrote nasty poems about them. He called these poems "erpigrams."

5. Pushkin spent the summer of 1829 out in the country. He woke up early each morning, drank a jug of warm milk fresh from the cow, and ran to the river to bathe. After bathing in the river, Pushkin lay on the grass and slept until lunch. After lunch, Pushkin slept in a hammock. Whenever he met a smelly peasant, Pushkin nodded to him and held his nose with his fingers. The smelly peasant doffed his cap and said, "It's nothin'."

6. Pushkin loved to throw rocks. Whenever he saw some rocks, he would begin to throw them. Sometimes he would get all red in the face, waving his arms, throwing rocks—truly awful!

7. Pushkin had four sons, all idiots. One of them didn't know how to sit on a chair, and always fell off. Pushkin himself did not sit too well on chairs. It was a real laugh. They'd sit at the table—at one end Pushkin always falling from his chair, and at the other end, his son. Oh my! Turn Saint Mary's picture to the wall!

1930s
Translated by Ian Frazier

CALVIN TOMKINS

History in the Balance

One afternoon recently, I took, as they say, a personal loan from a friendly bank. When I came home and added this sum to the previous balance in my checkbook, the figure that materialized in the left-hand balance column was $1492.16. Ignoring the sixteen cents, I suddenly realized, gave this figure a new significance. It seemed a marvelous omen for me to be setting out on a sea of bills with such a promising number on my ship, linking the hopes of my creditors with the discovery of America. This auspicious beginning to the monthly chore served to put me in a pleasant historical frame of mind and to postpone the painful business of actually writing checks. What other great events, I wondered idly, had taken place in $1492?

I went into the living room and found, on the bottom shelf of the bookcase, the *Encyclopedia of World History*, which my wife's Boston aunt gave us as a wedding present twelve years ago. After leafing through the Preface, Foreword, Introduction, Index, and Genealogical Tables, I plunged into Later Middle Ages, Western Europe, and learned that this crucial year also marked the death of Lorenzo the Magnificent and of Pope Innocent VIII ("the first pope to recognize his children and dine publicly with ladies"). What else? The Russians, under Ivan III, were invading Lithuania, as usual. Over in England, Henry VII had just signed the Peace of Etaples. I was about to dig into Far Eastern history when my wife called to me from the kitchen that she needed ten dollars for the cleaning woman. There being no ready cash in the house, I was forced to write out a check. This, of course, spoiled the balance, so I went ahead and paid the gas company and the mortgage installment, and sadly subtracted the total from $1492.16. The new balance, carried over to the following page, was $1394.29.

My curiosity still aroused (how can we understand the present without understanding the past?), I returned to the encyclopedia and found, with a surge of relief, that I was still in the interesting Later Middle Ages. In $1394, it turned out, a twenty-year truce had been signed between the Swiss Confederation and the Duke of Austria, whereupon Austria abandoned its claims to Zug and Glarus. Not quite up to $1492, admittedly, but it was something. Hopefully, I veered into Eastern Europe, only to learn that I had missed by nine years the capture of Sofia by the Ottoman Turks ($1385), and by five years the battle of Kossovo ($1389)—"a decisive date in all Balkan history." The ground here seemed unpromising, so I drifted back to our side of the Iron Curtain, looking for $1394s. In $1400, I noted with some surprise, King Wenceslas of Bohemia was deposed "for drunkenness and incompetence." (*Good* King Wenceslas?) Back I coursed through Medicis and Holy Roman Emperors, Guelfs and Ghibellines, Neapolitan Anjous, and neglected figures like Joanna II ($1415–$1435), sister of Ladislas, an amorous widow whose "amazing intrigues . . . with her favorites, successors designate, and rival claimants to the throne kept Italian diplomacy in a turmoil" for many years. But only precise dates would do if I was going to play the game right, and Italy, Portugal, Spain, France, and England didn't seem to have made significant history in $1394. I shut the book with a snap, snagging a hangnail between the Black Death and the Battle of Agincourt, and applied myself once more to my own rival claimants.

Checks to the plumber, the fuel company, and the consulting tree surgeon reduced the balance to $1235.61—a disappointing figure in all respects. The only incident worth mention in European history in that year was an expedition sent by John Vatatzes against the Venetians, which "failed to achieve anything." Earlier (later, that is), in $1305, another Wenceslas (Wenceslas I), challenged by claimants of the Piast family, had resigned and gone home to die, and in $1234 there was "unrest in southern Italy," but mere unrest no longer interested me. I hurried on, paying the exterminator, the garbage man, and the newspaper-delivery service, and looking for other small bills. I felt a sharp joy when a bill for a renewed magazine subscription enabled me to pause for a moment on the field of Runnymede and hail the signing of the Magna Carta at $1215.39.

Down I dropped through the Crusades and the Rise of the Towns, through the reigns of Louis the Young and Louis the Fat, coming finally, by way of Altman's, Bloomingdale's, and Bonwit Teller, to the $1076 Synod of Worms. Frankly, I would have preferred $1077 and Henry IV's dash across the Alps to the melodramatic penance at Canossa, beloved by modern newspaper correspondents, but I refused to tinker with history. At $1001.02 (coronation of St. Stephen, greatest ruler of the Arpad dynasty), I stopped for dinner, postponing the dreary descent into three figures and the early Middle Ages.

During the meal, I astonished my wife and our two older children by references to the Battle of Bouvines ($1214), in which Philip II and Frederick the something had completed the defeat of Otto and the Welfs. "You mean wolves?" asked my daughter, who is in the fourth grade. "Of course not," I shot back, and went on quickly to a discussion of Manegold of Lautenbach, who developed the theory that an evil ruler violates his contract with his subjects and may therefore be deposed. My wife said she would bear this in mind.

Actually, it was the next morning before I returned to the checkbook and the encyclopedia, where I immediately became bogged down in the Abbasid Caliphate ("Spain never recognized it, nor did Morocco") and the Danish kings, from Knut the Great back to Harold Bluetooth. Still searching for bills of small denomination, so as to prolong the Middle Ages, I paid McDermott's Dairy, Oak Tree Pharmacy, and the waterworks. This brought me to $929.91, the year in which St. Wenceslas (*this* must have been the good one!) had the bad luck to be murdered by his younger brother, who thereupon ascended the Bohemian throne as Boleslav I. I had a strange feeling that this would mark my last encounter with the Wenceslases (of the House of Premsyl), and I was right. The scene was darkening. As my balance declined, history grew less splendid.

Charles the Fat (who blocked Charles the Bald's advance to the Rhine) reigned for the exact number of years, or dollars, it took to satisfy Bide-A-Wee Diaper Service. The disintegration of the Carolingian Empire, played out in reverse, led me, via Andy's Meats, Tots' Togs, and a place called Twig, Ltd., to the start of the reign of Charlemagne ($771.05)—that "typical German" who "understood Greek, spoke Latin, but could not learn to write."

Just as the pile of bills at my right elbow seemed to be shrinking, I uncovered a quarterly notice from the Internal Revenue Service, plainly marked "Do Not Fold or Spindle." The thought of missing out entirely on the Merovingian kings so distressed me that I nearly lost my temper and spindled the notice, but instead I sighed and paid up, reeling back through Vandals and Visigoths to the birth of Emperor Jovianus ($331.33), who "surrendered Mesopotamia to the Persians and died soon after." Battered and full of foreboding, I was borne down by two MDs and a DDS into the third century, "characterized by the complete collapse of government and economics throughout the Mediterranean." The Dark Ages were upon me. I was now twelve centuries from that jubilant start in $1492.16, and there remained four or five inches of unpaid bills. A few more big ones, I knew, would push me over the brink into overdraft, or BC.

Writing in a cramped, unwilling hand, I slogged through the Antonines and the Flavians toward Augustus Caesar, hoping that the rest of the bills would stay in two figures, but long before the end I knew the game was up. My balance stood at $54.06 (death of the Emperor Claudius, "reputedly from poison administered by Agrippina in a dish of mushrooms"). The bill I had just opened was from the insurance company, for $118.54 (the year Hadrian took his oath not to execute senators without trial). Smothering a Latin oath, I shut the encyclopedia on insolvent Rome and bankrupt Greece, and went downtown to see about another loan. After all, I reminded myself, Columbus himself had managed to raise the money for three voyages to the New World before they sent him home in chains.

1958

MIKHAIL ZOSHCHENKO

The Bathhouse

I hear tell, citizens, they have some excellent bathhouses in America.

For example, a citizen just drives in, drops his linen in a special box, then off he'll go to wash himself. He won't even worry, they say, about loss or theft. He doesn't even need a ticket.

Well, let's suppose it's some other, nervous-type American, and he'll say to the attendant, "Goot-bye," so to speak, "keep an eye out."

And that's all there is to it.

This American will wash himself, come back, and they'll give him clean linen—washed and pressed. Foot-wrappings, no doubt, whiter than snow. Underdrawers mended and sewed. That's the life!

Well, we have bathhouses, too. But not as good. Though it's possible to wash yourself.

Only in ours, there's trouble with the tickets. Last Saturday I went to one of our bathhouses (after all, I can't go all the way to America), and they give me two tickets. One for my linen, the other for my hat and coat.

But where is a naked man going to put tickets? To say it straight—no place. No pockets. Look around—all stomach and legs. The only trouble's with the tickets. Can't tie them to your beard.

Well, I tied a ticket to each leg so as not to lose them both at once. I went into the bath.

The tickets are flapping about on my legs now. Annoying to walk like that. But you've got to walk. Because you've got to have a bucket. Without a bucket, how can you wash? That's the only trouble.

I look for a bucket. I see one citizen washing himself with three buckets. He is standing in one, washing his head in another, and holding the third with his left hand so no one would take it away.

I pulled at the third bucket; among other things, I wanted to take it for myself. But the citizen won't let go.

"What are you up to," says he, "stealing other people's buckets?" As I pull, he says, "I'll give you a bucket between the eyes, then you won't be so damn happy."

I say: "This isn't the tsarist regime," I say, "to go around hitting people with buckets. Egotism," I say, "sheer egotism. Other people," I say, "have to wash themselves too. You're not in a theater," I say.

But he turned his back and starts washing himself again.

"I can't just stand around," think I, "waiting his pleasure. He's likely to go on washing himself," think I, "for another three days."

I moved along.

After an hour I see some old joker gaping around, no hands on his bucket. Looking for soap or just dreaming, I don't know. I just lifted his bucket and made off with it.

So now there's a bucket, but no place to sit down. And to wash standing—what kind of washing is that? That's the only trouble.

All right. So I'm standing. I'm holding the bucket in my hand and I'm washing myself.

But all around me everyone's scrubbing clothes like mad. One is washing his trousers, another's rubbing his drawers, a third's wringing something out. You no sooner get yourself all washed up than you're dirty again. They're splattering me, the bastards. And such a noise from all the scrubbing—it takes all the joy out of washing. You can't even hear where the soap squeaks. That's the only trouble.

"To hell with them," I think. "I'll finish washing at home."

I go back to the locker room. I give them one ticket, they give me my linen. I look. Everything's mine, but the trousers aren't mine.

"Citizens," I say, "mine didn't have a hole here. Mine had a hole over there."

But the attendant says: "We aren't here," he says, "just to watch for your holes. You're not in a theater," he says.

All right. I put these pants on, and I'm about to go get my coat. They won't give me my coat. They want the ticket. I'd forgotten the ticket on my leg. I had to undress. I took off my pants. I look for the ticket. No ticket. There's the string tied around my leg, but no ticket. The ticket had been washed away.

I give the attendant the string. He doesn't want it.

"You don't get anything for a string," he says. "Anybody can cut off a bit of string," he says. "Wouldn't be enough coats to go around. Wait," he says, "till everyone leaves. We'll give you what's left over."

I say: "Look here, brother, suppose there's nothing left but crud? This isn't a theater," I say. "I'll identify it for you. One pocket," I say, "is torn, and there's no other. As for the buttons," I say, "the top one's there, the rest are not to be seen."

Anyhow, he gave it to me. But he wouldn't take the string.

I dressed, and went out on the street. Suddenly I remembered: I forgot my soap.

I went back again. They won't let me in, in my coat.

"Undress," they say.

I say, "Look, citizens. I can't undress for the third time. This isn't a theater," I say. "At least give me what the soap costs."

Nothing doing.

Nothing doing—all right. I went without the soap.

Of course, the reader who is accustomed to formalities might be curious to know: what kind of a bathhouse was this? Where was it located? What was the address?

What kind of a bathhouse? The usual kind. Where it costs ten kopecks to get in.

1961

MICHAEL O'DONOGHUE

❊ ❊ ❊

How to Write Good

If I could not earn a penny from my writing, I would earn my livelihood at something else and continue to write at night.

—IRVING WALLACE

Financial success is not the only reward of good writing. It brings to the writer rich inner satisfaction as well.

—ELIOT FOSTER, DIRECTOR OF ADMISSIONS,
FAMOUS WRITERS SCHOOL

INTRODUCTION

A long time ago, when I was just starting out, I had the good fortune to meet the great Willa Cather. With all the audacity of youth, I asked her what advice she would give the would-be-writer and she replied:

"My advice to the would-be-writer is that he start slowly, writing short undemanding things, things such as telegrams, flip-books, crank letters, signature scarves, spot quizzes, capsule summaries, fortune cookies, and errata. Then, when he feels he's ready, move up to the more challenging items such as mandates, objective correlatives, passion plays, pointless diatribes, minor classics, manifestos, mezzotints, oxymora, exposés, broadsides, and papal bulls.

And above all, never forget that the pen is mightier than the plowshare. By this I mean that writing, all in all, is a hell of a lot more fun than farming. For one thing, writers seldom, if ever, have to get up at five o'clock in the morning and shovel manure. As far as I'm concerned, that gives them the edge right there."

She went on to tell me many things, both wonderful and wise, probing the secrets of her craft, showing how to weave a net of words and capture the fleeting stuff of life.

Unfortunately, I've forgotten every bit of it.

I do recall, however, her answer when I asked "If you could only give me one rule to follow, what would it be?" She paused, looked down for a moment, and finally said, "Never wear brown shoes with a blue suit."

There's very little I could add to that except to say "Go to it and good luck!"

LESSON 1—THE GRABBER

The "grabber" is the initial sentence of a novel or short story designed to jolt the reader out of his complacency and arouse his curiosity, forcing him to press onward. For example:

"It's no good, Alex," she rejoined. "Even if I did love you, my father would never let me marry an alligator."

The reader is immediately bombarded with questions, questions such as "Why won't her father let her marry an alligator?" "How come she doesn't love him?" and "Can she learn to love him in time?" The reader's interest has been "grabbed"!

Just so there'll be no misunderstanding about grabbers, I've listed a few more below:

"I'm afraid you're too late," sneered Zoltan. "The fireplace has already flown south for the winter!"

Sylvia lay sick among the silverware . . .

Chinese vegetables mean more to me than you do, my dear," Charles remarked to his wife, adding injury to insult by lodging a grapefruit knife in her neck.

"I have in my hands," Professor Willobee exclaimed, clutching a sheaf of papers in his trembling fingers and pacing in circles about the carpet while I stood at the window, barely able to make out the Capitol Dome through the thick, churning fog that rolled in off the Potomac, wondering to myself what matter could possibly be so urgent as to bring the distinguished historian bursting into my State Department office at the unseemly hour, "definitive proof that Abraham Lincoln was a homo!"

These are just a handful of the possible grabbers. Needless to say, there are thousands of others, but if you fail to think of them, feel free to use any or all of these.

LESSON 2—THE ENDING

All too often, the budding author finds that his tale has run its course and yet he sees no way to satisfactorily end it, or, in literary parlance, "wrap it up." Observe how easily I resolve this problem:

Suddenly, everyone was run over by a truck.

-the end-

If the story happens to be set in England, use the same ending, slightly modified:

Suddenly, everyone was run over by a lorry.

-the end-

If set in France:

Soudainement, tout le monde était écrasé par un camion.

-finis-

You'll be surprised at how many different settings and situations this ending applies to.

For instance, if you were writing a story about ants, it would end "Suddenly, everyone was run over by a centipede." In fact, this is the only ending you ever need use.*

Warning—if you are writing a story about trucks, do not have the trucks run over by a truck. Have the trucks run over by a mammoth truck.

LESSON 3—CHOOSING A TITLE

A friend of mine recently had a bunch of articles rejected by the *Reader's Digest* and, unable to understand why, he turned to me for advice. I spotted the problem at a glance. His titles were all wrong. By calling his pieces such things as "Unwed Mothers—A Head Start on Life," "Cancer—The Incurable Disease," "A Leading Psychologist Explains Why There Should Be More Violence on Television," "Dognappers I Have Known and Loved," "My Baby Was Born Dead and I Couldn't Care Less," and "Pleasantville—Last of the Wide-Open Towns," he had seriously misjudged his market. To steer him straight, I drew up this list of all-purpose surefire titles:

_____ *at the Crossroads*

The Case for _____

The Role of _____

Coping with Changing _____

A Realistic Look at _____

The _____ *Experience*

Bridging the _____ *Gap*

A _____ *for All Seasons*

Simply fill in the blanks with the topic of your choice and, if that doesn't work, you can always resort to the one title that never fails:

South America, the Sleeping Giant on Our Doorstep

LESSON 4—EXPOSITION

Perhaps the most difficult technique for the fledgling writer to master is proper treatment of exposition. Yet watch the sly, subtle way I "set the scene" of my smash play, *The Last to Know*, with a minimum of words and effort.

(The curtain opens on a tastefully appointed dining room, the table ringed by men in tuxedos and women in costly gowns. There is a knock at the door.)

LORD OVERBROOKE: Oh, come in, Lydia. Allow me to introduce my dinner guests to you. This is Cheryl Heatherton, the madcap soybean heiress whose zany antics actually mask a heart broken by her inability to meaningfully communicate with her father, E. J. Heatherton, seated to her left, who is too caught up in the heady world of high finance to sit down and have a quiet chat with his own daughter, unwanted to begin with, disposing of his paternal obligations by giving her everything, everything but love, that is.

Next to them sits Geoffrey Drake, a seemingly successful merchant banker trapped in an unfortunate marriage with a woman half his age, who wistfully looks back upon his days as the raffish Group Captain of an R.A.F. bomber squadron that flew eighty-one missions over Berlin, his tortured psyche refusing to admit, despite frequent nightmares in which, dripping with sweat, he wakes screaming, "Pull it up! Pull it up, I say! I can't hold her any longer! We're losing altitude! We're going down! Jerry at three o'clock! Aaaaaaaaaaaaaaaagggh!" that his cowardice and his cowardice alone was responsible for the loss of his crew and "Digger," the little Manchester terrier who was their mascot. The empty chair to his right was vacated just five minutes ago by Geoffrey's stunning wife, twenty-three-year-old, golden-tressed Edwina Drake, who, claiming a severe migraine, begged to be excused that she might return home and rest, whereas, in reality, she is, at this moment, speeding to the arms of another man, convinced that if she can steal a little happiness now, it doesn't matter who she hurts later on. The elderly servant preparing the Caviar en Socle is Andrew who's been with my family for over forty years although he hasn't received a salary for the last two, even going on so far as to loan me his life's savings to cover my spiraling gambling debts but it's only a matter of time before I am exposed as a penniless fraud and high society turns its back on me.

The dark woman opposite me is Yvonne de Zenobia, the fading Mexican film star, who speaks of her last movie as though it was shot only yesterday, unwilling to face the fact that she hasn't been before the cameras in nearly fifteen years; unwilling to confess that her life has been little more than a tarnished dream.

As for her companion, Desmond Trelawney, he is an unmitigated scoundrel about whom the less said, the better. And, of course, you know your father, the ruthless war profiteer, and your hopelessly alcoholic mother, who never quite escaped her checkered past, realizing, all too late, that despite her jewels and limousines, she was still just a taxidancer who belonged to any man for a drink and a few cigarettes.

Please take a seat. We were just talking about you.

This example demonstrates everything you'll ever need to know about exposition. Study it carefully.

LESSON 5—FINDING THE RAW MATERIAL

As any professional writer will tell you, the richest source of material is one's relatives, one's neighbors, and, more often than not, total strangers. A day doesn't go by without at least one person, upon learning that I'm a professional writer, offering me some terrific idea for a story. And I'm sure it will come as no shock when I say that most of the ideas are pretty damn good!

Only last week, a pipe fitter of my acquaintance came up with a surprise ending guaranteed to unnerve the most jaded reader. What you do is tell this really weird story that keeps on getting weirder and weirder until, just when the reader is muttering, "How in the heck is he going to get himself out of this one? He's really painted himself into a corner!" you spring the "mind-blower": "But then he woke up. It had all been a dream!" (which I, professional writer that I am, honed down to: "But then the alarm clock rang. It had all been a dream!"). And this came from a common, run-of-the-mill pipe fitter! For free!

Cabdrivers, another great wealth of material, will often remark, "Boy, lemme tell ya! Some of the characters I get in this cab would fill a book! Real kooks, ya know what I mean?" And then, without my having to coax even the slightest, they tell me about them, and they would fill a book. Perhaps two or three books. In addition, if you're at all interested in social science, cabdrivers are able to provide countless examples of the failures of the welfare state.

To illustrate just how valid these unsolicited suggestions can be, I shall print a few lines from a newly completed play inspired by my aunt, who had the idea as far back as when she was attending grade school. It's called *If an Old House Could Talk, What Tales It Would Tell*:

THE FLOOR: Do you remember the time the middle-aged lady who always wore the stiletto heels tripped over an extension cord while running to answer the phone and spilled the Ovaltine all over me and they spent the next 20 minutes mopping it up?

THE WALL: No.

Of course, I can't print too much here because I don't want to spoil the ending (although I will give you a hint: It involves a truck . . .).

I just wanted to show you how much the world would have missed had I rejected my aunt's suggestion out of hand simply because she is not a professional writer like myself.

LESSON 6—QUOTING OTHER AUTHORS

If placed in a situation where you must quote another author, always write "[sic]" after any word that may be misspelled or looks the least bit questionable in any way. If there are no misspellings or curious words, toss in a few "[sic]"s just to break up the flow. By doing this, you will appear to be knowledgeable and "on your toes," while the one quoted will seem suspect and vaguely discredited. Two examples will suffice:

> O Sleepless as the river under thee,
> Vaulting the sea, the prairies' dreaming sod,
> Unto us lowliest sometime sweep, descend
> And of the curveship [sic], lend a myth to God.
> —HART CRANE

> Beauty is but a flowre [sic],
> Which wrinckles [sic] will devoure [sic]
> Brightnesse [sic] falls from the ayre [sic]
> Queenes [sic] have died yong [sic] and faire [sic]
> Dust hath closde [sic] Helens [sic] eye [sic]
> I am sick [sic], I must dye [sic]: Lord, have mercy on us.
> —THOMAS NASHE

Note how only one small "[sic]" makes Crane's entire stanza trivial and worthless, which, in his case, takes less doing that Nashe, on the other hand, has been rendered virtually unreadable. Anyone having to choose between you and Nashe would pick you every time! And, when it's all said and done, isn't that the name of the game?

LESSON 7—MAKING THE READER FEEL INADEQUATE

Without question, the surest way to make a reader feel inadequate is through casual erudition, and there is no better way to achieve casual erudition than by putting the punchline of an anecdote in a little foreign language. Here's a sample:

One crisp October morning, while taking my usual stroll down the Kurfurstenstrasse, I spied my old friend Casimir Malevitch, the renowned Suprematist painter, sitting on a bench. Noting that he had a banana in his ear, I said to him, "Excuse me, Casimir, but I believe you have a banana in your ear."

"What?" he asked.

Moving closer and speaking quite distinctly, I repeated my previous observation, saying, "I said, 'You have a banana in your ear!' "

"What's that you say?" came the reply.

By now I was a trifle piqued at this awkward situation and, seeking to make myself plain, once and for all, I fairly screamed, "I SAID THAT YOU HAVE A BANANA IN YOUR EAR, YOU DOLT!!!"

Imagine my chagrin when Casimir looked at me blankly and quipped,

১৯০২ বেড়েই চন্দ্রো এবর পরর্রাজ্জাঙ্গা প্রোসডেন্ট র্জে ১৯৩৭) কিংগ, বাতে.

Oh, what a laugh we had over that one.

With one stroke, the reader has been made to feel not only that his education was second-rate, but that you are getting far more out of life than he. This is precisely why this device is best used in memoirs, whose sole purpose is to make the reader feel that you have lived life to the fullest, while his existence, in comparison, has been meaningless and shabby . . .

LESSON 8—COVERING THE NEWS

Have you ever wondered how reporters are able to turn out a dozen or so news articles day after day, year after year, and still keep their copy so fresh, so vital, so alive? It's because they know the Ten Magic Phrases of Journalism, key constructions with which one can express *every known human emotion*! As one might suppose, the Phrases, discovered only after centuries of trial and error, are a closely guarded secret, available to no one but accredited members of the press. However, at the risk of being cashiered from the Newspaper Guild, I am now going to reveal them to you:

THE TEN MAGIC PHRASES OF JOURNALISM

- "violence flared"
- "limped into port"
- "according to informed sources"
- "wholesale destruction"
- "no immediate comment"
- "student unrest"
- "riot-torn"
- "flatly denied"
- "gutted by fire"
- "roving bands of Negro youths"

Let's try putting the Phrases to work in a sample news story:

NEWARK, NJ, Aug. 22 (UPI)—*Violence flared yesterday when roving bands of Negro youths broke windows and looted shops in riot-torn Newark. Mayor Kenneth Gibson had no immediate comment but, according to informed sources, he flatly denied saying that student unrest was behind the wholesale destruction that resulted in scores of buildings being gutted by fire, and added, "If this city were a Liberian freighter,* we just may have limped into port."*

**Whenever needed, "Norwegian tanker" can always be substituted for "Liberian freighter." Consider them interchangeable.*

Proof positive that the Ten Magic Phrases of Journalism can express every known human emotion and then some!

LESSON 9—TRICKS OF THE TRADE

Just as homemakers have their hints (e.g., a ball of cotton, dipped in vanilla extract and placed in the refrigerator, will absorb food odors), writers have their own bag of tricks, a bag of tricks, I might hasten to point out, you won't learn at any Bread Loaf Conference. Most writers, ivory tower idealists that they are, prefer to play up the mystique of their "art" (visitations from the Muse, *l'ecriture automatique*, talking in tongues, et cetera, et cetera), and sweep the hard-nosed practicalities under the rug. Keeping in mind, however, that a good workman doesn't curse his tools, I am now going to make public these long suppressed tricks of the trade.

Suppose you've written a dreadful chapter (we'll dub it Chapter Six for our purposes here), utterly without merit, tedious and boring beyond belief, and you just can't find the energy to rewrite it. Since it's obvious that the reader, once he realizes how dull and shoddy Chapter Six really is, will refuse to read any further, you must provide some strong ulterior motive for completing the chapter. I've always found lust effective:

Artfully concealed within the next chapter is the astounding secret of an ancient Bhutanese love cult that will increase your sexual satisfaction by at least 60% and *possibly more*—

(Print Chapter Six.)

Pretty wild, huh? Bet you can hardly wait to try it! And don't show your appreciation by reading Chapter Seven!*

*This ensures that the reader reads Chapter Six not once but several times. Possibly, he may even read Chapter Seven.

Fear also works:

Dear Reader,
This message is printed on Chinese poison paper which is made
from deadly herbs that are instantly absorbed by the fingertips so it
won't do any good to wash your hands because you will die a hor-
rible and lingering death in about an hour unless you take the spe-
cial antidote which is revealed in Chapter Six and you'll be saved.

Sincerely,
(Your name)

Or even:

Dear Reader,
You are obviously one of those rare people who are immune to
Chinese paper so this message is printed on Bavarian poison
paper which is about a thousand times more powerful and even if
you're wearing gloves you're dead for sure unless you read Chap-
ter Six very carefully and find the special antidote.

Sincerely,
(Your name)

Appealing to vanity, greed, sloth, and whatever, you can keep this
up, chapter by chapter, until they finish the book. In fact, the number of appeals is limited only by human frailty itself . . .

LESSON 10—MORE WRITING HINTS
There are many more writing hints I could share with you, but suddenly I am run over by a truck.

1971

DONALD BARTHELME

❋ ❋ ❋

Thailand

Yes, said the old soldier, I remember a time. It was during the Krian War.

Bless you and keep you, said his hearer, silently.

It was during the Krian War, said the old soldier. We were up there on the 38th parallel, my division, round about the Chorwon Valley. This was in '52.

Oh God, said the listener to himself. Enchiladas in green sauce. Dos Equis. Maybe a burrito or two.

We had this battalion of Thais attached to us, said the old sergeant. Nicest people you'd ever want to meet. We used to call their area Thailand, like it was a whole country. They are small of stature. We used to party with them a lot. What they drink is Mekong, it'll curl your teeth. In Kria we weren't too particular.

Enchiladas in green sauce and Gilda. Gilda in her sizzling blouse.

This time I'm talking about, we were partying at Thailand, there was this Thai second john who was a personal friend of mine, named Sutchai. Tall fellow, thin, he was an exception to the rule. We were right tight, even went on R & R together, you're too young to know what that is, it's Rest and Recreation where you zip off to Tokyo and sample the delights of that great city for a week.

I am young, thought the listener, young, young, praise the Lord I am young.

This time I am talking about, said the old sarge, we were on the side of a hill, they held this hill which sort of anchored the MLR—that's Main Line of Resistance—at that point, pretty good-sized hill I forget what the designation was, and it was a feast day, some Thai feast, a big holiday, and the skies were sunny, sunny. They had set out thirty-seven washtubs full of curry I never saw anything like it. Thirty-seven washtubs full of curry and a different curry in every one. They even had eel curry.

I cannot believe I am sitting here listening to this demento carry on about eel curry.

It was a golden revel, said the sergeant, if you liked curry and I did and do. Beef curry, chicken curry, the delicate Thai worm curry, all your various fish curries and vegetable curries. The Thai cooks were number one, even in the sergeant's mess which I was the treasurer of for a year and a half we didn't eat like that. Well, you're too young to know what a quad-fifty is but it's four fifty-caliber machine guns mounted on a half-track and they had quad-fifties dug in on various parts of their hill as well as tanks which was just about all you could do with a tank in that terrain, and toward evening they were firing off tracer bursts from the quad-fifties to make fireworks and it was just very festive, very festive. They had fighting with wooden swords at which the Thais excel, it's like a ballet dance, and the whole battalion was putting away the Mekong and beer pretty good as were the invited guests such as me and my buddy Nick Pirelli who was my good buddy in the motor pool, anytime I wanted a vehicle of any type for any purpose all I had to do was call Nick and he'd redline that vehicle and send it over to me with a driver—

I too have a life, thought the listener, but it is motes of dust in the air.

They had this pretty interesting, actually highly interesting, ceremony, said the sargie-san, as part of the feast, on that night on that hill in Kria, where everybody lined up and their colonel, that was Colonel Parti, I knew him, a wise and handsome man, stripped to the waist and the men, one by one, passed before him and poured water on his head, half a cupful per man. The Colonel sat there and they poured water on his head, it had some kind of religious significance—they're Buddhists—the whole battalion, that's six hundred men more or less, passed in front of him and poured water on his head, it was a blessing or something, it was spring. Colonel Parti always used to say to me, his English wasn't too good but it was a hell of a lot better than my Thai which didn't exist, he always used to say "Sergeant, after the war I come to Big PX"—that's what they called America, the Big PX—"I come to Big PX and we play golf." I didn't even know they had golf in Thailand but he was supposed to be some kind of hot-shot golf player, I heard he'd been on their Olympic golf team at one time, funny to think of them having one but they were surprising and beautiful people, our houseboy Kim, we had these Krian houseboys who kept the tent policed up and cleaned your rifle and did the laundry, pretty near everybody in Kria is named Kim by the way, Kim had been with the division from the beginning and had gone to the Yalu with the division in '50 when the Chinese came in and kicked our asses all the way back to the 38th and Kim had been in a six-by-six firing some guy's M-1 all the way through the retreat which was a nightmare and therefore everybody was always very respectful of him even though he was only a houseboy. . . . Anyhow, Kim had told me Colonel Parti was a high-ranked champion golfer. That's how I knew it.

He reminds me of poor people, thought the young man, poor people whom I hate.

The Chinese pulled all these night attacks, said the sergeant.

The babble of God-given senility, said the listener to his inner ear.

It was terrifying. There'd be these terrifying bugles, you'd sit up in your sleeping bag hearing the bugles which sounded like they were coming from every which way, all around you, everybody grabbing his weapon and running around like a chicken with his head cut off, DivArty would be putting down a barrage you could hear it but God knows what they thought they were firing at, your communications trenches would be full of insane Chinese, flares popping in the sky—

I consign you to history, said his hearer. I close, forever, the book.

Once, they wanted to send me to cooks-and-bakers school, said the sergeant who was wearing a dull-red bathrobe, but I told them no, I couldn't feature myself a cook, that's why I was in heavy weapons. This party at Thailand was the high point of that tour. I never before or since saw thirty-seven washtubs full of curry and I would like to go to that country someday and talk to those people some more, they were great people. Sutchai wanted to be Prime Minister of Thailand, that was his ambition, never made it to my knowledge but I keep looking for him in the newspaper, you never know. I was on this plane going from Atlanta to Brooke Medical Center in San Antonio, I had to have some scans, there were all these young troopers on the plane, they were all little girls. Looked to be about sixteen. They all had these OD turtlenecks with Class A uniforms if you can imagine, they were the sloppiest soldiers I ever did see, the all-volunteer army I suppose I know I shouldn't criticize.

Go to cooks-and-bakers school, bake there, thought the young man. Bake a bathrobe of bread.

Thirty-seven damn washtubs, said the sergeant. If you can imagine.

Requiescat in pace.

They don't really have worm curry, said the sergeant. I just made that up to fool you.

HOWARD MOSS

The Ultimate Diary (Further Jottings of a Contemporary Composer)

MONDAY

Drinks here. Picasso, Colette, the inevitable Cocteau, Gide, Valéry, Ravel, and Larry. Chitchat. God, how absolutely dull the Great can be! I know at least a hundred friends who would have given their eyeteeth just to have had a *glimpse* of some of them, and there I was bored, incredible lassitude, *stymied*. Is it me? Is it them? Think latter. Happened to glance in mirror before going to bed. Am more beautiful than ever.

TUESDAY

Horrible. After organ lesson at C's, he burst into tears and confessed that he loved me. Was mad about me, is how he put it. I was embarrassed. I respect him, he is a great *maître* and all that, but how could I reciprocate when I, myself, am so involved with L? I tried to explain. He said he thought it would be better if we discontinued our lessons. How am I ever going to learn to play the organ? Came home upset. Finished *Barcarolles, Gigue, Danse Fantastique,* and *Cantata.* Writing better than ever. Careful of self-congratulations. So somebody said. John Donne? Fresh mushrooms. Delicious.

WEDNESDAY

Drunk at the dentist's. He removed a molar, and cried when I said it hurt. *Très gentil.* I think he has some feeling for me. The sky was like a red blister over the Dome. Streaks of carmine suffused the horizon. Sometimes I wonder if I shouldn't have been a writer. Drunk as I was, I caught a glimpse of myself in a bakery window. No wonder so many people love me!

THURSDAY

Arletty said something profound at lunch. "The trouble with homosexuals is that they like men." She sometimes gets to the heart of the matter with all her superficiality. She is leaving M. Talked and talked about it. I found my attention wandering, and kept seeing the unfinished pages of the *Symphony.* It is a great hymn to world peace, a kind of apotheosis of calmness, though it has a few fast sections. Drank a lot, and can't remember much after lunch. Woke up in Bois. Think something happened. But what? To relieve depression, dyed my hair again. Must say it looks ravishing. *Ravissant.*

FRIDAY

Calls from Mauriac and Claudel. Why don't they leave me alone?

FRIDAY, LATER

Larry back from Avignon. Seems changed. Felt vague feeling of disgust. To camouflage, worked all day and finished *Pavane, Song Cycles,* and *Sonata.* Dedicated latter—last?—to Princesse de N. She sent me a Russian egg for my name day. How know? Malraux, Auric, Poulenc, and Milhaud dropped by.

SATURDAY

Stravinsky angry with me, he said over phone. I must never stop working, working. What about sex? L has left. Should I call C? Thinking of it. Press clippings arrived. Is there any other composer under seventeen whose works are being played in every capital of Asia? Matisse said, jokingly at lunch, that I was too beautiful to live. Genius is not a gift; it is a loan.

SATURDAY, LATER

At state banquet for de Gaulle, misbehaved. Slapped his wife in face during coffee. Drunk. Terribly depressed, but am I not also not a little proud? Contrite but haughty, sorry but pleased? Can't remember issue. Something about Monteverdi? Sent her a dozen white roses as apology. The Princesse says I should get out of town for a while. I WILL NOT RUN AWAY! C back. We are both more gorgeous than ever. Finished *War and Peace*. A good book.

SUNDAY

Pneumatique from Mallarmé. I will not answer. C and I had pique-nique. Fell asleep on Seine bank. Dream: Mother in hippopotamus cage, crying. She said, "If music be the feast . . ." and then gobbled up by crowd of angry deer. What mean? Shaken. C bought me drink at Deux Magots. Sweet. Told me he thought there had never been a handsomer man placed on this earth. Forced to agree, after catching tiny glimpse of myself in café window. How often are genius and beauty united? They will hate me when they read this diary, but I tell the truth. How many can say as much?

MONDAY

A name even *I* cannot mention. . . . And he wants me to spend the summer in Africa with him! C angry. Finished *Concerto Grosso* and *Hymn to the Moon*, for female voices. Something new, a kind of rough susurration, here and there, a darkening of strings. It is raining. Sometimes I think we are more ourselves in wet weather than in dry. Bought linen hat.

TUESDAY

Gertrude, Alice, James, Joyce, Henry Green, Virginia Woolf, Eliot, Laforgue, Mallarmé (all is forgiven!), Rimbaud's nephew, Claudel's niece, Mistinguett, Nadia, Marais, Nijinska, Gabin, and the usual for drinks. I did it with Y in the pantry while the party was going on! Ashamed but exhilarated. I think if THEY knew they would have approved. Finished *Sixty Piano Pieces for Young Fingers*. Potboiler. But one has to live!

WEDNESDAY

Snow. Hideous hangover. Will never drink again. Deli dinner with Henry Miller.

THURSDAY

Half the Opéra-Comique seems to have fallen in love with me. I cannot stand any more importuning. Will go to Africa. How to break with C? Simone de Beauvoir, Simone Signoret, Simone Weil, and Simone Simon for drinks. They didn't get it!

FRIDAY

C left. Am bruised but elated. Dentist. I was right. I wonder if he'll dare send me a bill. *Now*, I mean. Tea with Anaïs. *Enchantant.*

SATURDAY

René Char and Dior for lunch. Interesting. Clothes are the camouflage of the soul. Leave for Africa with X tomorrow. Had fifty tiny Martinis. Nothing happened.

SUNDAY

Barrault, Braque, Seurat, Mayakovski, Honegger, and René Clair saw us off. Very gala. I think I am really in love for the first time. I must say I looked marvelous. Many comments. Wore green yachting cap and cinnamon plus fours. Happy.

WEDNESDAY

Dakar: Tangled in mosquito netting. Getting nowhere with *Chansons d'Afrique*.

SATURDAY

Back in Paris. God, what a fool I've been! Someday I will write down the whole hideous, unbelievable story. Not now. Not when I am so close to it. But I will forget *nothing*. Leaving tonight for Princesse de N's country place. Green trees, green leaves! The piercing but purifying wind of Provence! Or is it Normandy? Packed all afternoon. Long bath, many thoughts. Proust called. . . .

1975

ELIZABETH BISHOP

12 o'Clock News

gooseneck lamp	As you all know, tonight is the night of the full moon, half the world over. But here the moon seems to hang motionless in the sky. It gives very little light; it could be dead. Visibility is poor. Nevertheless, we shall try to give you some idea of the lay of the land and the present situation.
typewriter	The escapement that rises abruptly from the central plain is in heavy shadow, but the elaborate terracing of its southern glacis gleams faintly in the dim light, like fish scales. What endless labor those small, peculiarly shaped terraces represent! And yet, on them the welfare of this tiny principality depends.
pile of mss.	A slight landslide occurred in the northwest about an hour ago. The exposed soil appears to be of

poor quality: almost white, calcareous, and shaly. There are believed to have been no casualties.

typed sheet Almost due north, our aerial reconnaissance reports the discovery of a large rectangular "field," hitherto unknown to us, obviously man-made. It is dark-speckled. An airstrip? A cemetery?

envelopes In this small, backward country, one of the most backward left in the world today, communications are crude and "industrialization" and its products almost nonexistent. Strange to say, however, sign-boards are on a truly gigantic scale.

ink-bottle We have also received reports of a mysterious, oddly shaped, black structure, at an undisclosed distance to the east. Its presence was revealed only because its highly polished surface catches such feeble moonlight as prevails. The natural resources of the country being far from completely known to us, there is the possibility that this may be, or may contain, some powerful and terrifying "secret weapon." On the other hand, given what we do know, or have learned from our anthropologists and sociologists about this people, it may well be nothing more than a *numen*, or a great altar recently erected to one of their gods, to which, in their present historical state of superstition and helplessness, they attribute magical power, and may even regard as a "savior," one last hope of rescue from their grave difficulties.

typewriter eraser At last! One of the elusive natives has been spotted! He appears to be—rather, to have been—a unicyclist-courier, who may have met his end by falling from

the height of the escarpment because of the decep-
tive illumination. Alive, he would have been small,
but undoubtedly proud and erect, with the thick,
bristling black hair typical of the indigenes.

ashtray

From our superior vantage point, we can clearly
see into a sort of dugout, possibly a shell crater,
a "nest" of soldiers. They lie heaped together,
wearing the camouflage "battle dress" intended
for "winter warfare." They are in hideously con-
torted position, all dead. We can make out at least
eight bodies. These uniforms were designed to
be used in guerrilla warfare on the country's one
snow-covered mountain peak. The fact that these
poor soldiers are wearing them *here*, on the plain,
gives further proof, if proof were necessary, either
of the childishness and hopeless impracticality of
this inscrutable people, our opponents, or of the
sad corruption of their leaders.

1979

ABOUT THE CONTRIBUTORS

Henry Alford's work has appeared in the *New Yorker*, the *New York Times*, *Vanity Fair*, and *Spy*. He is the author of three works of investigative humor—*Municipal Bondage*, *Big Kiss*, and, most recently, *How to Live*.

Roger Angell is an editor at the *New Yorker*. He is the author of several books, including *Let Me Finish*, a collection of autobiographical essays. He is considered one of the best baseball writers of his generation.

Donald Barthelme (1931–1989) began his writing career as a news reporter for the *Houston Post*. He was a longtime contributor to the *New Yorker*, which published dozens of Barthelme's unsigned Notes and Comment pieces, some film criticism, and 128 stories.

Elizabeth Bishop (1911–1979) was the Poet Laureate of the United States from 1949 to 1950, and won the Pulitzer Prize for *Poems—North & South*.

Roy Blount, Jr., is the author of many books, covering subjects from the Pittsburgh Steelers to Robert E. Lee to what dogs are thinking. He is a regular panelist on NPR's *Wait, Wait . . . Don't Tell Me!* and is a member of the American Heritage Dictionary Usage Panel.

Andy Borowitz is a comedian, writer, and creator of the award-winning humor site BorowitzReport.com. He has published in the *New Yorker* and the *New York Times*, and is a commentator on National Public Radio. His most recent book is *Who Moved My Soap? The CEO's Guide to Surviving in Prison: The Bernie Madoff Edition.*

Lynn Caraganis is the author of two books, *Garish Days* and *Cousin It*. Her writing has appeared in the *New Yorker* and the *Atlantic*.

Rich Cohen is the author of *Tough Jews*, *Sweet and Low*, and most recently *Israel is Real*. A contributing editor at *Rolling Stone*, his work has been featured in several publications, including the *New Yorker* and *Vanity Fair*.

Prudence Crowther is on the editorial staff of *Business Week*.

Larry Doyle, a former writer for *The Simpsons*, works in show biz and writes funny things for the *New Yorker*. He is the author of *I Love You, Beth Cooper* and *Go, Mutants!*

A former editor for *National Lampoon*, **Glenn Eichler** has written, produced, and created television programs for networks like MTV and VH1. He currently writes for the Emmy-winning show *The Colbert Report*, on Comedy Central.

Bill Franzen is the author of a collection of short fiction, *Hearing From Wayne and Other Stories*.

Ian Frazier is the author of several books, including *Great Plains*, *On the Rez*, *Coyote v. Acme*, *Lamentations of the Father*, and *Travels in Siberia*. His work has appeared in the *New Yorker*, the *Atlantic*, and the *Washington Post Magazine*, among many others.

Novelist, screenwriter, and playwright **Bruce Jay Friedman** is the author of numerous works of fiction and nonfiction. His original screenplay, *Splash*, was nominated for an Academy Award in the category of Best Original Screenplay.

Polly Frost's works of fiction, drama, and journalism have been featured in *Grin & Tonic*, the *Barnes and Noble Review*, *Narrative Magazine*, and the *Atlantic*.

Frank Gannon is the author of *Midlife Irish*, a memoir. A frequent contributor to the *New Yorker* and *GQ*, he has written for *Harper's*, *Atlantic Monthly*, *New York Times Magazine*, *National Review*, and *Vogue*.

Veronica Geng was a longtime editor and writer for the *New Yorker*. Her books include *Partners* and *Love Trouble*, a collection of her essays.

Scott Gutterman is deputy director of Neue Galerie New York.

Jack Handey, a former writer for *Saturday Night Live*, is the author of several books, including *Deep Thoughts, Deeper Thoughts, Deepest Thoughts, Fuzzy Memories,* and *The Lost Deep Thoughts.*

Bret Harte (1836–1902) arrived in California in 1854, where he worked as a school teacher, drugstore clerk, express messenger, typesetter, and journalist before becoming the editor of the *Overland Monthy.* He is the author of several books about the American West, including *The Luck of the Roaring Camp, The Outcasts of Poker Flat,* and *Plain Language from Truthful James.*

Larry Heinemann is the author of *Close Quarters, Cooler by the Lake,* and *Paco's Story,* which won the National Book Award for fiction. His stories and essays have appeared in the *Atlantic, Harper's,* and *Playboy.*

Garrison Keillor has been the host of *A Prairie Home Companion* for over thirty years. He is the author of many books and a frequent contributor to *Time* and the *New Yorker.* He has been awarded a National Humanities Medal from the National Endowment of the Humanities.

Dan Kennedy is the author of *Rock On: An Office Power Ballad* and a regular contributor to *McSweeney's.*

As a leader of the literary group OBERIU, **Daniil Kharms** (1905-1942) influenced a generation of Russian writers. His darkly humorous vignettes and prose captured the absurdities of life under Soviet rule. He is the author of *Today I Wrote Nothing,* a selection of his collected works.

Jamaica Kincaid was born in St. John's, Antigua. Her books include *At the Bottom of the River, Annie John, Lucy, The Autobiography of My Mother, My Brother,* and *Mr. Potter.*

David Mamet is the award-winning author of many novels, plays, and screenplays, including *Oleanna; Speed-the-Plow; Glengarry Glen Ross,* which won the Pulitzer Prize for drama; *The Untouchables;* the Oscar-nominated *The Verdict;* and *Wag the Dog.* He is a contributor to the *Huffington Post.*

Steve Martin is an actor, director, and writer. He has starred in such films as *The Jerk, L.A. Story,* and *Bowfinger,* for which he wrote the screenplays. He is the author of *Pure Drivel,* the novella *Shopgirl,* and the memoir *Born Standing Up.*

Patricia Marx is a former writer for *Saturday Night Live* whose work has appeared in the *New Yorker, Time,* and the *New York Times,* among other publications. She is the author of several children's books and humor books, most recently, *Him Her Him Again the End of Him.* She was the first woman elected to the *Harvard Lampoon.*

Bobbie Ann Mason is the author of *In Country, Clear Springs, Shiloh & Other Stories,* and *An Atomic Romance.* She is the winner of the PEN/Hemingway Award, and has been a finalist for the National Book Critics Circle Award, the American Book Award, the PEN/Faulkner Award, and the Pulitzer Prize.

Ian Maxtone-Graham writes for *The Simpsons,* where he is also an executive producer. He has also written for *Saturday Night Live.*

Bruce McCall is best known for his work as a writer and illustrator for the *New Yorker, Car and Driver,* and *National Lampoon.* He is the author, most recently, of *Marveltown.*

Patrick F. McManus is a renowned outdoor writer, humorist, and longtime columnist for *Outdoor Life* and *Field & Stream.* He is the author of many books, including the *New York Times* bestsellers *The Grasshopper Trap, The Night the Bear Ate Goombaw,* and *Real Ponies Don't Go Oink!*

George Meyer is a producer and writer for *The Simpsons.* In 2000, Meyer was called "the funniest man behind the funniest show on TV" by the *New Yorker.*

Howard Moss (1922–1987) was an American poet, dramatist, and critic, and he was poetry editor of the *New Yorker* from 1948 until his death. He won the Pulitzer Prize and the National Book Award for *Selected Poems.*

Mark O'Donnell is the author of *Getting Over Homer,* as well as two comic collections, *Elementary Education* and *Vertigo Park and Other Tall Tales.* His humor writing, cartoons, and poetry have appeared in the *New Yorker, Spy, Atlantic Monthly,* and the *New York Times Magazine,* and several of his plays have been produced off Broadway.

Michael O'Donoghue (1940–1994) was a contributor for *National Lampoon.* He was the first head writer for *Saturday Night Live.*

David Owen has been a staff writer at the *New Yorker* since 1991. Before joining the *New Yorker,* Owen was a contributing editor at the *Atlantic Monthly.* His most recent book is *Sheetrock & Shellac: A Thinking Person's Guide to the Art and Science of Home Improvement.*

Born in the Bronx, **Grace Paley** (1922–2007) was a renowned writer and activist. Her *Collected Stories* was a finalist for both the Pulitzer Prize and the National Book Award.

Charles Portis lives in Arkansas, where he was born and educated. He served in the Marine Corps during the Korean War. As a reporter, he wrote for the *New York Herald-Tribune*, and was also its London bureau chief. He is the author of *True Grit* and *Dog of the South*.

Padgett Powell is the author of *The Interrogative Mood* as well as four other novels including *Edisto*, which was nominated for the National Book Award. His writing has appeared in the *New Yorker*, *Harper's*, the *Paris Review*, *Esquire*, and other publications, as well as in the anthologies *Best American Short Stories* and *Best American Sports Writing*.

Simon Rich is the author of *Ant Farm* and *Free-Range Chickens*. He is a graduate of Harvard University, where he was president of the *Harvard Lampoon*. He writes for *Saturday Night Live*.

George Saunders is the author of the story collections *Pastoralia* and *Civil-WarLand in Bad Decline*, *The Very Persistent Gappers of Frip* (a children's book), and *The Braindead Megaphone*, a collection of essays.

Cathleen Schine is the author of seven novels, including *Rameau's Niece*, *The Love Letter*, *She is Me*, *The New Yorkers*, and *The Three Weissmanns of Westport*. She is a frequent contributor to the *New York Review of Books*.

David Sedaris is the author of several collections of essays, including *Naked*, *Me Talk Pretty One Day*, and *When You Are Engulfed In Flames*, each of which has been a bestseller.

Susan Shapiro is the author of the memoirs *Five Men Who Broke My Heart*, which was optioned by Paramount Pictures, and *Lighting Up*, and is the co-editor of the anthology *Food for the Soul*.

Paul Simms began his career in television writing for *Late Night with David Letterman*. Simms later wrote for *The Larry Sanders Show* and created the NBC sitcom, *NewsRadio*. More recently, he has directed and produced the HBO series *The Flight of the Conchords*.

Mark Singer has been a staff writer for the *New Yorker* since 1974. He is the author of *Funny Money*, *Mr. Personality*, *Citizen K*, and *Somewhere in America*.

A reporter for BNET, **Jake Swearingen** has written for *Wired*, *Business 2.0*, and *McSweeney's*, covering everything from locative technology to high-definition online video.

Calvin Tomkins has written more than a dozen books, including *The Bride and the Bachelors*, *Living Well is the Best Revenge*, and *Duchamp*. He is the winner of the Clark Prize for art writing, a subject that he covers as a staff writer for the *New Yorker*, in addition to profiles and humor pieces.

Calvin Trillin has been a staff writer for the *New Yorker* since 1963. Before joining the *New Yorker*, he served in the army and worked for *Time* as a reporter in the South and as a writer in New York. His most recent book is *Deciding the Next Decider: The 2008 Presidential Race in Rhyme*.

George W. S. Trow (1943–2006) was a writer and social critic at the *New Yorker* for thirty years. Trow, who joined the magazine in 1966, was best known as the author of *Within the Context of No Context*, an analysis of contemporary American culture.

Samuel Langhorne Clemens (1835–1910) adopted the pen name **Mark Twain** to author some of the most popular works in the history of American humor. He wrote many novels and short stories, including *The Adventures of Tom Sawyer*, *Adventures of Huckleberry Finn*, and *A Connecticut Yankee in King Arthur's Court*.

John Updike (1932–2009) was a member of the staff of the *New Yorker* for a half century. He wrote more than fifty books, including collections of short stories, poems, essays, and criticism. His novels have won the Pulitzer Prize, the National Book Award, the American Book Award, and the National Book Critics Circle Award.

Mikhail Zoshchenko (1895–1958) was one of the most popular Russian writers of the 1920s and 1930s. His comic sketches and short stories appeared in Soviet newspapers throughout the period. His translated work includes *Nervous People and Other Satires*, *Scenes from the Bathhouse*, and *The Galosh*, among others.

ABOUT 826 SEATTLE

826 Seattle is a nonprofit writing and tutoring center dedicated to helping youth, ages six to eighteen, improve their creative and expository writing skills and to helping teachers inspire their students to write. Our services are structured around our belief that great leaps in learning can happen with one-on-one attention and that strong writing skills are fundamental to a child's future success.

826 Seattle is one of seven chapters of 826 National, which was founded by author and *McSweeney's* publisher Dave Eggers. Like the other chapters, 826 Seattle offers students after-school homework help, as well as creative and expository writing workshops. We also invite school groups to our writing lab for field trips and send trained tutors to help in classrooms. All 826 Seattle services are available to both students and teachers free of charge.

For more information, please visit www.826seattle.org or www.826 national.org.

PERMISSIONS